THE THREAD THAT

BINDS US

The Scottish novelist Joan Fallon, currently lives and works in the south of Spain. She writes both contemporary and historical fiction, and almost all her books have a strong female protagonist. She is the author of the following books:

Fiction:
Loving Harry
The House on the Beach
Santiago Tales
Spanish Lavender
The Only Blue Door
Palette of Secrets
The al-Andalus trilogy:
The Shining City
The Eye of the Falcon

Non-fiction:
Daughters of Spain

Connect with Joan Fallon online at:

http:// www.joanfallon.co.uk

Joan Fallon

THE THREAD THAT BINDS US

Scott Publishing

ISBN 978 0 9931797 8 5
First published in 2017
Scott Publishing
Windsor, England

ACKNOWLEDGMENTS

Once again my sincere thanks to my editor Sara Starbuck, whose advice and support have been invaluable, as always.

All happy families resemble each other
Each unhappy family is unhappy in its own way.

Anna Karenina by Leo Tolstoy

CHAPTER 1

She sat on the rickety wooden bench by the water's edge, still feeling shaky from the night before—delicate, as though she would crack into pieces at the slightest loud noise. It was the first time they had been burgled. She had read of people saying what a traumatic experience it was, how they felt that they, not just their homes, had been violated, how they couldn't sleep at night. She always thought it an exaggeration, but now, having experienced it herself, she understood something of that invasion of home and spirit. But that wasn't all that was making her feel as though her life had been turned upside down. No, the house would eventually be back to normal, the insurance company would pay for the damage and last night's trauma would fade into something that was brought up occasionally at dinner parties. But her parents' lies—how would she recover from them?

*

They knew something was wrong the minute they drove up the drive; the light over the porch, which was invariably lit when they went out at night, was off and the house was in darkness. From somewhere inside they could hear the faint sound of Jess barking. They parked the car, leaving the headlights shining on the front of the house, its white facade spotlighted eerily. As Susan got out of the car and climbed the steps to the front door, she felt something crunch under her feet.

'Someone's smashed the light,' she said to her husband, her voice dropping to a whisper and she began to tremble slightly. 'Do you think they're in the house?'

'There's no sign of a car.'

'They could have left it in the lane.'

'Hang on, Susan, wait here a minute. Let me see what's going on,' Graham said, his voice harsher than normal—either from nerves or anger— and instinctively she felt she should stop him, but by then he had opened the boot of his car, taken one of his clubs from his golf bag and was striding towards the house.

'No, wait. Maybe I should I ring the police,' she said nervously, but he was already at the front door. It opened at his touch, swinging back to reveal the smashed frame and splintered wood.

'Someone has certainly been here,' he said. 'Yes, we'd better ring 999. Let's find Jess, first. I hope they haven't done anything to her.'

Susan switched on the hall lights and walked into the lounge. She stopped in astonishment at the scene of devastation before her. 'My God. What the hell happened here? They've taken the lot, TV, video player, my new iPad.'

'Is Jess okay?' Graham was beginning to panic. 'I hope they haven't hurt her.

'She's all right. She's in here. They shut her in the downstairs loo,' Susan said, opening the toilet door. 'Oh no. Look at the mess she's made of the door.' She bent down and examined the damage. 'We'll need a new door.'

Nearly four stone of Golden Labrador rushed past her and flung itself at her husband, almost knocking him off his feet. 'Okay, girl, we're back. It's okay now. Hush now, calm down. Good girl,' he said, soothingly as he bent down and put his arms around the excited animal.'Thank God they didn't hurt you,' he murmured.

'Have you seen the mess?' she asked, staring about her in dismay. 'What the hell were they after? I can't believe anyone could do so much damage.' The books had been swept off the bookshelves and lay scattered across the carpet, some open as though dropped carelessly in the moment of being read, others torn, their spines bent back as though someone had searched inside them. But for what? Money? What did they expect to find inside a pile of old books? CDs had fallen out of their casings and lay where they fell. The doors to their ancient oak sideboard, which always looked as though it could withstand any onslaught, stood open and the contents of the drawers were tipped in a pile on the floor.

Graham picked his way through the debris to the George III console table where he kept a few decanters of whisky and poured himself a large glass. 'Looks as though the thieves knew their Scotch,' he said, rather bitterly. 'They've drunk the McCallum and left the Bells.'

'Looking for a safe, I suppose. They probably thought there was one behind the book shelves,' she said, still unable to believe what was before her eyes, and then added sadly, 'My jewellery will have gone.'

This had never happened to them before and they had lived in this house for almost thirty years. The thought of strangers ransacking her home, pulling out drawers and going through her personal things made her feel sick. 'I'm going upstairs,' she said, heading for the hallway.

'Wait, I'll come with you,' her husband called after her. 'You never know, they might still be here.'

She looked at him standing there leaning on his golf club—it was more like a walking stick than a dangerous weapon. She prayed that there was no-one still in the house because Graham would be no match for any burglar. He was approaching his seventy-second birthday, and although he was pretty active for his age, his knees bothered him and he suffered from angina. Nothing to worry about, the doctor had assured them but she doubted that he would be able to tackle an intruder, not that it would stop him from trying. 'I'm sure there's no-one here now and if there was, I doubt if you'd be much match for them. Why don't you ring the police and tell them what's happened. The sooner we do it, the sooner we can get to bed,' she snapped. She felt so tired. The shock of finding her home invaded by strangers had drained her of any energy.

While Graham dialled 999 and explained about the break-in, Susan went to check on her office. Just as she had expected, her computer had gone, together with the printer, scanner and her laptop. The drawers of her desk hung open and their contents scattered on the floor. Her notes for the next day, so meticulously prepared, had been swept onto the floor along with everything else. She knelt down and picked them up, sorting them carefully back into order before replacing them in their file. The burglars had gone through everything, had touched all aspects of her life. She felt violated. In a minute she would have to go into her bedroom and see what damage they had done in there.

Then she saw it, open, under the table where they'd thrown it. Her father's wallet. When she had cleared out his belongings after he died, she couldn't bring herself to throw it out, and it had been at the back of her desk drawer ever since. It was old and battered, black leather worn with use, and contained only an old library card, a photo of her as an eight-year-old and a ten-shilling note—a relic from pre-decimalisation days. Not surprisingly, the burglars had taken nothing from it. She picked the wallet up and held it to her face. It still smelled of her father, that distinctive tang of cigarettes and after-shave. Idly she undid each compartment, unzipping the purse section, looking carefully for anything she had missed. The photo was still there, more faded than ever and the plastic covering that protected it was dirty, stained brown from nicotine, like so many other things in her parents' house had been, so she gently pulled it out, curious to see if she could recognise her younger self. As she did so, another photograph fell to the ground. She picked it up and peered at it. Against a woodland background stood two smiling people, one clearly identifiable as her father and the other a woman. Was that her mother? No, impossible. This woman had long blonde hair and her mother's had been as black as a raven's wing, that was how her father had described it once. Her aunt maybe? She too had been dark-haired, as were all her father's family.

Susan sat down at her desk and looked out of the window. Now, in the darkness, the lights of the town sparkled, strung out like a necklace of diamonds. She picked up the photograph again and held it under the reading lamp to examine it more closely but the faded image gave no clue to the woman's identity. So who was she? Someone he'd met on one of his courses? A friend? A neighbour? A girlfriend? According to her mother, he was always a bit of a womaniser. A vague memory stirred in the back of her mind but it refused to reveal itself. She put the photograph into her coat pocket and dropped the wallet back into the drawer.

Each morning she would sit there at her desk and look at Brunel's railway bridge in the distance, close enough to admire its unobtrusive lines as it spanned the Thames, yet far enough away for her not to be disturbed by the sound of passing trains. She loved that view of the water meadows and the curving sweep of the river as it headed downstream towards Windsor and beyond. She loved the room. When Aidan had gone off to university they had rearranged the house and this, the old play-room, had become hers. She had lined the walls with bookshelves and placed an old pine table under the window so that, when inspiration failed her and her computer lay silent, she could just sit and gaze at the river.

'The police'll be up in half an hour,' Graham called up to her. 'We're not to touch anything until they come.'

'All right.'

'Did they take your jewellery?'

'I don't know. I'm still in my office. They've taken the computer and my external hard drive. All my work was on it. God knows what I'll do now.' She still couldn't believe it. The months of work lost made her feel sick. 'They've been up in the loft, too. The trap door is open and there's stuff all over the landing.'

She could hear Graham's slow, heavy steps as he climbed the stairs to their bedroom so she went down to join him. It was even worse than she expected. Their room had been trashed. There was no other word for it. The mattress had been upturned in the search, and the bedding lay in an untidy heap on the floor. Drawers had been emptied out and clothes lay scattered everywhere. Even a box of Yves St Laurent talcum powder had been overturned, leaving a powdery coating on her dressing table and on the floor. She picked up her open jewellery box. It was empty. Everything had gone: the earrings that Graham bought her for their last anniversary, the gold bracelet he gave her when Aidan was born, brooches that belonged to her mother, a double string of pearls that she bought in Majorca and never wore anymore, all of it gone. She felt devastated with their loss and the memories that were associated with each and every piece.

'What, do they think we keep our valuables under the mattress? Haven't these guys heard of banks?' Graham said with a dry laugh, as he pulled the mattress back onto the bed.

'Maybe they just get off on trashing someone else's house,' she said, pulling a tissue out of her pocket.

'Did they find your jewellery?'

She nodded silently, tears gliding down her cheeks. Now that the shock of finding her home invaded was receding, the realisation of what had happened to them was becoming clear and it made her angry. It wasn't the monetary worth of the things the thieves had taken that mattered—they were well insured—as much as the value to them personally. The files on her computer represented months, in some cases years of work; the jewellery, not excessively expensive because she didn't like flashy jewellery, had mostly been gifts from Graham or left to her by her grandmother. None of it was replaceable. But beyond that was this dreadful feeling of violation, that her beautiful home—always considered so safe—her haven after a hard day's work, had been entered and turned upside down by person or persons unknown. No matter what the police said when they eventually arrived, they would never retrieve their possessions, and she would never be able to get rid of this overwhelming sensation of vulnerability.

'Why didn't the alarm go off?' she asked, looking at her husband. 'Shouldn't the alarm have gone off? Isn't that why we pay all that money every month?'

'I forgot to set it,' he said, looking embarrassed. 'I'm sorry, Susan. You were telling me to get a move on and Jess was up to her usual tricks of demanding a biscuit before we left, and I suppose it just slipped my mind.'

'Slipped your mind? Just slipped your mind? Graham how could you have been so careless?' She wanted to shout at him and tell him that all this could have been avoided, but what was the point? Graham was starting to show his age and, lately, he was becoming more and more forgetful. It drove her to distraction.

'I know, I'm sorry.'

'Sorry won't get my laptop back or my mother's jewellery,' she snapped. 'Oh, Graham. This isn't the first time you've left the house unsecured.' It was only a few weeks ago that he had gone to play golf and forgot to lock up the house. She had come home early to find the front door wide open and Jess sitting on the doorstep. How many other times had it happened that she didn't know about?

'I'm getting a bit forgetful, that's all,' he said.

'I should have set the alarm, myself,' she said, pulling out a handkerchief and wiping her eyes. 'You know they took my mother's wedding ring. My father gave it to me when she died. And all her brooches. I've nothing of hers now.'

'I'm sorry, darling. Really I am. Please don't cry. It's not like you to let things get the better of you,' he said, putting his arm around her and hugging her to him. 'We may get some of it back, you know. Look, once the police have been, and we've cleaned up the mess, you'll feel better.'

She sighed. Her beautiful house would never feel the same again, but she couldn't tell him that. As she surveyed her wrecked bedroom she thought of what her son Aidan would say when he found out what had happened. She sighed again, pushing her thick brown hair back from her face. She could remember quite clearly her last conversation with her son.

'So, what are you saying Aidan? You think we should move?' she'd asked, knowing that that was exactly what he had been saying. A quiet stubbornness had made her want to disagree with him, although she knew he was probably right. The house was far too large for them. And now, after the burglary? She left the thought unfinished.

'I know you love this house, we all do. After all I was only five when we moved here remember. It's my home too, my childhood,' her son had continued. She could hear his voice, raised in an attempt to get through to her. 'But it's a rambling old place now. Six bedrooms, three bathrooms. What do two people want with three bathrooms, for heaven's sake? The upkeep is enormous. You haven't had the outside painted in ten years and even the inside is starting to look tatty. No, Mum. It's time to move on. Dad needs somewhere with less stairs and less garden.' She had mildly protested, but there was no stopping him. 'You're always telling me to be practical. Now it's your turn. This house is too isolated. Think about the garden, two acres of it and no gardener. Look how long it takes Dad to mow the lawn, and then there're the fruit trees, the bloody herbaceous borders, the roses. It's endless. And right on the river's edge like that. It's a wonder you haven't been flooded.'

The tirade had continued but she'd stopped listening. He didn't understand how much the house meant to them. After all they'd lived there for most of their married life. There were so many memories. But tonight's events had made her realise that he was right in one respect; the house was isolated. Maybe they were too old to be living here, right by the river, at the end of an un-made road, surrounded by trees and with their nearest neighbour half a mile away.

'Did you say they'd been in the attic?' Graham asked. 'Why would they do that?'

She took off her coat and wearily followed her husband up the stairs. She tried to imagine him tackling an intruder. True he was pretty fit for his age and his tall, sparse frame carried only the hint of a stoop, but she had noticed him stopping to catch his breath more than once when he walked back up from the river with Jess.

'That's the police now,' he said as a car with a blue flashing light sped up their drive and stopped outside. 'I'd better go down. Should I mention about the alarm?'

'Wait until they ask you.'

She stared at the mess on the landing. The burglars had obviously expected to find something more interesting than the junk that they had thrown down—a few old books and a couple of boxes. One she recognised immediately. It was a wooden box that had belonged to her mother, for storing old letters and photographs. Susan had meant to sort them out after her parents died, but hadn't given them a thought for years. Now the box lay on the floor, its metal clasp broken in the fall and its contents spread across the carpet. She stooped to pick up the letters and was about to replace them in the box when she noticed a bulky, brown envelope underneath everything. She pulled it out and opened it. Inside were some small black and white photographs, faded and slightly out of focus. They were mostly of her as a child, two as a baby and some of when she started school. There was a hand-tinted one too, obviously taken in a studio. A three-year-old Susan was wearing a velvet hat and bore an uncanny resemblance to Winston Churchill, with a double chin and dimples in her fat, round cheeks. Then she noticed another photograph, slightly newer than the rest and in colour. It was of a baby wearing a blue knitted bonnet; his eyes were closed and his face wore the red, wrinkled expression of the newly born. The photograph was mounted on a piece of white card and there was a hand written inscription on the back. It was badly faded, but she was able to make out the words: *'To my darling David. All my love Anthea,'* and the baby's name was clearly printed at the bottom: Michael David. Susan looked at the date, 16th May 1962. She suddenly felt sick. Was this what she thought it was? Had her father had another child? How was that possible? And did her mother know about? She felt unable to breath, Of course she must have known. How could she not have known? The photograph was here in *her* box.

Susan felt stunned. Why hadn't her parents told her about the baby? Maybe not when she was a child, but surely they could have told her when she was a grown woman. Did this mean she had a step-brother? All these years she'd had a brother and they had never said anything? She felt her legs give way under her and collapsed into a sitting position. Why had they kept it from her? What else had they been hiding? What other lies had her parents told her?

CHAPTER 2

The next day, Sunday, Susan and Graham started to clean up the mess left by the burglars. The kitchen was the worst area, so she'd phoned Mrs Barnes, who normally came in on Fridays to clean the windows and run a hoover over the carpets, and asked her to come and help them.

'What a mess,' Mrs Barnes exclaimed when she walked in and saw the normally pristine kitchen looking as though a tornado had blown through it. 'Don't you worry, Mrs Masters. I'll soon have this sorted for you. You go and see to those books of yours.' She bustled Susan out of the kitchen and shut the door behind her.

Graham was already busy replacing the books on the bookshelves, so Susan decided to put the boxes back in the attic. It would be interesting to see exactly how much junk they had accumulated in the twenty-seven years they'd lived there. She couldn't remember the last time she'd been up there. Usually she asked Graham or Aidan to go up, and she just handed them the things she wanted stored, old magazines that might be useful for research, empty suitcases, clothes that were too good to throw out but never seemed to get worn, Aidan's old toys, golf clubs that had more antique value than practical use, in short, the overspill of their lives.

She pulled down the ladder and climbed up into the tiny space they called the attic. 'My God. Where do I start?' she muttered to herself, looking around.

She picked up an old wooden tennis racquet that had belonged to Aidan. Its strings were broken. She thought of the games they had played on warm summer evenings, Graham and him. Well that could go out for a start. And these books. Where on earth had they come from? She sat down on a Victorian nursing chair that was badly in need of reupholstering, and began to flick through the books: '18th Century Verse,' 'How Green is My Valley,' 'Shakespeare's Sonnets,' a heavy volume of the plays of George Bernard Shaw, with a tattered cover. They were her father's. She had forgotten all about them.

Her father had been an avid reader—many people were in those days when only a privileged few owned television sets. She could see him now, sitting in the armchair by the fire, a cigarette in one hand and a book in the other, with a cooling cup of tea on the floor beside him. She would pester him to read to her, usually something from 'Grimms' Fairy Tales' or 'Black Beauty'—she didn't mind which— she just loved to sit at his feet, listening to his deep voice as he swept her into the realms of childhood imagination. She had been quite small then. Ten, perhaps? Maybe only eight? She couldn't remember. Those details had become buried with all the other memories. But she did remember that feeling of being loved and wanted, pampered even. Her mother, who preferred to listen to the radio, would call to them from the kitchen, wanting to know if she wanted a cup of cocoa before she went to bed, and whether her father had let his tea go cold, again. But then everything changed.

She collected up her father's books and climbed down to put them with those that the burglars had thrown down. It was a shame to leave them in the attic, mouldering in the dark. They could go on the bookshelf in her office. But she wasn't really interested in the books, or anything else in the attic; she wanted to know more about that baby. She sat on the bottom rung of the ladder and pulled her mother's wooden box towards her and opened it. Her mother had kept all the letters they had ever written to each other, and after her death nobody had liked to dispose of them. Most of them were written during the war when her father was in the army. Susan had had a cursory look at them once before, intending some day to read them carefully and put them in chronological order but then forgot about them, just as she had forgotten about her father's books. She hadn't wanted to know about her parents' private lives, and she especially didn't want to remember the events of her childhood. She'd shut those memories away in her mind as securely as if they too were in a wooden box. But now she was curious. It was seeing the photographs that had aroused her curiosity; she hadn't been able to get them out of her mind. She needed to identify the woman in the photograph, the one he had kept hidden, tucked behind a younger Susan and, more than that, she needed to find out about the baby.

Susan had never had a brother nor a sister. She didn't really know the reason she remained an only child; she assumed it was because her father was always changing his job and her mother had to keep working. To be honest, she never gave it much thought when she was a child; it was not something that really bothered her, although she was sometimes envious of friends with siblings. Now and again she would imagine having an older brother and how he would take her to the cinema, or swimming in the sea when her parents were busy. She imagined her friends saying, 'Have you seen Susie's brother? He's so handsome.' Or maybe having an older sister, like her friend Ann, who would teach her how to put on make-up and paint her nails, even tell her about her boyfriend. Later, when Susan was older, there was no way she could ask her mother why she'd had no more children, without opening up a past they both wanted to remain closed.

She leaned back against the ladder, a handful of letters in her lap, and shut her eyes, trying to understand why her father had changed, why he had stopped being the loving husband who had written those letters. A feeling of sadness engulfed her as she thought of their wasted lives.

'Susie.' It was Graham. 'Aidan's on the phone. He says have we remembered we promised to go for lunch today.'

'What? Today? Did you tell him about the burglary?'

'Yes. But it's Jason's birthday on Tuesday. Don't you remember they wanted us to go over today to celebrate it? Anyway he says it will do us good to get out of the house.' Her husband's head appeared over the bannister. 'I said, of course we hadn't forgotten.'

Susan looked at him blankly. She'd totally forgotten it was her youngest grandson's sixth birthday next week.

'But what about the mess?'

'We can clear that up tomorrow. We can't disappoint Jason just because the house is in a mess. I'll tell him we'll be over by one. All right?'

'Oh, I suppose so. But I'll have to take some time off work tomorrow.'

'We'll take Jason the football I got him,' her husband added, heading back to reassure his son.

*

Aidan was surprised that his mother had agreed to come for lunch in the circumstances, but he decided not to comment.

'Hi Granddad. Hi Nan,' Jason said the minute Susan and Graham stepped through the door. 'Are you going to play football with us, Granddad?'

'I'd love to Jason, but I don't have a ball,' Graham said, hiding the boy's present behind his back.

'Yes, you do, Granddad. What's that?' the boy asked, jumping up at him.

'This? Oh, my goodness. How did that get there?' Graham said, feigning surprise at the package in his hands, which, despite the elaborate layers of wrapping paper, was so obviously a football. 'Is this a football? Well I never.'

'You know it is Granddad,' said Jason, jumping up and down in excitement. 'Is it for us? Can we play with it?'

'Hang on Jason, give your grandfather a minute to get in,' Aidan said.

'Well there's no keeping secrets from you, is there. Here you are then my lad, this is for you. An early birthday present,' Graham said, handing over the football.

'Look Daddy,' the excited child said, ripping off the wrapping paper. 'A proper football. Stitching as well. Cool. Just what I wanted Granddad.'

He rushed to his grandfather and threw his arms around him, saying, 'Thanks Granddad.'

Graham bent down, caught him in his arms and swung him into the air. 'You're going to score a lot of goals with that, my lad,' he said.

'Mind your back, Graham. He's not a baby any more,' Susan said and her husband dutifully put Jason down, but not before giving the boy a secret wink, which caused him to giggle and run to his grandmother. He threw his chubby arms around her legs, and said politely, 'Thanks Nan.'

'You're welcome Jason,' she said, bending down to kiss him on the cheek, then looked down at her immaculate black trousers and began flicking away imaginary specks of dirt.

'Come on then, my lad. Let's go down to the Common and try it out before lunch,' Graham said, taking Jason by the hand and skilfully manoeuvring both boy and ball down the hall and out of the door.

Aidan could swear he saw his mother heave a sigh of relief as she went into the kitchen to talk to Judy. Why couldn't she relax for once? She was still wearing her outdoor jacket, even though the temperature that day was around twenty-eight degrees. It was as though she'd just called in to drop off the present and then be on her way. She always gave him the impression that she couldn't bear to be in his house a moment longer than was necessary.

'Mum, let me take your jacket. You must be far too warm,' he said. 'You *are* staying to lunch, aren't you?'

His mother was perched on a kitchen stool, her handbag clutched tightly on her knees. She looked unsettled, like a bird that would take flight at any moment, but she obediently handed over her jacket. 'Yes, of course we're staying to lunch,' she replied politely. 'You did invite us, didn't you?'

That was the word for his mother: polite. She was always so polite to Judy. He imagined her speaking to her delegates in the same way, with a slightly forced bonhomie and a professional interest in what they were doing, but no real warmth. She'd never said she didn't like his wife, and to be honest, there was no reason for her to dislike her. Judy was always very amenable with his mother, although she often commented afterwards how difficult she found their relationship.

'I'll call Zak and Ben. They're in the bedroom playing with the Playstation,' he suggested.

'No. Leave them be. Don't interrupt them. I'll see them when they've finished. We've got all afternoon,' his mother said, with a rather forced smile.

She made it sound as though the afternoon stretched endlessly ahead of her, and maybe she felt that it did. He couldn't ever remember seeing her play with his children. It was always Graham who read them stories or played football. It was Graham who suggested they get out the Scrabble board or play Crazy Eights. He tried to remember whether she had played with him when he was a child. Maybe when he was small, but not later. He remembered her saying how she believed in giving children their freedom, so they could express themselves. She didn't want to stultify him. Was that why she'd sent him to a boarding school when he was only eight-years-old?

'Well, let me get you a drink then,' he said, feeling that even if she didn't want one, he certainly did. He took a bottle of gin from the refrigerator and poured out three large glasses of gin and tonic.

Lunch was excellent, as usual. The chicken pie was delicious, its crust a deep golden brown and the salad and new potatoes a perfect accompaniment. For dessert Judy produced her birthday special, a chocolate sponge cake, with an icing sugar model of Buzz Lightyear and 'Happy Birthday Jason' traced across the top in white chocolate.

'But it's not Jason's birthday today,' objected Zak. 'It's not until Tuesday.'

'It's 'cos Nan and Granddad are here, silly,' said Ben. 'Anyway you don't have to eat it, if you don't want to.'

For once the boys behaved well, no squabbles, no refusing to eat their salad, no sudden food allergies that meant they could not possibly eat chicken today, and no rushing away from the table before they were told.

'Any more cake anyone?' Judy asked.

'Not for me, thanks. That was all delicious,' Susan replied, carefully wiping her mouth with her napkin.

Aidan couldn't help noticing that most of her dessert still lay on her plate. His mother was always counting the calories, and he was sure she had found it difficult to even eat a little of the rich chocolate cake, but her innate sense of politeness made her at least try some.

'Coffee?' he asked.

'Well,' his mother hesitated, looking at her husband.

'Yes, please,' Graham replied. 'And I'll have a bit more of that delicious cake, if I may Judy.'

Aidan looked up in time to see his mother giving his father an irritated look.

'Mum?'

'Well, all right. Do you have any decaf?' Susan replied. 'Then we must be going, I'm afraid.'

'So soon?'

'I'm sorry darling, but you know what the traffic is like on a Sunday, and your Dad likes to get back to give Jess a bit of a walk before it gets dark,' his mother explained. 'Besides which, we've still got a mountain of clearing up to do.'

'But you've only just got here Mum,' Aidan said, the wine he had drunk with the meal, loosening his tongue. 'And anyway Jess doesn't need a walk. She's got acres of garden to run around in. At least stay until Jason's bedtime.'

Why did they always seem to be on the verge of a row? he thought, angrily. Why was she always in such a hurry to leave?

Judy put her hand on his arm. 'Your mum is right Aidan, the traffic on the M4 is awful on a Sunday evening. They'll have a much clearer run if they leave early. You stay here and chat to your mum and dad and I'll make the coffee.'

'Thanks, Judy. Two sugars for me, please,' his father said.

As soon as they could politely do so, his parents made their departure.

'It's been lovely to see you both, even if it wasn't for long. And thank you for Jason's football,' Judy said, hugging first her mother-in-law and then her father-in-law.

Susan smiled and kissed her lightly on the cheek. 'Lovely lunch Judy. You're such a good cook. You must show me how to make that delicious sauce some time.' She was gushing now, in her haste to be gone.

Aidan was on the point of making a sharp retort to this last remark, but caught himself just in time. After all he should be used to his mother by now. Instead he just said, 'Nice to see you Dad, Mum. Drive carefully now.'

*

All the way home Susan kept thinking about the photographs. She couldn't get them out of her mind. There were so many questions to be answered. Why was there a photograph of a baby with a blue bonnet amongst her parents' letters? Were there any more photographs of him in that brown envelope? Was David the father? Why did Susan know nothing about this child? Who was Anthea and where was she now? She wanted to get home to go through the letters and see if she could find anything to shed some light on this mystery.

'Delicious lunch,' Graham said, as they pulled off the motorway and headed down the familiar road that led to the river and their house. 'Judy's an excellent cook. And such a lovely girl. Aidan's a lucky man.'

'Not exactly a girl any more,' Susan said.

'Maybe not, but she seems like it to me,' he said, with a smile. 'That's what happens when you get to my age, everyone seems so young. Still you must agree, she's a good cook.'

'Of course she is. After all, that's what she teaches.'

'What's the matter, Susie? You've been in a bitchy mood all afternoon. Is it because of the burglary? It's not the end of the world, you know. Nobody was hurt. Okay, so you lost a bit of jewellery, but you didn't wear much of it anyway.'

'So that makes it all right, does it?'

'Look sweetheart, we were lucky. Goodness knows what could have happened if we'd been home,' Graham said, trying to mollify her.

'Maybe you're right. On the other hand, maybe it wouldn't have happened if we'd been at home, instead of at that stupid golf club dinner,' she snapped.

She hated going to the golf club. Graham's friends were all elderly and all they could talk about was golf. Even their wives played the game and had little else in the way of conversation. If she managed to draw the conversation away from golf, the women started to talk about their grandchildren. These were the only two topics on the table. She always came away from the golf club feeling bored and irritated.

'I'm sorry you feel like that. I thought you'd enjoy a night out and I wanted you to meet my friends,' he said.

She knew she was being unreasonable but how could she tell him what was really troubling her? First she had to find out more for herself. Why had her parents kept this secret from her? Her head was reeling as she tried to come to terms with what she had discovered in her mother's box of letters. She wasn't sure which upset her more, the thought that she might have a brother or the fact that they had lied to her for years. In whichever case, she needed to know more.

CHAPTER 3

Susan took out a bundle of loose sheets of cheap, lined paper covered in a fine italic script from the box. A sudden gust of wind threatened to snatch the papers from her hand, so she chose one and pushed the rest back into the box. A large white swan, glided past, heading downstream as stately as a Spanish galleon, faint ripples in its wake like glints of silver in the early evening light. Behind her she could hear the rasping whine of the lawn mower. Suddenly it went silent and then coughed into action again. She imagined Graham's muttered oaths at the erratic machine, and without turning round she could see him tinkering with its ancient engine.

She put on her reading glasses and began to read:

6th February 1943

My darling Mary,

Well dearest, I received your sweet letter today, and am glad to hear all is well with you. I'm sending you a postal order; it's not much and I'm sorry I can't manage any more this week. I have been looking for a book by Dylan Thomas for you but haven't had much luck so far. I hope you enjoyed the Daphne du Maurier one; I picked it up in an old booksellers for three pence. It seemed just the sort of book you'd like, lots of love and romance. Is your mum feeling better? Tell her I hope her bronchitis improves soon. She is lucky to have you there to help her with the little ones. It's good practice for you, for when we have one of our own. Has your dad been called up for the Home Guard yet? If they haven't been in touch by now they will probably leave him where he is. His work is just as important on the farm. The country desperately needs food.

Please give your parents my best wishes and tell them I hope to visit next month when I get some leave.

I love you Mary and miss you so much. I can't wait until we are together again.

All my love

Your loving husband David

Susan read letter after letter, until the light began to fade and she could read no more. They were touching in their simplicity and the paucity of the news they contained. They had written to each other every day for two years, consequently many of the letters had little to communicate save a repetition of their mutual love and a fervent longing to be together again. She learnt of her father's search for accommodation, of their plans for a house of their own, of money worries, of the tedium of waiting to be assigned to a regiment, of his promises to give up drinking and control his temper, of books that he had read. She learnt of her mother's doubts, of her boredom, of her fear of having an accident in the munitions factory and being injured or worse, of her concern for her mother-in-law, of her passion, of her restless days and sleepless nights. She learnt little of the war but, as she read on, she began to learn more about her parents and their love for each other and realised, rather sadly, that she had not really known them at all.

'Aren't you cold?' asked Graham, coming over to her, his hands black with grease from his attempts at repairing the lawn mower.

'No.'

'What are you reading?'

'Nothing important. Just some old letters I found in the attic,' she replied, bundling the letters into the box and closing it.

'Your parents?'

'Yes. Wartime stuff. Not very interesting really but it's made me think that perhaps they did love each other after all.'

'Did you think that they didn't then?' her husband asked.

'Oh, I don't know.'

'Well, I'd always thought they were a bit cold towards each other. Your mother had quite a tongue on her,' Graham said, sitting down beside her. 'But that doesn't mean they didn't love each other, at least in the early days. People change as they get older, you know.'

She looked at him in surprise. Graham had never mentioned her parents' marriage before. It was so unlike him. Maybe the robbery had unsettled him as well.

'Aidan said he'd come over tomorrow and give us a hand,' he said, sitting down beside her.

'There's no need. I told him we can manage quite well without him,' she said, picking up the box and heading for the house. 'You're right. It is cold.'

'The lawn mower's buggered,' her husband said. 'I'll have to take it into Joe's. See if he can fix it.'

Susan didn't reply. As she walked across Graham's immaculate lawn, she thought about her father. Why had he changed? Was it all to do with that woman in the photograph?

She had gone to check up on her father one afternoon after work, and found him asleep in the chair, sunbeams streaming through the lace curtains, daubing him with light. Sleep had relaxed the muscles in his face, removing the years and revealing traces of the handsome young man he had once been. She remembered some lines she had once read:

'Old men's faces often hide
the younger man that's still inside.'

She looked down at him and stroked his hair gently, reluctant to wake him. For a moment the inevitability of growing old overwhelmed her. Dust motes floated gently across her father's bedroom, caught in the sunlight. The ashes from the previous night's fire lay untouched in the grate and on the table a greasy plate contained the remains of her father's lunch, congealed and un-appetising.

Her father stirred. 'Susie, is that you?' he asked drowsily, pulling himself into a sitting position.

'Hello Dad. How are you feeling?'

'I've just had the strangest dream. Your mum was here. She was standing right there, by the window, wearing that green dress you bought for her last Christmas. And she beckoned me. "Come on Davy,'" she said. "I'm waiting for you." What do you think of that Susie?'

'Don't be silly, Dad. It was just a dream. I expect it's because you miss her. Why don't I make you some tea?'

He had died three days later. She couldn't believe it when his neighbour telephoned with the news. 'Susan, I'm so sorry. He was fine last night. Quite his old self. I had made him a bite of dinner, and when I took it round he had already lit the fire and was watching the news. I thought he was okay, or I wouldn't have left him. I'm so sorry. So soon after poor Mary too.'

Graham had been his usual stalwart self. He'd dealt with all the funeral arrangements, telephoning her father's elderly sister and a distant cousin in Northumbria—the only relatives that still remained—and arranging for them to be collected from the station. She'd wanted them to stay with her, at least until the next day, but they'd insisted on staying in a hotel in the town so that they could catch the early train home. Her mother had quite a few surviving relatives, but when Graham rang them with the bad news no one had been able to make it to the funeral. She didn't know what she would have done without Graham. He had been by her side all the time.

A gust of wind blew across the lawn. For a moment she felt old and vulnerable. What if something happened to Graham and she was left alone? He was twelve years older than her, after all. It was only last month that one of his golfing friends had dropped dead on the golf course. A stroke they said. It could happen to anyone, they said. He had been only seventy-three and left a widow just two years younger than him. Understandably, Graham had been very shaken by the news. If Graham died would she be able to cope on her own in this big house? Would she want to? She was sure this was what was behind Aidan's concerns. If she was widowed, he would feel that it was his responsibility to take care of her. She didn't relish the thought of anyone having to take care of her. Luckily she'd never had to take care of her own parents. They were both still independent until they died. Had they felt like her, valuing their independence above all else?

She remembered how she'd felt when she went to her father's small flat to sort out his possessions the week after the funeral. It made no difference that he was no longer alive, she still hadn't been able to shake the feeling, as she handled his underwear and opened the drawers of his dressing table, that she was prying into things that were not hers, that she was violating his privacy. When she had stripped the sheets from his bed and bundled them into her arms a smell of stale sweat and cigarette smoke had brought him instantly into the room with her. It was the same in the bathroom. As she removed his hairbrush and his razor, and threw the Lifebuoy soap into the bin, she seemed to be erasing all sight and smell of his existence. Her father had been a very private person and that strong sense of individual privacy had extended to other aspects of his life too, and to her mother. Maybe what she now viewed as secrets was just a need to keep their private life just that, private.

She'd looked around the room one last time, remembering the last time she had seen him, sitting in his armchair, with an open book in his hand as usual, and his reading glasses, grimy from the constant cigarettes he smoked, balanced on the end of his nose. The wooden box, where her mother kept family documents, birth certificates, their marriage certificate, their old ration cards— unneeded for years—and their rent book, and more than that, their love letters, sat on the old desk by the window. It was all that remained of her parents' lives. She'd picked it up, little realising then the impact those letters were going to have on her own life.

CHAPTER 4

It was days since she had found the photographs and she still hadn't mentioned anything to Graham. What was the point? She had no intention of doing anything about them. Why the hell should she worry about her father's bastard child? If he had wanted her to know about him he would have told her. All right, maybe not when she was young, but later he could have explained to her what had happened, who the baby was, what had become of him. But no, her father had said nothing. All her mother ever told her was in the form of cryptic remarks about their lack of money because her father was spending it on other things. No summer holiday. No new car. There was never enough money and it was all because of *her*, the mysterious woman that dogged their lives.

She wondered where the child was now. Michael. Was he a big-shot in the city? Or a journalist, a politician, a teacher? Whatever he was doing, it didn't concern her. She felt an irrational resentment towards him. Why hadn't her father told her? Or her mother for that fact?

There was one memory which had returned to her when she was in that nether world halfway between sleep and waking. She had been about twelve. No she had been exactly twelve years and five months old.

*

She knew something was wrong as soon as she got home from school that day. Her mother had been crying, her face was blotchy and her eyes were red and swollen; streaks of mascara had run down her cheeks, and there were dark smudges in the corners of her eyes. Her father wore his grim, controlled face, his mouth a tight, thin line and his eyes expressionless blue glass.

Two days later her father had gone. Her mother wouldn't talk about it. She just turned away angrily whenever Susan tried to ask her where he was. Had her father left them? Why hadn't he said anything to her? Why wouldn't her mother tell her where he was? She could hear her crying all night long, and in the mornings, when Susan got up to go to school, she found her on the sofa, in an exhausted sleep.

Her mother would still be lying there when she returned in the afternoon, so Susan prepared the supper—beans on toast or fish paste sandwiches—but her mother would not eat. She existed on cups of tea and endless cigarettes. After a week of this, Susan was about to ask her neighbour for some help, when her father reappeared. He wasn't pleased to be home. He looked around him and said to his wife, 'Mary. This can't go on. Think about Susie, for God's sake. Has she had any food? Does she have any clean clothes?' He opened the refrigerator door. 'There's nothing in the fridge. What the hell have you been doing? Look at the state of this place. It's filthy,' he shouted at her, looking in disgust at the overflowing ashtrays, the dust, the cluttered living room, the sink piled high with dirty dishes and the ants crawling in the bread bin.

His wife lay on the sofa, her uncombed hair, once so black and shiny, was dirty and bedraggled. She hadn't washed in three days, and her body stank of cigarette smoke and BO. She looked up at him through bloodshot eyes and managed a faint smile as she whispered, 'Davy, you're back.' That was all she had been waiting for.

The next day her mother rose early and cooked Susan breakfast before sending her off to school. Life returned to normal, except that now, normal was not the same as before. Susan's mother was a kind woman. Her father was a vicar, and she had inherited all the generosity of spirit that a strictly Protestant upbringing had given her, but somehow it had missed a beat when it came to forgiveness. She could neither forgive nor forget. On the surface Susan's family were happy, but that was the daytime face, the face that her mother showed to the world. Susan lay in her bedroom as before, listening to her parents through the thin walls, but not to their laughter. There was no laughter any more in their house; it had left that day with her father and had never returned.

*

Despite drinking at least half a bottle of wine, Susan could not sleep. She turned onto her left side and tried to think of something pleasant: the view across the garden, how pretty the apple tree had been that year. Nothing worked. She adjusted her position, lying first on her back and then on her side, but scenes from the day continued to replay themselves over and over in her head. The house was almost a century old now, and at night it played its own symphony of sounds. She could never precisely identify them. Was that creak a window hinge or a floorboard? Was that the wind squeezing its way in through some minute crack? Sometimes she heard a sudden snap as though a switch had been thrown, or dripping water when no tap was running. There had been occasions when she'd got up and stood in the middle of the room in an attempt to hear more clearly, but then the ghosts of the house became silent until she returned once more to her bed. Now the sounds had a more ominous significance. Were those someone's footsteps she could hear creaking up the stairs? Was that a shutter swinging open, when she had been sure that she had closed them all? Had someone got into her home again?

'Are you all right, Susie?' Graham asked.

'You're awake?'

'Well it's hard to sleep with you tossing and turning all the time.'

'I'm sorry. Just got a lot on my mind.'

'Work?' he asked, with a yawn.

'Yes. You go back to sleep. I might as well get up and sort out my notes for today.'

'Okay. Let Jess into the garden when you go down, will you.'

Susan pulled on her dressing gown and climbed the stairs to her office. Outside her window she could see the slowly moving river, like a slick of dark oil in the half light. It was too soon for the glow of sunrise but there was a whiteness along the horizon where the first rays of daylight struggled to push back the night. In a short while, the river and the sky would be mirror images of rose tinted clouds and the trees would glitter and gleam in the sunshine. She sat down at her desk and breathed in the view, just as a small flock of barnacle geese flew past, honking loudly, on their way to the water meadows further west.

It was strange, Susan had not thought about the night her father left in almost fifty years. Now she couldn't stop thinking about it. It must have been about another woman. Was that when he went off with his mistress? The one in the photograph? But he had come back and, as far as she knew, he'd never left again. But despite that, something or someone had destroyed her parents' marriage, because things were never the same again. She knew they weren't happy. She had known it then and she knew it now. Was it about the child? According to the photograph, the baby had been born about that time. The child, her half-brother, would be forty-eight now. How strange to think that after all those years as an only child she might have a brother. It made her feel uncomfortable and, if she were honest with herself, angry.

The box of letters lay on her desk. It had to contain something that could clear this up for her, something that could explain why nobody had ever spoken of Michael. She switched on the reading lamp and opened the box. First she removed the neat pile of letters that she'd already read—there were still dozens more to look at. She would read them all and look for any clues. The first one she opened was dated 1943. There was no point reading that. Michael hadn't been born until 1962. She decided to save some time by only reading the letters written post-1961. The first few contained nothing new, just general news and questions about the progress of baby Susan; there were letters from her aunts, her grandparents and someone called Gilly, who had worked with her mother in the munitions factory. She skimmed them and put them in a pile to be read later. Then she picked up an envelope addressed to her grandmother. It had obviously never been posted; the stamp with its picture of the young queen Elizabeth was unfranked. She opened it. All it contained was a black and white photograph of a small boy. Was this Michael? It was hard to tell. She held the photo closer to the light. The boy was about two years old and had curly hair. No, it couldn't be Michael.He didn't look at all like her father. It was almost as though he were … No, this wasn't Michael. She looked at the envelope again. It was definitely her father's writing so why would he be sending a photograph of a little boy to his mother if it wasn't Michael?

*

The next day she phoned the office and told them that she'd be in at lunchtime. She had to have another look in the attic to see if there was anything she had missed. She waited until Graham had gone off to walk Jess, then pulled down the loft ladder again and climbed into the loft.

'Mum. Are you up there?' a voice called.

It was Aidan. Since the burglary he'd taken to visiting them at least once a week, usually calling in on his way to a meeting. Aidan was like his father in many ways, but he had inherited his mother's round grey eyes and lop-sided smile. He also had her sharp tongue.

'So, you're having a clear-out then,' he said, looking around. 'About time.'

She registered, with a touch of resentment, his rather self satisfied grin. 'Forced upon us, I'm afraid.'

'So what are you doing?'

'I just thought I 'd have a look at what was up here. We've collected such a lot of junk over the years,' she said. 'Here give me a hand to get down.'

'Do you want me to take anything for you?'

'Not really,' she replied. 'I'd only just got up here. I thought you'd come round later in the day, after work.'

'Well I had a gap this morning, so I thought I'd see how you were. You know I've always said that this house was too remote. They could empty the place and nobody would be any the wiser,' her son said.

Susan didn't want to get into yet another argument with Aidan about the house and how they should move to something smaller. She wanted to be by herself, to think through what she'd discovered. Seeing the photographs had stirred something in her memory. She needed time alone to work it all out. But Aidan was here now and she could hear his voice, droning on and on about security and being isolated and how it was time to face up to the fact that they were no longer young.

She forced herself to concentrate on what he was saying.

'So why were you in the loft?' he persisted.

He could never leave things alone. Always wanting to know everything. Always wanting them to do what he wanted. He hadn't been like that as a boy, as far as she could remember, but then he'd been away a lot of the time at boarding school.

'I told you. I was putting back the stuff the burglars had chucked out. And then I just thought I'd have a look and see how much junk we'd got up there.' She wasn't going to give him the satisfaction of knowing just how much the burglary had upset her. He'd already suggested that he come over and stay with them for a bit. That was the last thing she wanted.

'And was it as bad as you expected?' he asked with a smile.

'Was what as bad?'

'The state of the loft?'

'Oh. Yes, actually, it was even worse than I thought.'

'I can give you a hand, if you want,' he said.

'Not today. One day, maybe.'

'Okay. Did you see my old tennis racquet up there?' he asked. 'I thought I'd take it for the boys to play with.'

'It's not worth taking. The strings have all gone. I was going to throw it out, but take it if you want.'

'So does this clearing out the attic mean you're taking my suggestion seriously? Are you going to down-size?' he asked.

'Down-size. What a ridiculous term. It sounds as though we've both shrunk in the wash. If you mean are we going to move to a smaller house, the answer is still no. I don't know how many times I have to tell you. I can understand that you're worried about us, but really Aidan, there's no need. We're not likely to get burgled again. They took it all the first time,' she said.

'God, there's no talking to you,' he said and slammed the loft door back into position. She watched her son go in search of his father. He'd always had a better relationship with Graham than with her. Graham said it was nonsense; he was just a man's man, whatever that meant. Aidan had also got on really well with her own father and been devastated when he'd died.

She remembered Aidan standing by the graveside, his shoulders shaking and tears running down his cheeks. Afterwards, at the wake, he drank too much and staggered up to her, waving his glass in her face. 'You're a cold fish mother. Not a tear. Can't you even show some emotion at your own father's funeral,' he'd said. 'You're an orphan now you know. Doesn't that hurt?'

It was true, Susan hadn't cried at the funeral. She had felt numb. Graham had tactfully led Aidan away before the other mourners heard him. She watched him put his arm around his son's shoulders and talk to him in a low, comforting voice. She would have liked to have done that. She understood how fond Aidan had been of his grandparents. He had been very upset when his grandmother died, and now, so soon afterwards to lose his grandfather. No wonder he was angry, and he was taking his grief out on her. Why couldn't she explain to him how hard it was for her to let go, to cry and grieve openly? But then she'd have to explain what lay behind her coldness, and she didn't want to do that. It would feel like betrayal. Aidan had loved his grandparents. He wouldn't recognise the self-destructive woman that she knew was her mother, or the feckless, womaniser that was her father. He wouldn't believe her, and if he did what would that achieve? She would be destroying his memories of childhood forever.

CHAPTER 5

Judy chopped at the basil until it was fine then tipped it into the salad dressing she was preparing for their evening meal. She selected a couple of ripe tomatoes from the dish on the table and expertly sliced them, the sharp knife flashing rhythmically as the fleshy red fruit fell in perfect rounds on the chopping board, then she arranged them on top of the salad. Judy loved cooking and everything to do with food; she made jams and preserves, cooked cakes and made her own bread. She was never happier than when she was in the kitchen. As she often told her students, and always at the start of each school year, 'The kitchen is the heart of a house. It needs to work smoothly and efficiently. It is where you can prepare wonderful food for the people you love.'

She knew the students sniggered at this but that was what she believed. Her own kitchen was a large, airy, square room where she could prepare her family's meals and talk to them at the same time. There was a round wooden table where they ate together each evening, where the children did homework, school projects, painted, made Christmas cards, where she sewed on missing buttons, planned their holidays, wrapped presents, turned up hems or, like now, simply prepared the evening meal.

Judy was a domestic science teacher at a comprehensive school in Putney. Home Economics they called it now. Even as a child she'd always loved food and its preparation. But the real advantage of Judy's job was the long school holidays. She and Aidan had always known they would have a family and, from the moment she'd met Aidan's mother, she realised that she wouldn't be able to rely on the elegant Susan to look after any children during school holidays. Susan was a career woman, through and through and her own mother, being much older and living three hundred miles away, could only be relied upon in an emergency. So she and Aidan knew from the start that they would have to manage more or less, on their own.

Judy loved her job but lately she felt she was spending more time struggling to keep control than actually teaching anything. There was one class who were particularly disruptive, especially the boys. She had spoken to the Head about the problems they caused and suggested that maybe they shouldn't be doing Home Economics but the headmaster—who liked to think of himself as progressive—wouldn't consider it. He believed that in the 21st century all children should learn Home Economics, not just the girls. She tried to tell him that the girls, in trying to gain the approbation of the boys, were equally disruptive, but he wasn't listening. The situation was getting intolerable, and after an afternoon with that particular class she would arrive home, exhausted and frustrated. She sipped her tea and looked out of the window, trying to empty her mind of the latest altercation she'd had with Darren Brown, the biggest and loudest of the boys. He was the ring-leader, she knew. If only there was some way of getting rid of him then she was sure that the others would settle down. But nothing worked. Detention, trips to the Headmaster, letters to his parents, they only seemed to raise his standing with the rest of the class. To make it worse he was a good-looking kid and the girls all vied with each other for his attention. Well, he'd be moving to another class at the end of the year and then he'd become someone else's problem.

Their flat, which was actually the top floor of a converted two-storey Edwardian house, was close to the Windmill Nature Trail. From the kitchen window she had a view of a small green area with an enormous oak tree in the centre. Today the late afternoon sun was shining through its branches, dappling the ground beneath it and casting blue shadows over the front of the house. They'd been so happy when they bought the flat. It had been wonderful to have a place of their own. Although the flat was small, the high ceilings gave an illusion of space, and it had been discretely modernised, with some of the rooms retaining their original mouldings on the ceilings. At first it had been ideal. Everything was within walking distance: the tube station, the shops, the pubs, even her school was only a short cycle ride away. But by now of course they had three growing children, and what had seemed luxuriously roomy for two of them, had started to feel crowded and often stifling. She longed for somewhere where the boys could just walk out into the garden to play, where they could have the dog they kept asking for each Christmas, where they could make as much noise as they wanted without disturbing the neighbours below them, where they could each have a room of their own, but she knew they could never afford it—not in London, anyway. Despite the fact that they were both working, their mortgage was already at the maximum, and London prices just kept going up and up. There was no way they could afford to buy a house in the same area.

She heard her husband's key in the lock and, before he could make it into the kitchen, a small figure had dashed through the door and hurled himself at his father.

'Daddy, come on. You said we could go to the Common when you got home. C'me on.'

'Okay Zak, just give me a minute. I've only just got in,' his father replied, lifting up his small son and swinging him round. 'God, you're getting heavy.'

'Why don't you go and get your boots on, Zak and then round up the others. By that time Daddy will have changed. Okay?' Judy said.

The boy didn't bother to reply. He rushed off, shouting for his brothers to come and join him.

Aidan put down his briefcase and bent over to kiss his wife. 'Had a good day?' he asked.

'Not really.'

'Not the dreaded Darren again?'

'I'm afraid so. And you?'

'I popped into Mum and Dad's today.'

'Really. I didn't know you were out that way.'

'Well, I wasn't supposed to be. I had a meeting in Windsor, and it's not much of a detour to call in at Maidenhead on the way, you know.'

'Are you worried about them or something? You only saw them last week,' his wife asked, feeling puzzled that he should complicate what was already a tedious journey.

'Not really. Oh, I suppose I am, just a bit, especially after the burglary. They're getting on now, and that house is so big and isolated. I just wish they lived a bit closer, then we could pop round whenever we felt like it. They'd see more of the kids too.'

His wife stifled a smile. She got up and switched on the oven. 'I'm not sure your mother would welcome us popping in whenever we felt like it. Nor treating her like she has one foot in the grave.'

She could just imagine Susan's face if she were to overhear their conversation. To say that Judy liked her mother-in-law was a stretch of the imagination; they moved around each other like combatants in an uneasy truce.

'You're probably right,' he admitted. 'But I think she may be considering it now, after the burglary. I caught her clearing out the loft today.'

'That doesn't mean anything. Anyway I doubt if she'd want to move out to Wimbledon. So don't get your hopes up. What's your dad got to say about it all, anyway?'

'Dad? Well, you know Dad. He doesn't say much.'

While Aidan went into the bedroom to change out of his business suit, Judy put the fish pie in the oven and set the timer. Everything was ready. All she had to do was lay the table and that could wait until they got back from the park. She leaned her head on the back of the armchair and closed her eyes for a moment. Some stray wisps of blonde hair that had escaped from the headband she always wore when cooking, curled around her ear.

Judy had just celebrated her thirty-eighth birthday and she felt old. She and Aidan had met while they were both at university. They'd lived together for a while, but hadn't considered marriage until the day Judy had come home and announced that she was pregnant.

Aidan had been delighted. 'Well, we'd better get married then,' he'd proposed in his distinctly matter-of-fact way.

By the time Ben was born Judy was almost thirty, and the other two boys followed in close succession. It was having three lively sons that had kept Judy fit. Her skin was taut and clear, the only wrinkles a few laughter lines around her eyes, and she was still as trim as when Aidan first met her, without the need to resort to diets, liposuction or the gym, and those persistent grey hairs were dealt with by regular visits to her hairdresser. She was happy. Well so she told everyone. The truth was that there were times when she felt that life was running away from her. The boys were growing up so quickly and it made her feel old. Maybe she should have another baby. She knew Aidan was keen to have a daughter and if they didn't do something soon she would be too old.

'We're off. Back in about an hour.'

'Okay. What about a kiss then boys?'

Judy got up to receive three dutiful pecks on the cheek as the excited boys made a detour past her on their way to the front door. She listened as the door slammed behind them. She could hear them clattering down the stairs and the rhythmic thud of the football as Ben bounced it off the wall as he ran. If she moved to the window she would be able to see their small figures hurrying towards the Common, Jason holding tightly to his father's hand and the other two racing ahead, passing the football between them. Ben was wearing his Arsenal strip today, and Zak the royal blue and white colours of Chelsea. But this evening she didn't bother to get up to spy on her family, and was content to enjoy this brief respite from their boisterousness. No, how could she even contemplate another child unless they moved somewhere bigger. That's what

Aidan should be worrying about, finding them a larger house, not pestering his parents to move somewhere smaller.

CHAPTER 6

Aidan sat on a wooden bench and watched his sons argue about how they were going to play. In a few minutes they would be shouting for him to join them but until then he was content to sit, enjoy the cool breeze that always seemed to blow across the Common and smoke an illicit cigarette. He'd told Judy he would stop smoking, and in fact he virtually had stopped. He didn't smoke at home; it wasn't allowed any more at work nor could he smoke on the train and she hated him smoking in the car. So this was one of the few remaining opportunities open to him, but he knew Judy would be angry if she found out. She would say it was a bad example to set the children. He lit the Marlboro and inhaled deeply.

His mother hadn't said much to him that afternoon. He wondered if she were really considering a move. You could never tell with her. She kept things close to her chest, never confided in anybody as far as he knew. It was as though you couldn't reach the real Susan. She was encased in glass, the perfect wife, mother and business woman, immaculate, elegant, poised, polite but not real and certainly not warm. He loved his mother, but doubted that she felt the same about him. He wondered if there was anyone she did love. He couldn't even remember seeing her show any affection to his father, apart from a perfunctory kiss on the cheek occasionally.

Although he knew how distant his mother could be, he'd still been shocked to see how unemotional she'd been at his grandfather's funeral. Her own father and she hadn't shed a single tear. He couldn't believe she didn't feel anything for her father, but she refused to show it. Was it more important to keep it all bottled up inside her? Everything tightly under control? Was no-one allowed to see the elegant Susan cry, even at her own father's funeral?

Aidan had been very upset when his grandparents died. As a child, he had spent many happy hours with them, especially in the summer holidays when his parents were both working. It was his grandfather who'd taught him to ride a bike, one wet day just after his seventh birthday. The weather had been so awful that summer that it was impossible to play outside, and Aidan was bored. On one particularly miserable day, when the rain had been coming down in sheets for hours, he was sitting at the window of his grandparents' living room, watching the raindrops sliding down the glass, when he heard his grandfather calling him.

'Come on, my lad. You can't sit there moping all day. Let's go out and get some fresh air,' he called.

His grandfather was waiting for him in the hallway, wearing his old gardening coat and a felt hat. He held a battered fishing umbrella in his hand.

'Right then youngster, get your raincoat on and here, take this old cap of mine. It'll keep those curls of yours dry,' he said. 'Today you're going to learn to ride a bike.'

'A bike, Granddad? But I don't have a bike.'

'No, but I do. It'll be just the job for you,' he said and ushered Aidan out of the house and along the path that led to the garden shed.

His grandfather's shed was packed with gardening tools. Spades and forks hung from makeshift hooks, a rusty hoe leaned arrogantly in the corner, while dozens of flowerpots of assorted sizes were stacked on most of the available floor space. There were cartons of fertiliser propped up against compost accelerator and insecticides, open packets of seeds with their contents spilling across the shelves, gardening magazines, damp and mouldy with age, piled on the top shelf. At first glance Aidan couldn't see any bicycle. Then he spotted a wheel sticking out from underneath a stack of old garden cushions with half a dozen strings of onions laid carefully on top of them.

'Is that it Granddad?' he asked, feeling excited at the prospect of riding his first bike.

'It is, lad. It's a good bike, a Raleigh. Hardly been used. It's not one of those BMXs of course, but it'll do for you to learn on,' his grandfather said, wiping the dust off it.

He carefully wheeled the bicycle out into the garden. 'Yes, just about the right size for you, I'd say.'

It was perfect. The leather saddle had to be adjusted a little, so that he could reach the pedals, and his grandfather had to pump up the tyres, but otherwise it might have been bought for him.

'Oh Granddad, it's brill,' he said, running his small fingers along the pristine paintwork.

'Good, now let's see how it goes. You put your leg over the crossbar and I'll hold the bike steady.'

His grandfather took hold of the seat in one hand and the handlebars in the other, while the excited boy climbed on. After a few tentative turns up and down the driveway, they were off down the lane. His grandfather, with the umbrella held aloft in one hand and guiding the back of the bike with the other, ran alongside him, up and down the quiet lane outside his grandparents' house. Aidan couldn't remember if the rain had continued or if it had stopped, all he remembered was that magical moment when he realised that his grandfather was no longer running beside him. He had let go of the bicycle and Aidan was on his own, pedalling unaided, solo. What a wonderful moment. At first he'd wobbled alarmingly then he had cycled back to the house looking for his grandmother.

'Granny, Granny. Look. I'm cycling. This is just brill,' he shouted as he spotted her in the doorway. But his grandmother looked annoyed, and went in and shut the door with a bang. 'What's the matter with Granny? Is she cross with me? I want her to see me cycling, Granddad.'

'Don't worry Aidan, it's nothing to do with you. It's me she's annoyed with. I should have told her what we were going to do. She doesn't like surprises you know,' his grandfather explained.

He had loved that bike. Whenever he went to stay with his grandparents he would spend hours exploring the quiet Buckinghamshire lanes, a bottle of water and some of his grandmother's special paste sandwiches in his saddle bag.

Living here in Wimbledon, this was a simple pleasure his own boys couldn't experience. There was far too much traffic and he knew Judy would never allow it. He could see his sons hunkered down on the ground, Jason sitting on the ball, listening intently to his older brothers.

As a teenager he'd gone every Saturday afternoon to his grandfather's house to watch the football. His grandfather was a Nottingham Forest supporter, but Aidan had never held that against him, even though he was less than complementary about Aidan's team, Leeds United. 'Time they got some new players. Or got rid of that manager. He's a waste of space,' he repeated every time they came on the television. He would look sideways at Aidan to see if he would rise to the bait, but Aidan was used to his tactics and never replied. He often wondered at his grandfather's passion for football. From what his mother had told him, his grandfather, a rather bookish man, had not been much of a sportsman in his youth, with neither the inclination to play nor be a spectator.

Aidan's father, on the other hand, was not at all interested in football and although he never complained when Aidan wanted to watch a particular match on the television, it was never as much fun as watching it with his grandfather. One day Aidan asked his father why he didn't like football.

'It's not that I don't like football Aidan. It's just that I've got too much to worry about already,' was his reply. 'Look at your Granddad and his neighbour Harry, all they do is worry about what's happening to their teams. Are they selling this player, or buying that one, is he worth the transfer fee, should they sack the manager, who's been injured, will they be relegated, where did they get that referee from? They're endless, the problems that you accumulate when you support a football team.' His father had laughed his deep throaty laugh and added, 'I don't need all those problems, Aidan. I'll stick to my golf.'

Over the years Aidan's loyalty had held firm, He'd supported his team through the good years and the lean. Even now, with the twin responsibilities of fatherhood and work, he could still find the time to drive up to Elland Road for a particularly important match, and he always bought tickets for the London games. Sometimes he thought Judy resented the time and money he spent on his hobby, but she'd never actually said anything. It was after all, he reasoned to himself, something he could share with their sons. The boys loved the game, although he'd been unable to convince them that Leeds United was worth their support. All their schoolmates were mad on football and, of course, the older two boys were London supporters like them, whilst Jason, still a bit of a baby at six, joined in whatever was going.

A whoop from his sons dragged him out of the past. He took one last drag on his cigarette and stubbed it out on the sole of his shoe—cowboy style—just as the boys came rushing up to him.

'Come on Dad. You're on my side, 'gainst Zak and Ben.'

They always put Jason with him, because Jason was the smallest, but despite that Ben still liked to discuss other possibilities although the outcome was inevitably the same. Maybe he should talk to Judy about having another baby so they could even the teams up, then he could be the referee instead of charging up and down the pitch. He wondered what she'd say to that.

CHAPTER 7

The gentle motion of the early morning train made Susan relax. She felt herself drifting off into the past. That was where the answer lay, she was sure—in her past. There were memories of those days, but she had buried them a long time ago. Now was the time for them to resurface.

She had loved her father once, in that semi-hero-worshipping way that most little girls did. She remembered walking along the promenade, holding his hand, looking up into his thin, handsome face, his dark, curly hair falling across his forehead as he bent to tell her a special secret, his blue eyes sparkling with amusement. She remembered him too, not many years later, slamming the door and shouting abuse as he stormed out of the house, foul words spilling from his lips and her mother crying, her body shaking with loud ugly sobs.

'Excuse me. Is anyone sitting there?' a voice interrupted her reverie.

She sat up abruptly and said, 'No, help yourself.'

She pulled out her iPhone and checked her emails. It was time she concentrated on work, instead of dwelling in the past. After all, if her parents hadn't wanted to confide in her, what could she do about it now?

*

As she went into her office, Susan found her thoughts returning again to the photograph of the baby, which now lay tucked in a pocket of the bag that contained her laptop. The more she thought about it, the more she became convinced that the child was her father's. There was no other explanation. So what had happened to the boy? She needed to find out.

'Ah, Susan. There you are. I've just had a call from Beavis and Son, their HR chap can't make it today. Give him a ring, will you, and make another appointment. We don't want to lose this one do we. Could be quite a lot of work there, you know.' Susan's boss was standing in the doorway, a half empty coffee cup in his hand.

'Okay, John. Did he say why?'

'Something about car trouble, I think. Still sounds keen to meet you though,' he reassured her. He lingered by her desk, hoping to prolong the conversation, but Susan turned away and opened the file on her desk.

She had already done some preparation for the meeting by researching the company's background. Beavis and Son were a long established company that dated back to the early nineteenth century. The original factory had been located in High Wycombe, the heart of the furniture industry, and their only product had been beautifully hand-crafted beech wood chairs. Both Mr Beavis and his son had long since died, and now the company was part of an international conglomerate. They still produced the much prized chairs, but had also expanded the range to include rustic garden furniture, sofas and easy chairs. She had read with interest that the company had a new chairman who was seeking to diversify still further. It was, in fact, this chairman who was the impetus behind the new interest in management training. Susan had made an attempt to anticipate their requirements from the brief information she'd received from their Human Resources manager. She'd already prepared an outline proposal for a series of short courses on a number of personnel issues: interviewing, anger management, assertiveness and discipline techniques. She smiled as she looked at the last one. Graham always kidded her about that one, suggesting that if she wore her black boots and leather jacket she might get better results. Well it was all hypothetical until she had the chance to discuss it with Jim Brady, Beavis's HR manager. She put the file into her pending tray, and opened up her computer.

'Anne, how would you go about finding a missing person on the internet?' she asked her assistant, who had just come in, carrying the morning's post.

'A missing person. Well, you could try Google I suppose, and see what comes up.' Anne hovered near Susan's desk, looking over her shoulder at the screen.

'Actually, it's not really a missing person, just someone I've lost touch with,' Susan explained, acutely aware of Anne's curiosity and suddenly feeling very defensive.

'Oh well, in that case, I suppose Facebook is the best, but there's also a web site called Missing You and there's one for getting in touch with old school friends. I know that one works because my sister contacted a girl she was at school with once.' Susan could feel Anne's enthusiasm growing by the minute. 'Are you on Facebook?' Anne asked her.

Susan had heard of the site—it was impossible not to, as it seemed to be in the news almost daily—but she'd never felt the inclination to join. The thought of sharing her life with strangers didn't appeal to her. 'Isn't that for kids?' she asked.

'Yes, well maybe it was at first, but now everyone's on there. Even my mum has a Facebook page. She says it's the only way she can find out what my youngest brother is up to. I could give you a hand if you like,' Anne suggested, putting the post in Susan's in-tray.

'No. Thanks anyway. I'll give you a shout if I get stuck.' The last thing Susan wanted was Anne telling the whole office that she was looking for an illegitimate half-brother.

Sure enough Google produced nearly twenty million entries pertaining to missing persons. What on earth could she do with all those? She picked one web site from the list on the screen, Family Finder. She would start with that one. Within a few key strokes she managed to transfer to some American-based, world-wide search company that wanted to charge her a fortune to enrol. Maybe she was not going about this the right way. After all what did she know about this child? Only that he existed. She typed in 'register of births'. That was better, only two million sites to investigate there. This was it, the General Register Office. Now she had two options: find the information she needed on-line or find a telephone number and speak to someone. After twenty minutes of selecting various options, scrolling, and printing, she had what she needed to get started, the telephone number of the Contact Centre. However, printed alongside it was the caution that nobody would provide her with any information on missing persons until they knew why it was required. She stared at the words on the screen. Why was it required? What exactly did she want it for after all these years? Unfinished business? The need to know if he was still alive? Duty to her father? Guilt? She had no answers, just the feeling that this was something she had to do before it was too late.

Susan rang the number, and after negotiating with the ubiquitous automated answering service found herself speaking to a woman in the registry office who, sadly, was not very eager to help her.

'Yes, I realise it is a simple thing to order a certificate on-line, but I don't have very much information to go on,' Susan explained. 'Can't I come and speak to someone in person? I'm trying to trace a relative. No, I have no idea where he lives. All I have is his date of birth and his Christian name. Yes, I do realise it's not much to go on. No, I'm not even sure of his surname.' She continued to listen to the woman explain about current procedures, and then said, 'Yes, well maybe you're right. Very well. Thank you for your help.'

She put the phone down with a bang. What a stupid system. She knew she'd never find him like that. Perhaps the woman was right and she should find a private detective. After all they would know exactly where to start and how to negotiate this mire of information.

'Any luck?' Anne asked, coming into her office carrying two cups of Starbuck's coffee.

'No, nothing,' Susan said, closing her laptop and taking the coffee from her secretary's outstretched hand.

'Are you sure you don't want me to have a go? It can't be that difficult.'

'No thanks. I'll have another try later.'

'Well just shout if you need any help.'

'I will, thanks.'

She opened the proposal she'd been working on and skimmed through it. There was no more she could do until she had clearer information about the company's objectives. She put the file back in her drawer, and was about to start working on some new handouts for a leadership course for trainee managers, when she realised that she wouldn't be able to do anything productive until she'd discovered the whereabouts of her half-brother. She grabbed her coat and her bag and left the office, only stopping to put her head around Anne's door to say she wouldn't be long.

She knew where to go. There was a small bureau-fax office in one of the streets that she walked along every morning on her way from the underground station. Surely they could help her.

It took her barely ten minutes to get there and, to her delight, the office was almost empty except for a man—a student by the look of the pile of books on the floor beside him—using one of the computers. The bureau-fax assistant, a young man wearing jeans and an orange tee-shirt with the company's logo emblazoned on the front, sat behind the counter, working at another computer. He looked up at her and asked, 'Can I help you?'

'I don't know,' she said. 'I hope so.' She suddenly felt embarrassed. How could she admit to this young man that she felt overwhelmed by the internet, that she needed someone younger and with more agile fingers to find what she required. He would wonder why she didn't ask her son, or a friend, why she preferred to ask a complete stranger to help her find her half-brother.

'Well?' he asked, and she realised she'd been standing there for some minutes without saying anything. Now he would definitely think she was strange.

'Ah. It's just that I want to find out about someone, and everyone says it's easy to find people on the internet but I don't seem able to do it. Can you help me?'

There, she'd said it. But, instead of treating her as if she were an imbecile, the young man smiled pleasantly and said, 'We can have a try. It depends how much info you have on this person. A woman is it?'

Oh my God. He thought her husband was having an affair, and she was trying to trace the other woman. She wanted to laugh. The thought of Graham having an affair was absurd. That was one of the reasons she'd married him, because he was so loyal that she could never imagine him being unfaithful to her. She'd wanted a man as different from her father as was possible.

'A man actually, a relative in fact,' she said.

He pulled a chrome and plastic seat out from behind the desk and offered it to her. 'Why don't you sit down and tell me exactly what you know about this man and what you want to find out.'

Susan took a deep breath and began to tell him all she knew about her half-brother. As she did so, he tapped away at the keyboard, occasionally interrupting her for clarification or asking a question.

'Well, Miss ...'

'Mrs Masters,' she said. 'Susan Masters.'

'Well, Susan, you haven't given me a lot to go on. Are you sure you haven't got a surname or a place of birth?'

'I'm afraid it's all a bit speculative. It is possible the child was registered in my father's name. That was Thomas. It's also possible that the baby was born in Taunton, where we were living at the time, but I really don't know,' Susan explained. 'Look I'm sorry if I'm wasting your time.'

'No, no. I've found people with less,' he replied, scrolling quickly down the computer screen. 'Look, here's something. May 1962, you said?'

'Yes, the 16th. Have you found him?' Susan asked, her stomach tightening in anticipation.

'There's a Michael David Wright Thomas born on that date in Exeter Maternity Home, to an Anthea Wright Thomas. The father's name's not recorded. Could that be him?'

'My father's name was David,' she said absent-mindedly, as she tried to take it all in. So Anthea had taken Susan's father's surname. Did Susan's mother know about that? If their relationship was that serious why didn't her father leave her mother and marry Anthea?

'Thank you. Thank you very much,' she said, opening her bag to pay him.

'Is that all you want to know? Don't you want to know if he's still alive or where's he's living?'

She looked at him in surprise. 'Can you tell me all that?'

'Well I can try. Let's see if he's still alive first, although I don't see why he shouldn't be, how old is he, forty-eight? Look why don't you help yourself to some coffee from the machine, while I see what else I can find out.' He pointed to a jug of Cona coffee, stewing on a hotplate. It didn't look very appetising, but she took a plastic cup and poured herself some.

'No sign of his name in the Register of Deaths, although that doesn't mean that he hasn't died abroad of course. But let's assume that he's alive. The parents weren't married, you said. It could mean that the mother gave him up for adoption. Is that a possibility?'

If the reason for her parents' unhappiness and their constant rowing had been the birth of that child, then somehow she didn't think that the child had been adopted. Was that the reason her mother was so bitter? Had her father remained in contact with both Anthea and their son all those years? Did her father have two families?

'No, I don't think so,' she said. 'Something my mother said years ago, makes me think Anthea kept the baby.'

'Okay. Well, let's see if Michael David is married.'

Once again the computer screen flashed and changed its format. This seemed to take longer, but at last he said, 'No sign of this Michael David Wright Thomas getting married.'

She waited while he clicked on page after page but, in the end, the young man looked up and said, 'Sorry that's about all I can find for you. It's possible he's moved abroad.'

'So you can't find anything else?' she asked, biting back the disappointment.

'Not as much as you'd like, but you do know his full name and the name of his mother, now. Do you want me to try to find his mother?'

'She might not be still alive,' she said, biting back her disappointment.

'Hang on. Let's find her death certificate then.'

Susan sipped her bitter coffee and studied the dingy office. Posters listing their rates covered the back wall, where two wall clocks showed the local time, one in London and one in New York. A bank of computers lined one of the side walls. The student was gathering up his books, the screen of his computer now blank. He was leaving. She watched him lay some money on the desk and, with a brief nod in her direction and a grunt for the young man, he left.

'I've found her. You're right. She died in 2008, in Leicester. Cancer. Here, I'll print out a copy for you. You might know the name of the informant.'

So they were all dead now. Her parents and Anthea. The three protagonists who had played out their drama night after night during her childhood. There was just Michael left to find.

'Thank you for your help. I can't tell you how much I appreciate it,' she said, feeling quite emotional as she collected up the photocopies he had printed for her and paid him what she owed.

'No problem. If you think of anything else you need to look up, just call in. This is a good time of day. I'm never very busy just before lunchtime.'

As she retraced her steps along the street, she pulled the photograph of Michael out of her bag and studied it. She wasn't looking for a baby now. She was looking for a man, a middle-aged man who was out there somewhere, completely unaware that he had a sister who wanted to meet him. Finding her half-brother had suddenly become important to her. She wanted to know what he was like. What work did he do? If he was not married, was he living with someone? Did he have any children? Did he like art or music? Did he play sport? Did he look like her or her father? So many questions and none of them could be answered until she found him. The urgency transferred itself to her step and she found herself striding purposefully back towards her office.

*

Anne was putting a pile of new brochures on her desk, when she got back. 'John said to give you some of these. They've just arrived from the printers,' she said.

'Okay. I'll look at them later.'

'By the way, I'm not in tomorrow,' Anne added. 'Did John tell you?'

Susan looked at her and frowned. 'No, he didn't. Shouldn't you have mentioned it to me first?'

'Sorry. It's my Amy. She has an interview at Reading University, and I'm going along with her. You know, a bit of moral support and all that. I hope it's not inconvenient.'

'No, as it turns out I can manage without you tomorrow. But next time, speak to me first.'

She saw Anne shrug, probably thinking she was being a bit officious, and she was but it annoyed her when Anne went straight to John instead of discussing things with her. It had happened before.

While everyone in the office went to lunch, Susan remained behind. She bought herself a ham roll from the vending machine and made some instant coffee. She sat at her desk and sipped the tasteless coffee while she waited for her emails to appear on the screen, then skimmed down the list, her finger hitting the delete button as she went. She spotted one email with a sizeable attachment from Frost and French; she was hoping to run a number of team building courses for this company early next year. She read it quickly and then pressed the print key. There was also an email from her boss. Typical. Why on earth couldn't he just stick a note on her desk, like any normal person? He only worked in the office next door, after all.

Sue. Jim Brady is going on holiday on Friday. He wants to leave the meeting until he gets back. Says to phone him in two weeks. John

A two week delay at least, maybe even three. Well she had better reorganise her work schedule in that case. She opened up her electronic diary. The whole of the following week had been allocated to working on the post-meeting changes—the client always wanted to make some changes, no matter how carefully she'd planned it. The week after that, she was running a Presentation Skills course in Staines. It was a repeat course, the third of six that had been booked, so she had very little preparation to do for it. There didn't seem to be anything that could be moved forward a week. September was always a slow month because companies took a while to recover from the summer holidays. Maybe she should take this opportunity to have a few days' leave. She could use the time to make a determined effort to find Michael.

'Ah, Susan. You're back early I see.' John and Anne came in together. 'Have a nice lunch?' he asked. His hand slid nervously round his collar, pulling at it as if it were too tight.

'Yes, thanks,' Susan replied, pushing the remains of her ham roll into the desk drawer. 'And you?'

'Oh, yes. Went to that little pub round the corner, the Black something or other. Just for a change, you know. Bumped into Anne there. Quite a coincidence, eh?' He looked at Anne for corroboration. 'They do a nice Cornish pasty, I must say, and the John Smith's is first class,' he babbled on.

Anne murmured something as she squeezed past him to go to her desk.

'The Black Swan?' Susan looked down so he wouldn't see her smile. She'd suspected that something was going on between the two of them for some time.

'Yes, that's it. Nice little place, homely. Well did you get my message?' His embarrassment now over, John resumed his role as her manager.

Anne, meanwhile, was rifling through the filing cabinet, looking for non-existent papers.

'Yes, I did. The thing is John, now that this meeting has been postponed I have very little scheduled for next week,' she replied. Her boss looked up from examining the forward planning schedule that hung behind her desk. 'So I think I'll take a week's leave,' she continued before he had a chance to interrupt her and delegate some of his own work.

'Oh. Okay, if you're sure there's nothing pressing.'

Nothing more pressing than tracking down my half-brother, she thought but had no intention of telling him that. This was her chance. She would spend the week trying to find Michael. Where this would lead her and what she would do if she succeeded, she had no idea. One step at a time, she told herself. One step at a time.

CHAPTER 8

Graham was out with the dog when she got home. Susan went straight to her office and sat at her desk looking out at the river. She hated to start something and not finish it, and now she was becoming obsessed with the thought that this man was out there somewhere and she couldn't find him. She pulled out her parents' old box again and began searching through the more recent correspondence. Susan's mother had been very fond of her mother-in-law and there were a number of letters from her, all in a beautiful copperplate script on blue vellum paper. She picked up one and started to read it:

15th December 1961

Dear Mary

I am feeling much better these days. My cough has almost disappeared and I expect I shall go back to work soon. It's been five weeks now. I'm so worried that if I don't go back soon they will tell me not to bother.

Caitlin is coming over to stay next week. She's bringing little Betty with her too. They'll stay until after Christmas I hope, so that will be great company for me. I'm looking forward to seeing them, especially Betty; she must have grown a lot since last time they were here. She's almost twelve now. I'm busy knitting her a cardigan for school. I hope I have got the size right.

How are you and Davy and my lovely Susie? It's ages since I've seen any of you. I hope everything is all right. You didn't answer my last letter and you are usually such a good letter writer. Please write back and let me know how you are. If you have any problems you know I will help in any way I can.

Give Susie a big kiss from me,
Your loving mum-in-law
Margaret

Of course, why hadn't she thought of it before; her father's younger sister, her aunt Caitlin, was still alive. She had come to the funeral. She remembered talking to her and asking her about her daughter, Susan's cousin Betty. What had she said? Something about Betty having married a West Indian and living in Leicester. Surely one of them would be able to tell her something about Michael. Frantically she began searching through the remaining papers, looking for an address or telephone number. There had to be something or Graham would never have been able to contact them about her father's death.

Graham. She stopped searching. All she had to do was ask Graham. He would have the address. He never threw anything away and his memory was excellent. She didn't move. For a reason that she couldn't quite explain to herself, she didn't want to include Graham in this search. She didn't want to tell him about Michael. It was a secret. Her mother's secret. It would be like betraying her mother, a woman who had spent her whole life guarding this information from the world, and especially from her family. She knew now why they'd never visited her aunts and uncles, why she hadn't got to grow up with any of her cousins. When she'd given her mother the news that she and Graham were to be married, her mother had even then declined to invite any of the family.

'They won't be interested in coming all this way for a wedding. Besides you don't know any of them. It would just be a waste of money. You invite your own friends. Lots of young people, that's what you want,' her mother had said, her mouth set in a tight line that brooked no argument.

Susan hadn't argued with her. In fact she'd been secretly relieved. It was true, she couldn't remember any of her mother's family. The last time she'd seen them was just before her twelfth birthday and she didn't want her wedding day to be the occasion for getting to know them again. So she said nothing. She didn't even talk to Graham about it. When they sat together one evening in the local pub, over a pint of Old Speckled Hen and a half of Watney's bitter, with the guest list on the table between them, he asked how many of her relatives would be coming.

'Just my Mum and Dad,' she replied.

He made no comment, just wrote their names down on the list in his immaculate script. That was one of the things that had endeared him to her. He never probed into her life. If she told him anything about her past he seemed genuinely interested, but never pressed for more details. More from the habit of keeping things locked inside herself than from any intention to deceive him she had never talked about her childhood nor her parent's marital problems. So how could she tell Graham about Michael now? How could she tell him about her father's infidelity? And her mother's shame? It was still too hard to speak about her parents and their marriage, to Graham, to anyone. She couldn't put her feelings about those days into words; they just dried in her mouth.

She put the letter back in the box and took out another. This was also from her grandmother, but it was addressed to her father and dated June 1962. She must have written it not long after Michael was born.

My dear David,

I was so upset to receive your last letter. I cried all night. Oh, Davy, I don't know what's come over you. How can you talk about leaving your lovely wife and your beautiful daughter for a woman you have only known a few months. I know you think you're in love, but it will be like all the others, just infatuation. You have always let your heart rule your head, Davy, and that was all right when you were single, but you're a married man now, with responsibilities. You can't just throw everything away for this woman, no matter how much you think you love her. And why do you say that you still love Mary? If you loved her you wouldn't want to hurt her like this.

Oh Davy, you know how much I care for you. You were my first born and you will always be very special to me. You were all that kept me going when your father walked out on us, and surely you can remember how awful that was. Remember how you missed your father, and he was never the loving father to you that you have been to Susie. She will be devastated if you leave. I know you say that you will still see her, that you are not abandoning your daughter, but it won't work out like that. If you go off with this woman you will probably have other children, and then what? You won't be able to support two families, and in the end you will have to choose between them.

Please don't break my heart by rushing into something I'm sure you're going to regret, Davy. For Susie's sake, for Mary's sake, give your marriage another chance, I beg you.

Your loving mother xx

So her father had considered leaving them. She wondered why he had stayed in the end. It certainly wasn't because things improved between her parents, anything but. She could vividly recall their bitter fights, night after night, week in, week out. Maybe her grandmother would have given him different advice if she'd known how it was going to turn out, how her mother would change into a jealous harridan that ranted and raved at him all night long, how it hurt Susie to be caught in the middle of their personal war, watching them tear each other apart, how she had to distance herself from both of them and shut down her feelings, how she grew up unable to confide in her mother like other girls and unable to respond to her hugs and kisses. Would her grandmother have told him to go if she had known that by staying he would make both the women he loved unhappy because he was so unhappy himself?

Her parents had been caught in a macabre dance that neither had the strength to stop. Susan neither condemned her father nor consoled her mother. She remained impartial. She stopped crying herself to sleep and she put her head under the bedcovers, pressed her beloved transistor radio to her ear and switched on Radio Luxembourg to cut out the sound of their voices. She held her emotions deep inside herself. She squeezed them tighter and tighter until they shrivelled within her. She wasn't going to choose between her parents, so she chose neither. She gave up her old habit of cuddling up beside her father on the sofa and asking him to read to her. She no longer went for walks with him down the lanes, looking for mushrooms, nor helped him wash his car on Saturday mornings. She stopped sitting with her mother each evening to listen to the Archers, and refused to help her with the baking. She told them she had too much studying to do. She stayed in her room and kept to herself.

When she went to Bristol University her parents had a telephone installed so that Susan could call and let them know how she was progressing. Dutifully Susan phoned, but their talks were brief. She didn't want to extend the conversation to the point where her mother began to tell her, once again, how unhappy she was. She would listen to her room-mate Christine, chattering to her own mother for hours, casual chit chat about nothing in particular, laughing together, happy to be making contact. But Susan couldn't be like that with her mother. She could only go through the motions of being a dutiful daughter.

She picked up another letter. It was creased as if it had been screwed up in a ball, as if someone had been about to throw it away and then changed their mind. It was also from her grandmother.

Dear Mary,

I was so sorry to hear what happened. I've been lying awake all night, thinking of you and little Susie. I can't understand my son —and I told him so. Surely he realises what an impossible position he is in. I've told him he has to cut off all ties with this woman. If he continues like this it is only going to bring unhappiness to everyone who loves him, especially you, dear daughter-in-law— you must be heartbroken. I know how much you have always wanted a son and it's so sad that you were never able to have one. So it must hurt you terribly to know that Davy has a son with someone else. What can I say? It's not the poor child's fault that he was born and I understand why Davy feels he needs to do something for him. But that doesn't mean that he has to leave you and Susie. What does your mother say about it all? Is she going to come down and stay with you for a while?

If there is anything I can do to help, please write and tell me. As soon as I've got rid of this awful cough, I will come and visit you. Tell Susie I miss her and I'm looking forward to seeing her soon,

Fondest love,

Your mother-in-law,

Margaret

Susan folded the letter and placed it on the box with the others. There was another one, still screwed into a tight ball. She opened it and smoothed it out. It too was from her grandmother.

Dear Mary,

I know you're upset and angry, but I was so very sad to receive your last letter. Of course I won't mention your private life to anyone—as you rightly say, it's nobody's business but yours and Davy's. I'm sorry if you think I'm interfering and will not write about it again. But I think you're wrong to cut yourself off from your family. You should at least let your mother know what is happening. People need their families at times like this. You can't face it all on your own. If you won't let me help you, then please talk to your own mother. Remember you have nothing to be ashamed of. You have done nothing wrong. I know you're embarrassed and don't want people gossiping about you and Davy but your mother is your mother, after all. Surely you can confide in her?

I do hope Susie is all right. I know they are very close. I pray to God every night that he will help my son to see sense.

Your loving mother-in-law

Margaret

So her mother hadn't even told her own mother about the affair. How unhappy she must have been and how lonely. Susan looked at the dates on the last two letters, both July 1962. That was when her father was living with that woman and the baby.

She picked up another letter. This one was also addressed to her mother and it was from Caitlin.

August 1962

Dear Mary

I'm so sorry to tell you but Mum died yesterday. She had been ill for sometime but in the end it was very sudden. I don't think she told you—she never told me until the end—that she was suffering from lung cancer. She didn't want to worry us, she said. So like Mum. The funeral is next week at our local church. 2 o'clock on the Friday. I don't have an address for my brother, so I hope you can get in touch with him before then.

Your sister-in-law,

Caitlin

So that was why the photograph was never sent; her grandmother had died before her father could send it. How sad. Was that why her father had come back to live with them? Was he respecting his mother's wishes? She had to know more.

Susan went into her bedroom. Graham kept his wallet and his personal address book in the drawer of the bedside cabinet. She could hear someone downstairs in the kitchen and a dog barking excitedly. Graham must be back and feeding Jess. She opened the drawer and took out the address book. There was nothing under *T*, nor under *C*. Nothing at all. She carefully replaced it in the drawer, being sure to put it back exactly as it was. As she pushed the drawer shut, she felt the first pangs of guilt. Why was she behaving like this? Creeping about and going through her husband's things instead of asking him straight out?

'Hello, darling. Is that you?' Graham called up the stairs. 'Fancy a drink?'

Her husband was sitting on the sofa in front of the television when she entered the lounge. The dog lay at his feet, intently watching the flickering screen.

'I'm sure this dog is becoming a television addict. Look at her. You'd think she could understand what was happening. I thought we might just catch the end of the news,' he added, turning up the sound. A BBC news correspondent was standing in front of a crowd of emotional Chilean miners. 'They've got them all out,' Graham said. 'It's a miracle.'

'Thank God. Imagine being trapped down there for two months. I don't think I'd survive two days.'

He held out a glass of white wine to her. 'Thanks, I need this,' she said, taking a generous mouthful from the glass. 'This is nice. What is it?'

'It's one of those Spanish Alberiños that came from the Wine Society. Good, isn't it. Might have to buy some more,' he replied.

The picture on the television screen changed and was now showing close-ups of the families who'd come to greet their loved ones. So many emotions: relief, happiness, disbelief that they were once more above ground, euphoria and horror as they recounted their ordeal.

The dog stood up, stretched and walked over to her bed. 'See, now she's lost interest,' Graham said with a smile. 'It's the animal programmes she likes best, of course.' He turned the sound down and said, 'So, tell me, how was your day? You were pretty late tonight.'

'Yes, we've got a rush job on. A new client. Wants us to do some pilot Junior Management courses for them right away.'

'Mmn, sounds interesting.'

'Next week in fact. I was going to tell you later. I'll be away for a few days.' She hadn't planned to lie to him. It just happened and now, before she could stop herself the lies were tripping off her tongue, one after the other. 'It's a big company. There could be a lot of work there if the pilots go well.'

Why was she lying to him? Did she think Graham would tell her she was being ridiculous trying to find someone after all these years? Did she think he would resent her bringing someone else into their lives? She felt the blood rush to her face with embarrassment.

'Goodness, that wine has gone straight to my head,' she said, turning towards the television where the newly elected Chancellor of the Exchequer was now expounding on his proposed spending review, a smug look on his round face.

'Will those changes to child benefit affect Aidan?' her husband asked.

'I shouldn't think so. I don't think he's in the high-rate tax band. Depends whether they count Judy's salary as well.'

'Maybe we'll have to give them a hand,' her husband said, stroking Jess's head, lovingly. 'We can afford it. After all, there're only two of us now, and with all the work you're doing these days we're not exactly short of money. I'd like to help them out.'

'All right, if they need it,' she said. 'But you know Aidan, he can't bear to accept anything from us.'

'That new training sounds good. Where are you off to?' he asked.

'We're not sure yet, but they're talking about holding them in one of the Motorway Inns. I'll know more tomorrow. Anyway I won't be gone very long, just a couple of nights,' she continued, amazed that she was able to deceive her husband so readily.

'Are you doing it all on your own?'

'No. It's Paul Burton's area really. He'll be doing most of the training. I'll be there to make sure it goes all right. You know what John's like when he sees the pound signs flashing.'

Graham laughed. He knew her boss and his obsession with money. 'He should be well pleased then. That will be good for his bottom line,' Graham said.

'Yes. He wants me to negotiate the price,' she added.

'Let me know which days you'll be away and I'll organise an extra game of golf,' Graham said. 'Fills in the time a bit. I must admit, I miss you when you're off running those training courses. Still, not much longer until you retire. If you ever do, that is?' He looked at her, wistfully.

'Yes, and then you'll be moaning that I'm getting in the way of your golf, I suppose,' she said with a laugh. Retirement was something she didn't want to think about. She would soon be eligible for her pension, but she also had the option to stay on until she was sixty-five. Much as she loved her husband she wasn't ready to stay at home with him every day of the week, and she certainly wasn't ready to give up her career. 'Anyway, I should know tomorrow, for certain,' she added.

Her conscience was beginning to trouble her now. She wasn't in the habit of lying to Graham, but it was too late to retract what she'd said. Nevertheless, she knew she couldn't sit there in front of him any longer, not with those lies hanging between them like a heavy weight.

'Did you get anything for dinner?' she asked, getting up.

'I took a shepherd's pie out of the freezer this afternoon. It should have thawed out by now.'

'I'll go and put it in the oven then. We'll eat in half an hour. Okay?' she said, hurrying out before he could see the guilt that she knew was beginning to suffuse her face.

*

Later that evening as they sat eating at the small table in the corner of the living room, she decided to broach the subject of her father's funeral.

'Don't know why, but I was thinking a lot about my dad today,' she began.

'I thought you looked a bit distracted earlier,' her husband replied, looking up. 'Is it the anniversary or something?'

'No, nothing like that. I was just thinking about the funeral, and how wonderful you were, handling all the arrangements and everything. I don't think I ever really thanked you for all you did.' She reached across and took his hand.

'Oh, Susie, don't be silly. That was over five years ago. And anyway, isn't that what husbands are for? Broad shoulders and all that. Rising to the occasion. There in your hour of need.' He seemed embarrassed at this unexpected show of affection from her, and disengaging his hand, he picked up the wine bottle and poured the last of the wine into her glass. 'Here, you finish this. I've had enough.'

'Thanks. I didn't think anything of it at the time, but getting Aunt Caitlin to come to the funeral was lovely. I didn't even realise she was still alive. How did you find her?' The words were out before she knew it.

'Aunt Caitlin? I expect your mother's cousin told me, when I phoned to tell them about your father's death. You know, that one who lives in Durham, with lots of kids. Teresa, that's her name. Full of excuses about why they couldn't come down again so soon after your mother's funeral, then started to tell me I should contact your Aunt Caitlin, being your father's sister and all.'

'That's strange. I mean, I wonder why they kept in touch with her and my parents didn't.'

'Well, it's none of my business really, but I got the impression that your mother and father didn't want anything to do with the rest of the family. According to Teresa, none of them had heard from your parents in thirty-odd years, not since your grandmother died and they went to her funeral. Not even a Christmas card, she said.'

She looked at him. This was the moment when she could tell him. Explain to him that her mother was too ashamed to tell anyone in her family about her father's affair, and was constantly terrified that they would find out. She knew that her mother had done everything she could to keep her shameful secret hidden, even cutting herself off from her own family. How ridiculous it seemed now, and yet here was Susan still hiding that secret from her own husband. Why? It wasn't her shame, but in some way she felt it was. She was their daughter. Everybody believed that she was an only child, and now it seemed that she wasn't. She didn't want people to know that her father had had another family, that she and her mother hadn't been enough for him. She felt let down by him, and the only way she could cope with it was by burying it, by pretending that her parents'd had a perfectly ordinary marriage, by blotting out from her memory the woman and the child who had stolen her father's heart.

Graham pushed his plate away, with a sigh of contentment. 'That was delicious Susie.'

'So what did she say about Aunt Caitlin? You know I never got to speak to her for long at the funeral, and she wouldn't come back to the house because she was tired and wanted to get back to her hotel. Remember?' Susan tried not to seem too eager.

'God, Susie it was five years ago. My memory isn't what it was, you know. I think she said she was living in Bradford or was it Leicester. Not far from her daughter, anyway. She's a widow now of course. Her husband died years ago, in a car accident. I thought she looked pretty frail at the funeral, actually. I'm surprised she came at all, but then he was her big brother, wasn't he.'

'So did Teresa give you Caitlin's phone number? Did you ring her or write?' she asked, her impatience to get an answer starting to show.

'What is this, the third degree? I don't know. She must have said something, I suppose. Let me try to remember. Yes, I think she said she would ring Caitlin for me and tell her about the funeral. That's right. Then she phoned back that evening to say that Caitlin's phone had been disconnected so maybe I should write to her instead. So that's what I did. Sent it express delivery, but I never received a reply. Actually I was quite surprised to see her turn up at the church because I was sure the letter wouldn't arrive in time or that she would have moved. But there she was.' he explained.

Susan didn't ask any more questions. She had her answer. Graham was meticulous in everything he did. That was why he had been such a successful dentist, and why his golf handicap was so low. He was careful and thorough, and he left nothing to chance. She knew that her Aunt Caitlin's address would be neatly written in blue ink, on the appropriate page of their joint address book, and right now was sitting in the left hand drawer of their Sheridan hall table. It was all she could do to restrain herself from jumping up there and then to confirm it.

'Maybe we should send her a Christmas card this year. It seems a shame not to keep in touch with the few relatives that you have left,' he said.

Graham was the youngest of five brothers, but the only one still living. His parents had died many years before, and any other relatives had emigrated to Australia in the early fifties. Although he never said so, she often thought he missed his family. He'd liked Susan's parents and got on with them very well because they'd always treated him as their own son. Would he have viewed them in the same way, she wondered, if he had known about Anthea?

'I think her name is Jenson or Jennings. One of those. I expect I've written it down somewhere. Can't rely on my memory anymore. It used to be so good,' he complained. 'God, I hate growing old.'

'Okay, old man. You go and watch TV and I'll clear away. Fancy a coffee?' she asked.

'That would be great,' he said, moving back to the sofa. 'I think I'll put the golf on. I might just catch the re-run of the Portugal Masters.'

Susan waited until his attention was focused on the small screen. Richard Green marched down the fairway, a slight smile on his face; his caddie was hurrying behind him, his gait unstable, bent under the weight of Green's enormous bag. She heard a roar of applause from the crowd as the player approached the putting green, and took that opportunity to slip into the hall to look for the address book.

This time she turned straight to *'J'* and running her finger quickly down the list, soon came to a recent entry *'Caitlin Jennings, 45 Brickhouse Lane, Leicester.'* There was no post code, but that didn't matter. She copied the address on to a small piece of paper and put it into her trouser pocket.

CHAPTER 9

The next day was Friday. She thought she was going to escape John's invasive questioning about her plans for the following week because his office door had remained shut all morning. Nobody appeared to know his whereabouts. But then, at ten minutes to one, when she was considering what to do for her lunch, he arrived looking extremely pleased with himself.

'Susan. Good, I'm glad I've caught you. Got a minute to come into my office?' he asked, with no expectation of a refusal.

She knew what to expect and, grabbing a spiral notebook and pencil, followed him into his office. He had thought of some job for her to do, no doubt.

'Sit down, sit down,' he said waving her impatiently into a high-backed chair in front of his desk.

He was some twenty years younger than Susan, and could never quite decide how to approach her. His attitude vacillated between treating her like an aged aunt and a valued colleague that he hoped would soon be retiring.

'I've just had a very interesting meeting with Samuel Biggs from the Foreign Office. He has recently taken over from that chap Watkins, who was DS in charge of training and development.' He looked at her as though congratulations were in order, and when she said nothing, he continued, 'They've a new mandate for next year, and want to expand the range of one-day training programmes on offer. There may even be a few residential ones in the offing, though they still sound a bit vague on that score. You know how budget conscious they are. They want to do everything on a shoestring.'

Susan tried to look enthusiastic. On any other day she would have felt quite excited at the prospect of a new client, and especially one as prestigious as the Foreign Office, but today her head was full of plans for her trip to Leicester. Nevertheless she mustn't let John know that. He had a devious way of getting back at staff whom he felt were not fully committed to the company's objectives—this was how he liked to phrase it, when really they all knew that he meant those who were not prepared to drop everything at the drop of a hat and jump to his bidding. 'That sounds wonderful John. Exactly what type of training do they have in mind?' she asked. She prayed he wasn't going to use this as an excuse to prevent her from taking some leave.

'Well, that's the thing. They don't really know. You know the system there. This chap Biggs' last job was in the immigration department and before that he was in charge of sorting out staff housing in Harare, so what he knows about training you could write on the back of a postage stamp,' he explained, obviously delighted that his expertise was in demand.

'Really? I thought that nowadays the FO were offering staff the opportunity to sit professional exams in Personnel and Training, so that they could build up a cadre of qualified Human Resources staff instead of always relying on generalists,' she replied, fully aware that this was not the reply he'd hoped for.

He looked at her, his round face still glistening from the exertion of climbing the stairs, a routine he always insisted on, despite there being a very reliable lift. He wasn't exactly overweight, but there was a certain protuberance around his stomach that suggested the beginning of a beer gut. 'That's true and it's possible that this chap Biggs will end up staying on after the usual three-year stint, but in the meantime, he wants to outsource the training to a specialist company like ours,' he continued.

She could see that he was irritated that she should cast a shadow on his news, and waited as he carefully smoothed down his dark hair, which was slicked back with some sort of gel.

'So what is the plan? How do you want me to be involved?' she asked, knowing as soon as she saw his frown that she should try to placate him.

'Well, Susan, it occurred to me that as the Beavis project is on hold for a few weeks, you might like to get your teeth into this instead,' he replied as if the idea of her taking a few days leave had never been mentioned. 'Just ring Biggs' secretary and set up an appointment. If you phone the main FO switchboard they will put you right through. Tell her you work for me, and that I've briefed you on the meeting I had with her boss.' He leaned back in his chair, pressing his hands together to form a steeple that rested lightly on his ample stomach, and beamed at her as though everything was settled. The frown had been replaced with a look of smug satisfaction.

'Fine, John. I'll ring this afternoon and set up an appointment for when I get back from leave. In the meantime, if you have any papers that might be useful, I'll take them home with me and read them over the weekend.'

Susan was resolved not to give way but knew she should try to show that she was willing to be as accommodating as possible. It would be foolish to dampen his enthusiasm in case he decided to exclude her from the project. She'd had the feeling for a while now that John considered her too old for the front line. Given half a chance he'd replace her with someone younger and more attractive. She wasn't going to give him any excuse to bring in anyone new.

'Leave?' The frown had returned. 'Oh, yes, you did mention something about that yesterday but I didn't think you were serious. We don't want to delay on this one you know. It would be a shame if one of our rivals got in first.'

When he mentioned rivals, she knew he was thinking of Training Times, a company that specialised in cut-price, off the peg, one-day training courses in everything from Business Letter Writing to Improving your Interpersonal Skills. He loathed them with an intensity that was out of proportion to the competition they represented. Even as he spoke, she could see the frown intensify; it pulled his bushy eyebrows closer together, giving his eyes a rather crafty look and his fleshy lips tightened at the thought of them.

Susan had been in the management training business for many years and she knew how government departments worked. Decisions were not made overnight. 'Aren't they putting it out to tender? I believe they have to put all their work out to tender these days. As you said earlier, they are very budget conscious now.' John muttered something she didn't quite hear, so she continued, 'Usually they send a letter, specifying the date by which the tender has to be presented.'

John swivelled his chair back and forth, tapping his fingers on the desk, a sure sign he was thinking of how to couch his reply. 'Actually, yes. I think you're right. I do have the tender letter here somewhere.' He idly shuffled some papers that lay on his desk.

Susan spotted the Foreign Office logo and pounced. 'Here it is,' she said, and before he could stop her she had the letter in her hand and was skimming through it. 'Yes, I thought as much. All tenders to be submitted, with full costings, by November 27th. Good, that gives us plenty of time to prepare, almost two months in fact.' She read on, 'The lucky applicants will be asked to present their proposals on the 12th or 13th December.' She looked up and added, 'They're cutting it a bit fine there if they want the courses to start in February, aren't they? Still, first things first.' She beamed at him and sat patiently waiting for his reply.

'So,' he said, obviously wondering how to proceed.

Susan knew she'd disconcerted him. While he hesitated she continued, 'That's fine. Look, I'll get straight on to it when I get back. I'll set up a meeting with Biggs to see exactly what he wants, and how much he is prepared to spend and I'll get Paul involved too. He likes the one-day courses. Then we'll all sit down and go through it together at the end of the month. Shall we say the 30th? That will give us plenty of time to prepare some initial ideas first.' She knew that if she took the initiative, John would capitulate, grateful that the matter had been taken out of his hands.

'Great. Okay. Here take these,' he said, handing her a sheaf of papers, including the telltale letter.

She got up to leave.

'Oh, by the way, where are you off to next week?' he asked, trying to show some companionable interest in her plans.

'Nowhere much, just some family things I need to see to, spend some time with the grandchildren, things like that.' She was mumbling now, not inclined to involve herself in any complicated lie in case it backfired. She knew he was probably not listening anyway.

'Right, well have a good week then.' John seemed to have resigned himself, at last, to the fact that she would not be showing up for work on Monday. 'Oh, ask Anne to pop in on your way by, will you,' he added, his attention now moving on to other matters, Susan and the Foreign Office forgotten.

*

When Susan got home on Friday evening, Graham was in the garden, dead-heading the roses. He looked up when he heard her car come up the drive and waved. She parked in front of the garage and went to join him.

'Just about finished now,' he said, greeting her with a quick kiss on the cheek. 'Looks a lot tidier, doesn't it? Can't get rid of this black fly though.'

'Looks fine to me,' she said, picking one of the late-flowering roses and holding it to her nose. 'Wow this smells lovely, a bit like lychees.'

'Yes, the old Madame is a good sturdy rose. Shall I pick you some for the house?'

'Yes, why not,' she said, pleasantly surprised. Normally Graham didn't like picking his roses at this time of year because there were so few of them.

'I'm glad you're home on time,' he continued. 'I thought we might eat out tonight. Fancy trying that new Chinese place in Bray?'

'That sounds nice but I'm shattered. I'd just like a quiet night. Do you mind?'

'No, of course not.' He sounded disappointed.

She turned to walk up to the house then stopped to tell him, 'Oh, by the way, that training course is on. I'm driving up to Leicester on Sunday evening, in time for a Monday morning start.' It was so much easier to tell him out there in the garden, while his mind was still preoccupied with the roses, and now she could walk away before he questioned her, and before he could see the untruths hiding in her pale, grey eyes.

*

As she sat in her VW Golf, waiting for the lorry ahead of her to move, she began to doubt the wisdom of tackling the M1 on a Sunday evening. It was growing dark and had started to rain. After a while, the methodical clacking of the windscreen wipers began to irritate her, and she felt the old pain across the back of her neck as she strained to see the road. The rain was heavier now and it lashed against the car. Rivulets of water ran down the sides of the glass and the spray from the Sainsbury's lorry made it difficult to see the road in front. Susan told herself to relax. She hated driving in the dark, dazzled by approaching headlights and constantly peering at road signs she could barely read, and this heavy rain made it so much worse. She straightened her back, stretching her neck in the hope of getting some relief from the pain, and switched on the radio. It was set, as always, to Classic FM, perfect music for driving. The London Philharmonic Orchestra were already into the first movement of Sibelius's First Symphony, one of her favourites, and as she listened to it, her tension began to ebb away.

In a way, it had been her father who had introduced her to classical music. It was he who bought her an electric gramophone for her thirteenth birthday, and three records. She remembered them well: Debussy, Grieg's piano concerto and Ravel. Her mother had said he was just trying to bribe her with expensive presents that they couldn't afford, and would have sent it straight back to the shop, but Susan cried and begged her to let her keep it.

They were so different from each other, her parents. Her father was a romantic. He loved classical music and he read poetry, neither of which were to her mother's taste. Her mother was the practical one in the family, the one who paid the bills and eked out the meagre housekeeping allowance that he gave her. Of course now, with hindsight, Susan could see how difficult life must have been for both of them. He had told her grandmother that he was in love with both women. Was that possible? She supposed it was, otherwise surely he would have left one of them.

Her father had taken it hard when she left for university. He knew she would never live at home again. She remembered his lonely figure on the platform, waving sadly as her train pulled away, taking her to the start of a new life. She knew there were tears in his eyes, but she could feel no compassion for him, only an immense sense of relief, no more sleepless nights listening to their quarrels, no more piggy-in-the-middle. No, she decided she would never live at home again.

Her mother was very vindictive when she was angry and although Susan loved her, she never knew how to respond. She hated to see her mother upset, tears streaking her face and her mouth distorted in a perpetual cry of anguish, but somehow over the years she had gradually become inured to it. However it was even worse when she was alone with her father.

'Susie I can't stand much more of your mother's accusations,' he said to her one day. 'It's ruining my health. I can't sleep because she rants and raves all night. I don't know where she gets the energy from. This jealousy has turned her into a demon. I tell you, I'm frightened what I might do one day when she's in one of those rages. I'll hurt her, I know I will. Maybe I should just pack up and leave her for good, before I do something I regret.'

Her father had threatened to leave on many occasions, but he never had. Her mother had a set response to these threat, first she cried and pleaded with him to stay then, when he capitulated, as he always did, she was contrite and grateful, full of promises that she would forgive and forget and allow their life together to move forward. But always the jealousy returned and with it the renewed accusations and nightly rows, all the more virulent for their brief respite. Susan could not understand why her father was so weak, why he did not leave and start a new life, or why her mother did not throw him out and find a more faithful husband. Once, just before she left for university, she broached the subject with her mother. Her reply was simple and to the point, 'I love him, Susie. I've never loved anyone else and never could. We were so happy once, before that woman bewitched him. Everyone said we were the perfect couple. I can't live without him, and I'm not going to let any cheap tart take him away from me.'

Susan wondered what she would do if she found that Graham had another woman? She knew she wouldn't hesitate. It would be over between them. She would never be able to live with him after that, never able to trust him, always wondering where he was or who he was phoning. No, she wouldn't hesitate to end her marriage, even after all these years. She would feel betrayed. That was how her mother had felt—betrayed by the man she loved. But she hadn't wanted him to go. She hadn't been *able* to let him go. Regardless of the suffering, the jealousy, the hours spent wondering where he was and with whom, she preferred to still call him her husband. It was a pretence. Susan could see that now. Yes, her mother's heart had been broken but broken hearts could mend, if you let them. It seemed to her that her mother preferred the pain to the emptiness of life without her husband. But neither of them had thought about her, caught in the middle of their wrecked marriage.

A police car passed her in the outside lane, its blue light flashing. The rain was easing, and the traffic had picked up speed, at last. Another hour and she should be at the hotel. Thinking about her parents' marriage had depressed her and she felt the need to speak to someone. She punched her home number into the phone and after a few minutes, heard Graham's familiar voice.

'Hello, darling. It's me.'

'Susie. Are you there already?'

'No, the traffic has been very slow. I should get there before nine. Just hope the restaurant is still open. I'm starving.'

'Is everything all right?'

Susan wanted to say that no, it wasn't, that she missed him, that her memories were crowding in on her and that she was sorry she had lied to him. She wanted to tell him that she'd driven all that way, maybe on a fool's errand, to look for a half-brother that she hadn't known existed until a few days ago, but instead she said, 'Yes, it's fine. I just wanted to make sure you'd had something to eat.'

'I ate the remains of the curry and opened a bottle of Burgundy to go with it.'

'And now you're watching television?' Today there was something very comforting about Graham's love of routine.

'That's right. And then an early night, I think.'

'Well, I'll let you get back to it then. Bye darling.'

'Drive safely, Susie.'

*

Her hotel room was clean, warm and comfortable in an antiseptic sort of way. She knew, without having to check, that it was identical to the other thirty rooms on that floor and to the thirty rooms on all the other floors. What the Motorway Inn lacked in atmosphere, it made up for in dependability. But try as she might she couldn't sleep, and her thoughts kept returning to her father and the woman in the photograph.

Where had he met her? She didn't think she was a local woman. Maybe he had met her on one of those courses he was always attending. Twice a year he left her mother and her and went on a three-day course at one of the universities. He said it was to further his education, and make him more employable—get a better paid job, her mother explained—but even as a child she had understood that a three-day course on Renaissance literature had very little to do with selling insurance. The courses were his get-aways, his opportunity to forget about his family and, for a short time, to be a student again. The sudden disappearance of his father, and later the start of the war, had robbed him of his chance of a university education. The oldest child, in a family of eight, it had been her father's responsibility to go to work and support his brothers and sisters. Looking back now, she felt sorry for him. He had been an intelligent man, a scholarly man, who if given the chance, could have been a teacher or a journalist, but instead he'd had a series of boring, low-paid jobs. Surely that must have been at the root of his frustration and why he had insisted on Susan going to university, even though she was not a particularly brilliant student. Perhaps that was why he looked for satisfaction in other aspects of his life. She would never know for certain why he was so unhappy, but unhappy he definitely was and so was her mother. Did this woman have something to with it? And who was Anthea? Were the woman in the photograph and Anthea one and the same? So many questions. If only she could remember something about those days but she had spent the last fifty years successfully blotting them all from her mind.

CHAPTER 10

Saturday had opened wet and windy. When he woke that morning and saw the weather, Aidan decided to spend the afternoon in front of the television, watching some football, or even a bit of cricket beamed by satellite from the sunny West Indies, but Judy had other ideas.

'I've got to take Jason and Zak to a birthday party,' she told him over breakfast. 'Would you mind taking Ben shopping? He has to have some new shoes for school; his toes are coming through the old ones.'

'Can't it wait until next week?' he asked, knowing perfectly well what her answer would be. 'You know he hates shopping with me.'

'No it can't. You don't want your son going to school barefoot do you? He'll be all right. He'll probably enjoy the chance to have you to himself for a while, without the other two around. Just pick him up when he finishes school at twelve o'clock and go straight there.'

So it was decided. Maybe, if they found something he liked quickly, they would still be back in time for the match.

'What time's the party?' he asked.

'One-thirty,' she replied, pouring out some more coffee. 'We're going to the first performance.'

This was not just any birthday party, this was the birthday party of Lord Ripley's youngest son, a precocious seven-year-old called Arnold, who was oblivious to the fact that he was something like six-hundred and fifth in line to the throne. He was a friend of Zak and Jason, and attended the local Montessori school with them. His mother had invited the entire class to an afternoon performance of Freddy Wilde's circus. Afterwards all seventeen of them were going back to his home, a beautiful Georgian mansion on the expensive edge of the common, for a birthday tea.

All Aidan's sons attended the Montessori school. Its philosophy was very much in line with Aidan's own ideas on education: *educate .. to develop the faculties and powers of, by teaching, instruction or training, from the Latin educere, to lead out.* The Montessori teaching leaned far more towards the 'leading out' than the 'cramming in' that Aidan had experienced at school. It focused on the children as individuals, each child with its specific needs and talents. This was yet another area where he had disagreed with his mother.

'Why on earth do you want to send them to those middle-class, pretentious child-minders?' she said when she heard. 'All they do is play with felt numbers and feely bags. Why can't they go to the perfectly good primary school in the village?' His mother always referred to Wimbledon as the village, as though it were on a par with Bray, their own small, neighbouring village. 'And how do you know if they're achieving anything? They never have any tests or exams. And they treat competition as a dirty word. It's not fair to the children. How will they cope in the modern world if they don't know how to be competitive?' she'd continued.

But Judy agreed with Aidan and, on completion of their third birthdays, each boy had been enrolled at the Park Montessori school. Aidan and Judy had not regretted it for a single moment. All the boys had thrived in its atmosphere of self responsibility and independence. The school provided the parents with individual assessments on their children's progress in the form of lists of their achievements, their strengths and their weaknesses, which had shown that not only were they developing academically but also socially.

Soon, when the children reached prep school age, Arnold's class would disperse, the children drifting away like so many fallen leaves to their various futures. Zak's future would not include being Arnold's class mate, Aidan was sure of that. That young man was probably destined for Eton. He and Judy had not made any plans for their own sons yet, but he could guarantee that Eton would not be included, nor any other boarding school. He remembered a conversation he'd had with his mother, a few weeks earlier.

'Have you put their names down for a school, yet, Aidan?' she asked.

'No, we can't agree on which one we like best. The ones Judy likes are far too expensive, and she says the ones I like are not academic enough, too much emphasis on sport,' he replied reluctantly, knowing that she would think he was dragging his heels on this one.

'Well if you don't get a move on, you won't get them in anywhere decent. There's fierce competition for places in good schools, you know,' she said, looking at him as if she hadn't expected anything better from him. 'Lots of people put their children's names down as soon as they're born.'

She had sent him to boarding school just before his ninth birthday. He could still remember that day as if it were yesterday. Eight-years-old and small for his age, he had been totally overwhelmed by everything, the imposing school itself—a Georgian mansion converted into classrooms and dormitories— and the hundreds of boys that it contained. He knew it was a good school—many successful people had gone there—but at the time he had hated it. His mother had uprooted him from the local village school, with its three teachers and sixty-three pupils, from his friends and, it seemed at the time, thrown him to the wolves. He was sure it was done with the best of intentions, but it had not been a happy experience. Most of the children in his class were there because their fathers had jobs which involved them living abroad for long periods at a time and they wanted some stability for their sons. He was embarrassed to admit that his parents lived only fifty miles away and there was no reason why he couldn't go home at weekends. When he questioned her, his mother just said that he would be bored at home and that there were many more things to do if he stayed in the school with his friends. With time of course things changed; he grew taller and stronger; he made new friends; he excelled at cricket and he became used to living away from home. But, in his heart, he never forgave his mother. Even today he couldn't shake off that feeling of rejection. He loved his mother, he told himself repeatedly, so why couldn't they get on? Why was she so cold to him and his children? He couldn't understand it and the truth was that it hurt like hell to think that she hadn't wanted him. Perhaps she'd never wanted to have children. He imagined that was why she never had any more. It was something he'd missed when he was growing up, not having a brother or sister to play with, and now that he was an adult, with children of his own, he could better appreciate what he had missed out on.

He sometimes thought that the reason he married Judy was because she was so different from his mother. Judy was warm and affectionate. She made a point of speaking to the milkman instead of just leaving his money tucked into an empty bottle, of stopping her bike and having a word with the homeless man who hung about outside the supermarket, often slipping him a few coins, of talking to the mothers dropping their children off at school, even though she was in a hurry to get to her own classes. She had time for everyone, the old lady who lived on the floor below, the new mother opposite whose baby cried non-stop, her pupils, her children and most of all him. She made him … He struggled for the word that would best describe what Judy meant to him. It was simple. She made him feel loved. She and the boys were his family now.

Walking down Wimbledon High Street with his anorak hood giving him inadequate protection from the rain, Aidan felt sure that despite the discomfort, he had the best of the deal today. He wondered how Judy was coping with the smell and sounds of the circus and hundreds of noisy children. He shuddered at the thought. Ben didn't seem to mind being left out of this prestigious occasion. Perhaps Judy was right when she said he actually might enjoy the chance to be the only son for a short while. It was difficult to share out the time equally between the boys. Jason, being the baby, always demanded more of their attention, Zak was becoming quite independent these days and Ben, being the oldest, was expected to look out for the other two. He made a mental note to spend more time talking to him. Ben had recently moved into the top class at school in this, his final year, and already felt himself moving away from the others. Right now, as he splashed through the puddles in his Arsenal Wellingtons, his mind was set on some new football boots which Aidan had mentioned might be coming his way, once they'd bought the shoes for school.

'Hang on a minute, Ben. I just want to pop in here. We won't be long,' Aidan added when he saw disappointment creep into his son's face. They had stopped outside an estate agent's window. After scanning the photographs on display for a moment, they both went inside.

'Can I help you, sir?' A fresh faced young man of no more than twenty-two came from behind his desk to greet them.

'Yes. I'm looking for a two-bedroom flat in the area, but a large one, at least two hundred square metres. Do you have anything?' Aidan enquired.

'Oh, I'm sure we do. What sort of price range are you thinking of?' the young man asked smoothly.

'Well, I'm not too sure, exactly. What do you have?' Aidan continued.

The young man gave him a look which said quite clearly, 'I do hope you're not about to waste my valuable time.'

'It's not for me actually. It's for my parents. They have a big house in Maidenhead and are thinking of buying something smaller, a flat possibly,' Aidan explained.

At this amplification, the young man brightened noticeably and even managed a smile for Ben. 'Here young man, have a sweet,' he said, offering Ben a glass dish filled with boiled sweets.

'Thank you,' Ben said, politely, helping himself to as many sweets as he could grasp in one hand.

'This one looks promising,' said Aidan pointing to a single A4 sheet where the details of a luxurious flat were graphically laid out.

'Yes sir, that one is a very nice property and it is only five minutes away from the High Street. Would you like to view it?' The young man was already on his feet, in anticipation.

'Daddy,' a small voice said, in a somewhat plaintive tone. 'Aren't we going shopping? Mummy said we had to.'

'Yes Ben, just a minute, there's a good boy,' Aidan replied, then turning back to the estate agent said, 'No, not today, but I would like the details of it, and can you get out the details of a few more as well. I'd like to take them to show my parents, tomorrow.'

'Daddy, not tomorrow. We're going to Pat and Jenny's tomorrow,' his son interrupted.

'Well, next week then.'

The estate agent selected a few likely properties from his data base, printed them out then slipped them into a glossy folder with Paine's Estate Agency and Conveyancing emblazoned on it, which he handed to Aidan.

'Here's my card. Our web page address is there in case your parents want to look us up. And just give me a ring when they decide to view.'

Aidan looked at the name on the card and said, 'Thank you Stuart. I'll do that.'

*

Later that afternoon, while Ben clomped around the flat in his new football boots, Aidan poured himself a glass of Sauvignon from the half empty bottle in the fridge. He spread the estate agent's details out on the table in front of him.   Of the five properties on offer, only one had a view of the Common. This would be the only one that would tempt his mother. He knew she would not give up her uninterrupted view across the Thames for anything less. He placed it on top of the pile to show Judy later. It would certainly be much more manageable than their existing house. There was a lift and a caretaker. It had a twenty-four hour security system, and panic buttons in case of emergencies. All in all, it was much more suitable for two elderly people.

He heard the door to the flat open and his two younger children spilled into the kitchen, their faces flushed with excitement.

'Hi Dad. Where's Ben?' and without waiting for an answer they rushed off to find their brother to tell him all about their afternoon.

'What are those? Planning on moving without me?' Judy had spotted the estate agent's brochures strewn across the kitchen table.

'What and iron my own shirts? Don't be mad.' Aidan grabbed his wife around the waist and gave her a hug. 'I just popped into the estate agents in the High Street when I was out with Ben, and picked up a few details in case Mum and Dad were interested.'

'Oh, Aidan, why don't you just leave it alone. I think they're perfectly happy as they are. They're not that old, for goodness sake. Your mum's still working and your dad is very active. You're only going to cause more bad feeling between yourself and your mother if you continue with this.'

'Well there's no harm in them looking, is there. It would give them an idea of what's available. You know, possibilities for the future, for when they do have to move.' He picked up one of the brochures and offered it to her. 'Here, look at this one. It would be perfect for them, and it's just around the corner.'

Judy studied the details of the flat. It was certainly a beautiful place, and very spacious. She sat down, saying nothing.

'What is it?' Aidan asked. 'What's the matter?'

'Look Aidan,' she began, 'have you never considered the possibility that we might move away from here? I would love a house with a garden and a bit more space, and you know that the prices here are impossible. The only way we could have a bigger house is to move to a cheaper area. If you persuade your parents to move to Wimbledon, we'll be stuck here for ever.'

'Well, it doesn't have to be Wimbledon. I just think they need somewhere more manageable,' he argued, carefully avoiding any response to the idea that they might also look for a house.

He knew Judy was right about the flat being too small for them but he wasn't ready to move just yet. His salary wouldn't stretch to a bigger mortgage payment and there was no sign of any promotion on the horizon. It was all right for Judy to keep on about getting somewhere bigger, but how would they pay for it? He'd have to look for a better paid job, and if he was honest, he didn't really feel like going through all the hassle of job interviews again. He would be happy to stay exactly where he was until he was old enough to retire but he knew he couldn't say that to his wife. One of the things that he'd liked about Judy when they'd first met was that it didn't seem to matter to her that he wasn't ambitious. But ten years on, with three children and a crowded flat, her opinions were changing. This was not the first time she\d brought up the subject of moving to somewhere bigger.

'I think I'll show them what's available and then it's up to them,' he said, continuing to ignore his wife's comments.

'Yes well, I'm telling you now, your mother will not be interested.' Judy got up and reached for her handbag.

'Are you all right, Judy? You seem a bit strung up.'

'So would you be, if you'd just spent three hours with hundreds of screaming kids. I'm going to lie down.'

'Would you like me to bring you a cup of tea?' he asked, surprised to see his usually cool and collected wife on the verge of tears over a birthday party.

'A glass of wine would be better,' she said, but this time managed to give him a smile. 'And by the way, why is Ben wearing new football boots?'

'Ah, well. He said he needed them.'

'But you got his shoes for school?'

'Of course. Was the party okay?'

'Zak and Jason will tell you all about it,' she said, going into her bedroom and shutting the door firmly behind her.

Aidan put the papers into his briefcase. He would phone his parents later. He sighed. He shouldn't have left them out for Judy to see. It was foolish of him. Now she would want him to talk seriously about moving.

*

The sky looked grey and menacing on Sunday morning when they piled into the family Shogun to drive to their friends in South Oxfordshire. The Common was shrouded in low lying cloud, obscuring the Windmill entirely and leaving only a few trees visible, dark, shadowy shapes on the horizon.

'It looks like rain to me,' said Judy. 'Do you think it's worth going?'

'I don't see that we have much option. They're expecting us, aren't they? Anyway, it's a bit brighter over there,' replied Aidan, looking west to where the tiniest sliver of blue sky was trying to slip between the dark clouds.

It didn't take them long to reach the junction for the M40 and soon they were speeding up the motorway towards Oxfordshire. Their friends, Pat and Jenny, owned a small dairy farm outside Abingdon. They had fifty cows, two pigs, numerous chickens, an ancient donkey and a pony, not to mention a couple of dogs and various cats. Sunday lunch on the farm was a regular outing for Aidan's family, and the children loved it. There were so many things for them to do, and they had a freedom there that was denied them at home.

They arrived at the farmhouse just before lunch. The farm was in a small valley, set between two wooded hills and surrounded by thick pastureland: lush, green grass, studded with late cowslips. A small stream meandered between grassy banks lined with tall, stark bulrushes and wild irises, dividing the fields into two halves as it made its circuitous journey to join the Thames. Today the cows were in the field by the stream and, where they'd wandered down to drink, their heavy hooves had churned the water into a muddy soup. As they drove up a tarmac drive to the house, a short, thick-set man in his forties came striding towards them.

'Hi there kids, good to see you,' he said, as the children clambered out of the car. He picked Jason up and swung him through the air. 'And how are you, young man?'

'I'm okay Uncle Pat,' the boy replied, gasping for breath.

'Hello, Uncle Pat. Can we see the kittens?' asked Zak, who was already running towards the barn.

'They've grown quite a bit since you were last here. You'll have to look around for them. I'm sure they'll be getting into mischief somewhere,' he called after him.

'I'm going to see Toby. I've got a carrot for him, Uncle Pat,' Jason said, producing the largest carrot that he'd been able to find in his mother's kitchen.

'Okay, but don't go in her stall. I don't want you to get kicked. She's getting a bit crotchety lately. Must be her age.'

'She's not the only one,' Aidan said a bit sourly. Judy had been very tight-lipped that morning. He knew it was this house business.

Pat looked at his friend and smiled. 'Hi there. Good journey?'

'Yeah, fine. Bit slow on the M25 but then it always is.' He gave Pat a friendly punch on the arm. 'So, how's things?'

'Good. Much the same as always. Not a lot changes here.'

'That's what I like about coming here. It's so comforting and dependable. There're never any surprises,' Judy said, emerging from the car with a large carrier bag.

'Good to see you Judy,' Pat said, giving his friend a kiss and a bone crushing hug. 'What have you got there?'

'I've just brought a few things for lunch: some wine and a lemon meringue pie.'

'Lemon meringue pie, my favourite. Come on, let's go in and I'll get you a drink. Jenny's in the kitchen, putting the finishing touches to lunch. I think it's a bit too cold to sit outside. Better in the kitchen.'

'Jason. Ben. Boys come here,' Judy called.

'Don't worry about them, Judy. Let them run off some energy and then we'll call them in to eat when it's ready,' Pat said. 'I expect they've gone over to the orchard to do some more to the tree house.

*

Lunch, as usual, was traditional and filling. As soon as it was over, the children went off to play, leaving their parents free to talk to their friends in that relaxed way that often follows a good Sunday lunch and a couple of bottles of Bordeaux.

Later, whilst Judy was in the kitchen helping Jenny clear up, Aidan and Pat sat in the lounge, finishing the last of the wine. The windows offered a direct view over the valley and Aidan could see the rain clouds returning, darker and more menacing than ever. He leaned back into the soft cushions of the armchair, letting his body relax into its welcoming arms. It was warm and comfortable in the room and the heavy meal he had just eaten made him feel a little soporific. He felt like unburdening himself to his friend, but didn't know where to start.

'Are you having some work done, Pat?' When he'd arrived, Aidan had noticed that one of the outbuildings had scaffolding around it and pallets of bricks and sacks of yellow builder's sand leant against its walls.

'Yes, we're converting that old barn into a granny flat for Jenny's mum. It's never been used for much except storing bits and pieces.'

'Really. Is her mum tired of living alone then?' He knew that Jenny's mother had been a widow for many years and still lived in the family's original home in Salcoats.

'No not really. I think she would be happy to stay there until she pops her clogs but she's eighty-five and Jenny worries about her. She would be a lot more relaxed if her mother lived a bit closer. The farm keeps us so busy that there isn't a lot of time to go visiting and she hates the idea that her mother might be taken ill with no-one there to help her,' he explained. 'She always seems to be reading these obscure news reports about old people found dead in bed with nobody having missed them.'

'I see her point. It's a great idea if you have the space to do it,' he added, thinking of their own limited accommodation.

'Maybe you should think of selling that expensive flat of yours and moving out into the country. I know three young men that would love it,' Pat said watching Aidan's sons chasing the farm dog around the yard. He was used to Aidan complaining about the lack of space in their flat.

'Yes, maybe. I know Judy would like to move but, to be honest, I think it would be such an upheaval, changing schools and all that and then there's the expense. Anyway I'm not sure now is the time. We just can't afford to increase the mortgage.'

'But that's my point. If you moved away from that over-priced neighbourhood you wouldn't have to increase your mortgage. You'd have a bigger home and it might even cost you less.'

'Okay, I'll think about it. I know Judy would love to move. She's always giving me a hard time about it.' Aidan paused, sipping his wine thoughtfully, then continued, 'Actually I'm more concerned about my own parents at the moment.'

'What, Susan and Graham?' Pat knew Aidan's parents.

'Yes. I think their house is too big for them now and much too isolated; they're very vulnerable right on the river's edge like that. I'm hoping to persuade them to move but my mother is very resistant to the idea. You know how stubborn she can be,' he added.

'Has something happened to them? They looked fine last time I saw them and they're still pretty young you know,' his friend replied. 'Relatively speaking.'

'Well, Dad's seventy-two now but I suppose he's quite fit,' Aidan admitted. 'He's still playing golf and he walks a lot with Jess.'

'So? Susan isn't sixty yet, is she?'

'Next year. It's just that I think it would be better for them to make a move now, while they're both still in good health. Besides which they were burgled last week.'

'That's terrible. Were they out at the time?'

'Yes, thank goodness but I can't help wondering what would have happened if they'd been home. It's too isolated where they are. You can't even see their neighbour's house without going down the drive and through the woods.'

'I can see it's a worry, but look Aidan, you don't realise how lucky you are to have such active parents. They'll need your help soon enough, don't bring it forward unnecessarily. Tell them to install a burglar alarm and some security lights if you're that worried.'

Aidan sipped his wine, swirling it round in his mouth to savour the flavour. It was a South African Bordeaux and very smooth. 'If only it were that easy,' he said. 'You know my mother; she hates taking advice, especially from me. Anyway, they have a burglar alarm and a lot of use that was.'

'Look, if you want my opinion, stop worrying about them and their house and concentrate on your own family. It's you that should be making the move. Why don't you look for somewhere closer to Susan and Graham. Maidenhead is a nice area and a hell of a lot cheaper than Wimbledon. That way you'll kill two birds with one stone.' The confidence in their friendship always allowed Pat to speak openly to Aidan. He was looking at him now, glass in hand and just the glimmer of a smile on his lips.

'It's an idea. I said I'd think about it, and I will,' said Aidan reluctantly, drinking down the last of his wine. He'd always considered Pat to be the brother he'd never had and he supposed that was what brothers did, they sometimes told you what you didn't want to hear.

*

It was very late when they arrived home. They had to wake Ben and Zak, who were lying with their arms entwined around each other, reluctant to leave the warmth of the back seat. Judy guided her sleepy children to the front door, while Aidan carried Jason across his shoulder. He could feel his son's silky hair against his cheek and the warm breath that escaped from his parted lips. He took him into his bedroom and laid him on his bed; the child grunted gently and rolled onto his side without waking. Carefully Aidan removed his dressing gown and slippers and pulled the coverlet over him. He paused for a moment, looking down at his youngest son. He was a Giotto angel when he slept, pink cheeked and innocent. Aidan couldn't resist stroking his head gently and touching that soft, baby skin and then, filled with a sudden wave of love for this small person, he bent down and kissed him. He could hear his other sons in the bathroom, grumbling about being made to clean their teeth. Gently, so as not to wake the sleeping child, he picked up Jason's favourite, well-worn teddy bear from the end of the bed and tucked it in beside him.

He thought about what Pat had said and how annoyed Judy had been with him for going to the estate agents. Neither of them seemed to realise that he was only concerned about his parents' welfare. He just wanted what was best for them. He had always felt a responsibility for his parents that he knew was probably misplaced. He couldn't imagine his mother, so confident and independent, her life perfectly organised, ever asking him for his advice, never mind needing his help but Aidan believed in family life, in the strength of the family unit and because of that he felt the duties of an only son more acutely. If only his mother would reach out to him occasionally but the chances of that happening were as remote as him winning the football pools.

CHAPTER 11

Aidan was impatient to speak to his mother about the flats as soon as he could. He dialled her office number the moment he arrived at work. He knew if he didn't catch her early before she became involved in any training sessions, he'd have to wait until the evening.

'Good morning Anne. It's Aidan, can I speak to my mother please?' He knew Anne and a number of his mother's other colleagues because each summer Susan and Graham held a party on June 24th, the longest day of the year, and everyone: work colleagues, family and friends, was invited. Apart from Christmas morning, when they asked their neighbours in for a drink, it was almost the only entertaining his parents did these days.

'Hello Aidan. How are you?' Anne answered. She waited for the usual response before continuing, 'Susan isn't in this week. She's taken a week's leave. I thought she said she was going to spend some time with the grandchildren or something.'

There was a pause while he processed this new information. 'Oh, yes. Of course. I'd forgotten that it was this week. How stupid of me,' he babbled, trying his hardest not to sound surprised at this news. 'Oh, well I'll see her when she comes to collect the kids. Sorry to have bothered you.'

This was good news. If they were coming over to see the children, he could probably persuade them to have a look at the flat at the same time. He decided to telephone and find out their exact plans.

'Hi Dad. How are you?'

'Aidan, you've just caught me. I'm about to go to golf. Getting in some extra games while your mum's away.'

'Mum's away?'

'Yes, don't sound so surprised. She's always away these days.'

'On holiday?'

'Holiday? Of course not. She's running a training course in Leicester this week. Won't be back until Wednesday. You know your mother; she doesn't take holidays.'

'A training course? Really? She didn't mention it when I spoke to her last. Are you sure?'

'Sure about what, that she is running a course or that it's in Leicester? Of course I'm sure. She phoned me last night when she arrived. Had a hell of a journey, poor love, torrential rain and the M1 at a standstill but she arrived all right in the end. Did you want to talk to her then? You've got her mobile number haven't you? If not, I'm sure I've got it somewhere.'

'No, I was just curious.'

'Did you ring for something in particular?'

'No, just called for a chat, really. Maybe I'll ring Mum tonight. She'll be busy now, anyway,' Aidan replied. He was beginning to feel confused.

'Look son, I'd love to talk more but I have to go. I'm due on the tee in half an hour. Why don't you phone me later?'

'Okay, Dad, I'll do that. Bye.'

'Bye son.'

Aidan put the telephone back on its receiver. He didn't know what to think. Despite the sun streaming through his office window, he felt cold. Had he misunderstood Anne? He went over their brief conversation in his head. There was no doubt in his mind, Anne had definitely said Susan had taken a week's holiday. His mother had lied to his father and she had lied to her colleagues. She obviously wasn't running a training course in Leicester so where was she? What on earth was happening? What was she up to? He had to find out. Instinct had prevented him from saying anything to his father until he'd been sure but now he could only think of one reason for her behaviour. She was having an affair and had gone for a few days' holiday with her lover. But where? Surely she hadn't gone to Leicester. If he were to have an affair, and as he thought of Judy he thought it highly unlikely, he would take his lover somewhere much more romantic than Leicester.

He laughed aloud, a dry, bitter sound. What was he thinking? This was his mother. His mother didn't have affairs. And his mother didn't tell lies. She'd instilled in him from an early age the importance of always telling the truth, no matter how much it hurt. No, he couldn't imagine the cool, organised, perfect Susan lying to his father, just as he couldn't imagine her with a lover.

*

Judy was already in the kitchen, preparing the evening meal when he arrived home. She had just put a lasagne into the oven and was peering, short-sightedly at the timer.

'Hi, darling. Just look at this for me will you. Does it say twenty minutes or thirty? I can't see a thing without my specs and I've no idea where I've put them,' she said, straightening up and giving him a kiss on the cheek.

'Twenty minutes.'

'Oh, that's not enough. Turn it up to thirty, will you.'

She seemed to have forgiven him about going to the estate agents or at least forgotten about it, for the moment. He watched as she began to clear a space on the table, removing a large pile of exercise books that she'd brought home to mark and a papier-mâché model of a dinosaur.

'What's that?' Aidan asked, taking the model from her.

'It's Zak's history project. He got an A for it.'

'Did he, indeed?'

Aidan turned the model around in the light, admiring the rough texture of the papier-mâché and the fluorescent green paint. It looked like a Tyrannosaurus Rex with a headache.

'Don't laugh. He's very proud of it.'

'I'm not laughing, well not really. It's good. It's just the expression he has painted on its face. What is it? Fierce? Or constipated?' He stopped. Zak and Ben were coming into the kitchen.

'Hi, Dad. Have you seen my dinosaur?'

Aidan bent down to kiss his sons. 'Hi guys. Yes, it's great, Zak, very lifelike.'

'I copied it from a comic,' the child explained. 'It's actually Dino, the lonely dinosaur.'

'Well, it's very good, Zak,' Aidan assured him. So that explained the dinosaur's pained expression.

'Is dinner ready yet Mum?' Ben asked, opening the refrigerator.

'No, it'll be about half an hour. And come out of that fridge. You're not eating anything now or you won't eat your dinner.'

'Oh, Mum.'

Aidan went through to the lounge and closed the door behind him. He could still hear Ben's protestations and Judy's firm replies. He picked up the daily paper and started to glance through it but he couldn't concentrate. His thoughts kept returning to his conversation with his father. He wondered if he should telephone and see if he'd heard anything more from his mother. Perhaps that would be unwise; he didn't want to worry his father as well. He could always telephone his mother himself. But should he? Was it any of his business? He pulled out his mobile and skimmed through his list of contacts until he reached her number. All he had to do was press the call button.

'Darling. Are you all right? Why are you sitting in here in the dark?' Judy had opened the lounge door, letting a shaft of light spread across the parquet floor. The smell of the lasagne drifted into the room behind her, a mixture of savoury meat, wild herbs and garlic. Momentarily the gastric juices in his stomach responded.

'Yes, I'm fine. Just a bit of a headache, that's all.'

'I thought you might like a glass of wine, to unwind. It's Valpolicello.'

Aidan took the wine from her outstretched hand and sniffed it. 'Nice.'

'Yes, I thought so. It's from Sainsbury's. This week's special offer, only five ninety-five.'

'Mmm. It'll go well with the lasagne,' he said, swilling it around the glass and tasting it.

He watched his wife go round the room switching on the table lamps one by one. Warm pools of light suffused the room, bringing to life the soft reds and oranges with which the lounge had been decorated.

'Something strange happened today,' he said at last, sipping the wine.

Judy had sat down on the sofa next to him. She leaned back, sinking into the leather upholstery and rested her head on his shoulder. 'How do you mean, strange?'

He told her about his conversations, first with Anne and then his father.

'So? Perhaps Anne made a mistake. Maybe your mother made a sudden decision to go to Leicester and she didn't tell Anne about it.'

'No, I don't think so. Anne prepares all her course handouts and organises her diary. She would have to know.'

'Well if you're worried about your mother why don't you just telephone her? She has her mobile with her, doesn't she?'

'I'm not sure it's a good idea. What if she's not alone?' Aidan felt rather foolish admitting his fears to his wife. He knew she would scoff at the idea of Susan having a lover. Even as he spoke he could feel her body shaking with merriment at the idea.

'Don't be ridiculous. The perfect Susan having an affair. I don't believe it, not at her age. Look just ring her. I'm sure there's a perfectly plausible explanation.'

'Yes, I expect you're right. Maybe I'll ring her later on.'

'Well don't sit there moping about it. Dinner will be ready soon.' Judy sighed and pulled herself away from him, reluctantly, he thought. She looked tired. Even the soft glow from the lamp couldn't hide the shadows under her eyes.

'Okay, sweetheart. I'll come and give you a hand in a minute.'

His wife stood up, becoming once more the energetic wife and mother he was used to seeing bustling around their home. He drank a little more wine. It was ridiculous this antagonism that existed between his mother and him, but it was nothing new. She'd always seemed a little cold, he thought, even when he was a child. It was almost as if she didn't trust herself to love him fully, as if there was always something holding her back. And yet he was sure that she did love him, just as he loved her, only she seemed to have difficulty in expressing that love. Aidan was a very tactile person; he liked to touch and stroke and express his love through contact. His mother was quite different. Of course she had cuddled him when he was small. He was sure she would have read that this was the correct thing to do with a small child but, as he grew older, all physical contact, apart from a cursory kiss on his cheek in greeting, had ceased. As he thought about it now, with the heart of an adult, he wondered if she was afraid that if she loved him too much he would be taken away from her. On occasions, when he looked at his own sons, the sweetness of his love for them was so intense that he would experience an irrational fear that one day he would lose them. Maybe such fears had caused her to withdraw in some strange act of self-preservation.

The door opened a crack and a small head peered round it. 'Daddy. Can you hear me read please? Mummy says so.'

'Okay, Jason, just coming.'

He took up his mobile telephone and was about to press his mother's number then changed his mind, clicked it shut and replaced it in his pocket.

CHAPTER 12

Monday morning dawned bright and breezy. Susan woke early, aroused by the sound of a loose shutter banging in the wind. Despite her restless night, she felt no need to linger in bed and was soon showered and dressed and on her way down to breakfast.

The dining room was a well lit area of chrome and plastic, and a long table, covered in a white tablecloth, was laid with the usual range of breakfast cereals, pastries, jams and bread. She sat at a table set for one and looked around her. Apart from a family with three children seated around a large table by the window, all the other tables had single occupancy like hers. This was a popular hotel with businessmen. It seemed that a man wearing a dark suit, a crisply laundered shirt and a tie sat at each table. Some had their laptops open on the table beside them, others were busily scanning sheaves of paper; one was reading The Financial Times and all had their mobiles at the ready. Instead of the silence one would expect from a room of solitary eaters, there was the buzz of detached conversations as people talked to their absent colleagues or assuaged their wives' misgivings, all against a background of musical chirping which emanated from their digital companions.

Susan helped herself to a selection of fruit and a cup of tepid coffee. She'd bought a street map of Leicester the previous evening when she'd stopped at Leicester Forest service station and now she spread it out on the table in front of her. Caitlin Jennings lived in the north of the city, just off the Loughborough Road. If the traffic was light, it would probably take her about half an hour to get there.

*

The 1930's semi-detached houses that now lined Brickhouse Lane had removed all traces, save in a name, of the prosperous 19th century brick fields that used to lie to the north of the city. She drove slowly along the road and parked her car outside number forty-five. Her Aunt Caitlin's house was identical to all the others in this quiet lane: a modest red-brick semi, with a gabled porch and a bay window that curved out over a tiny patch of garden. The front door was partially glazed with an art deco stained-glass design of twisting vines and lilies and the early morning sun shone fully on the front of the house, illuminating and intensifying the colours in the glass. Everything was very neat and clean.

At first Susan thought the house was empty but when she rang the bell for the second time she noticed the curtain in the upstairs room move. A few moments later the door opened as wide as its safety chain would allow.

'Yes? What do you want?' an old woman enquired.

'Aunty Kate. It's me, Susan, your niece,' she replied.

'Susan? What, Davy's Susan? What are you doing here?'

'I'm working in Leicester this week, so I thought I'd look you up.' More lies, Susan thought ruefully.

'Well come in, my dear. Wait just a minute while I take this silly chain off.' The woman shut the door momentarily while she unhooked the safety chain, then opened it again. 'Bit of a nuisance these things but you can't be too careful you know. There, now I can see you. What a lovely surprise, my dear. Come on in.' Her aunt held the door open so Susan could enter.

She bent down and gave the old lady a kiss on her cheek. 'It's lovely to see you Aunty Kate. I hope I haven't come at an inconvenient time.' Underneath a blue housecoat, her aunt was still wearing her nightgown.

'No, my dear, that's all right. I've only just got up. I don't get up much before ten these days. Well no need really. I don't have much to do any more, and it only makes the day seem longer.' She closed the front door and replaced the security chain, then led Susan into the sitting room.

'I didn't have a telephone number for you so I couldn't let you know I was coming,' Susan added.

'Oh, I had the phone disconnected some time ago, too expensive. I have this little mobile thing now. You know, everyone has them. It's pay-as-you-go, so I don't have any bills. Much better for me,' explained her aunt. 'Well, my 'andsome, this is a nice surprise,' she continued looking at Susan and smiling happily. 'I don't get many visitors you know.   Well apart from the Social Services. They come round a couple of times a week but they don't come on Mondays. I used to get those meals-on-wheels people coming too, but I soon stopped them. I wasn't going to pay for that muck. Inedible it was. I'd sooner boil myself an egg, much healthier and cheaper.'

She bustled around the room, switching on a gas convector fire and pulling back the curtains.

'Would you like a cup of tea? I was just going to put the kettle on when you arrived.'

'That would be lovely. Can I help you?' Susan asked.

'No, you sit there and rest. You've come a long way,' her aunt replied.

Susan sat back on the moquette sofa, sinking into its deep cushions. The room was small and cosy to the point of being stifling. The windows, she noticed were double glazed and screwed shut, curtains of heavy velour hung to the floor and a draught excluder in the shape of a sausage dog lay behind the door. The heat from the fire was overpowering now. She leaned across and turned it down to its lowest setting; she would have liked to open a window. The room was crowded with furniture and ornaments, but everything shone brightly. Someone, most likely Caitlin, spent a lot of time cleaning and polishing. A number of framed photographs stood on top of the small television in the corner of the room. Susan picked one up. It was of her grandmother as a young woman. She had a baby on her knee; a boy of about fourteen and another of ten stood by her side and, at her feet, sat five more children, boys and girls of varying ages. A stern looking man in a stiff white collar had his hand on her shoulder as if claiming her as his own.

Her aunt came in, pushing a wooden tea trolley with small rubber wheels. 'That's a photo of my parents, with the family. That's me, sitting on my mother's knee, and Davy, he was the eldest, is there on the right. Wasn't he a handsome boy. And always so kind to me. Mind you, there was such a gap of years between us, by the time I was growing up he was off to the war. Then he married your mum, so I didn't see a lot of him after that.' She picked up the photograph and held it up so that Susan could see. 'This one is Ned, that's Bessy—she died of diphtheria when she was three—and that's Bronwen and Brynhey, the twins, both dead now and this is Dylan—named after the poet—and Angelica. There's only me left now.' She replaced the photograph on top of the television.

'You needn't have gone to so much trouble Aunty, really,' Susan protested, as her aunt poured some milk into her cup.

'It's no trouble my dear and, as I said, I don't get many visitors. I can't think when I last used this teapot. I never bring it out for Betty. She doesn't like tea. Only coffee. It's pretty, isn't it,' she added drawing Susan's attention to the intricate design of roses and gold leaf that covered the delicate porcelain.

Susan nodded her agreement then asked, 'And how is Betty? Do you see much of her?'

'Not so much now she has her new job, but she phones. It was her idea I get the mobile phone. That way she can check up on me.' She laughed. 'Not that I have much opportunity to get into mischief nowadays.'

'Is she still married?' Susan asked.

'Yes. She has a nice husband, West Indian chap. Lived here all his life.'

'Do they have any children?'

'No, Betty didn't want any. It's a shame really, I think Winston would have liked some. He'd be a great father,' she replied. She handed Susan a scone.

'What a pity. So no grandchildren then.'

As she said it, Susan regretted her words. A sadness descended on her aunt's face like a grey cloud and she seemed to become smaller and frailer. Her daughter's decision was obviously a great disappointment to her.

'No, well she didn't want to take the risk you know. She was frightened the baby would be handicapped. Some more tea, Susan?' She poured out a second cup for herself and then one for Susan.

As she sipped her tea, Susan wondered how to bring the conversation round to the topic of her illegitimate brother. 'Do you have any more photographs of my dad, Aunty Kate?' she asked.

'Yes, I've got dozens. My mother bought me a Brownie camera for my twelfth birthday and I just loved it. I took lots of pictures, well, snaps really. Some of them aren't very good but they'll give you an idea of what he was like when he was younger,' her aunt replied, her enthusiasm returning. 'You help yourself to another scone and I'll go and look them out.'

Her aunt disappeared into the room with the bay window and reappeared a few minutes later with a couple of battered photograph albums in her arms which she placed on the coffee table in front of Susan. Her round face, with its apple cheeks was very different from Susan's father's pale, gaunt features but nevertheless there was a strong family resemblance. As they started to look through the photographs, this became even more apparent.

'I hadn't realised you and Dad were so alike,' Susan said picking up a rather faded photograph of the two of them.

'When we were younger, yes, but not so much in later years. He was the lucky one, always so slim. I became quite plump when I reached my forties, although I've lost most of it again now. Here look at this one. See what I mean?'

Her aunt handed her a photograph of her uncle, with his arm around a middle-aged woman with wide hips and a full bosom that struggled to escape from her rather tight sweater. The woman was looking straight at the camera and laughing. 'That's me and Albert. He always said he liked a woman with plenty to hold onto.'

Susan smiled. Her uncle had died at sixty-five, just five days after he had retired. She remembered her mother saying at the time how unfair life was, how Caitlin and Albert had been a perfect couple and now Caitlin had to grow old alone.

'Do you have any of my mum?' Susan asked.

'Not that many. Like I said I didn't see much of them after they got married. Although after your grandmother died your dad used to write to me almost every month. Ah, here's one of their wedding but you've probably got this one at home.' She handed her the album. 'They were such a handsome couple and so much in love. It was wonderful to see them together, always finding excuses to touch each other in some little way, brushing against each other or letting their fingers touch under the table for a moment. Your dad used to write her poems, you know. Sometimes I would catch them looking at each other as though there was no one else in the room. I was just a kid then and a very romantic one at that. To me they seemed like a couple of film stars.'

Susan looked at the photograph. She knew it well. Her parents smiled blissfully at the camera. Her mother's dress was of a close fitting satin, embroidered with tiny pearls on the sleeves and neckline, its diaphanous train falling to the ground in a swirl of light. She carried a tiny bouquet of lily-of-the-valley. Susan's father held his bride's hand. He looked immaculate in his dark suit, a white carnation in his buttonhole, the love in his eyes still shining from the celluloid after all these years. She recognised the people standing around them: Granny Thomas, Nanny and Grandpa Taylor, a young Caitlin that looked no more than eleven-years-old, her mother's elder sister Gladys with her first husband, her uncles Tom and Christopher. 'Yes, I've got this in a frame at home,' Susan said. She turned the pages of the album. 'Why didn't we keep in contact with the family after Nanny and Grandpa Taylor died? Do you know?' she asked.

'People didn't travel about so much in those days you know, not when you were young. It's different now. Everyone has a car and a telephone and it's so much easier to keep in touch. Look at me with my little mobile,' her aunt replied, touching her mobile phone affectionately.

'Yes, I know that but something must have happened to my parents when we lived in Taunton. Before that my cousins used to come to stay for a week in the summer, or we would take the train to visit them at Christmas. Then nothing. Did they have a fight?' Susan was reluctant to tell her aunt what she remembered of those years.

'Didn't your mother ever say why that was?' her aunt asked.

'My mother didn't say anything but she even stopped sending them Christmas cards,' Susan replied. 'She said it was a waste of money. They'd only throw them in the bin.'

'But didn't she tell you anything later? When you'd grown up?' her aunt asked, getting up and putting the cups back onto the tray.

'Well I think my father had an affair when I was about twelve but my mother never spoke much about it. I think it hurt her too much.' It was a relief to say the words that she had never said to anyone before. She continued, 'But why would that stop her keeping in touch with her own brothers and her sister? They never even came to her funeral.'

'Your mother was a very proud woman. She idolised your father. I'm sure you know that.'

Susan nodded. Was she at last going to learn more about her mother?

'When Davy fell in love with someone else she just couldn't accept it. She didn't tell anyone about the affair, not her parents, not even her sister, and she was very close to her sister. She didn't want anyone to know that this fairytale love of theirs, that was going to last forever and ever, had already foundered after only fourteen years. She just couldn't face them. She was too ashamed.'

'But she had nothing to be ashamed about,' Susan said.

'Maybe not, but that wouldn't stop people talking. If a husband strayed in those days, people would say it was the wife's fault in some way. So she didn't want anyone to know. I don't know which she feared most, their condemnation or their pity?'

'So she just cut off all contact?' Susan asked.

'Yes. I didn't know anything about it at the time. I was only in my twenties then and had gone to London to work. But later, when your father started writing to me regularly, he told me the whole story. He was very unhappy, you know,' her aunt continued. 'I don't think he ever stopped loving your mother. He just loved someone else as well.'

'So her own family didn't know anything about the affair?' Susan was trying to make some sense of her parents' actions.

'Well, not at first. They were all very hurt when she severed contact, and annoyed with her too. Then of course it came out, like all secrets do eventually but by then it was too late. It had become one of those family skeletons that everybody was aware of but nobody spoke about. Anyway, why the sudden interest?' Her aunt turned her blue eyes, so like Susan's father's, directly on Susan.

'I was going through some things in the attic and I came across a box of old letters and photographs belonging to my parents. It got me thinking back to my childhood. You know I hadn't thought about it in years,' Susan replied.

Her aunt drank some more tea.

'So my 'andsome, why are you really here? It's lovely to see you, but you've never dropped in to see me before, and I've lived in this house for twenty-five years,' her aunt said.

Susan could see that it was about time that she came to the point. Her aunt was old but she wasn't senile and her mind was as sharp and clear as it had ever been—the pile of puzzle magazines and Sudoku books under the coffee table bore witness to this.

'Well, I found this in the box with the letters.' Susan took the photograph of the new-born baby out of her handbag and handed it to her aunt. 'It has an inscription to my father from a woman called Anthea. I want to find that baby. Baby. Goodness, he must be a man in his forties by now and I think he's my half-brother. I want to meet him.' Susan explained.

Her aunt looked at the photograph and said nothing. Then she leaned forward and put her head in her hands.

Susan continued, 'I've come to see you because I thought you might be able to help me find him. The only thing I've managed to find is his birth certificate and the fact that Anthea is dead. So I thought I'd ask the family next but there are only you and Betty left. I just hope you can help me.'

'I just don't understand why you want to stir this all up now, after nearly fifty years.' Her aunt stretched across and took Susan's hand. She looked bewildered.

'I don't really understand it myself, Aunty Kate, but I need to find out more about these people. My parents were never happy after that child was born and my own childhood came to an abrupt end. I have lived all these years with these secrets. Now I want them out in the open,' she said, for the first time realising why she was sitting there in that stifling room, when her husband thought she was at work. She was suddenly tired of all the lies, ashamed of deceiving Graham. She was as bad as her mother with all these secrets. She resolved to talk to her husband as soon as she returned home.

'Well my dear, I'll tell you what I can remember,' her aunt replied, leaning back in her chair and resting her feet, in their fluffy blue slippers, on the tapestry pouffe in front of her. 'I'm sure you know that in the fifties life was not easy for a woman who had a baby out of wedlock and especially when the father was a married man. But Anthea was a nice girl, by all accounts, only twenty-two when your father met her at some university course—on the Victorian novel, I think it was.' She paused. 'Anyway Anthea was there and when they met it was a revelation for both of them. I think their heads were full of all that Victorian romantic nonsense and they fell in love. Your father was considerably older than her, but he was a handsome man and he certainly had a way with words.' Her aunt smiled sadly.

Susan listened patiently as her aunt unravelled the tale of her father and his mistress for her. Anthea's Catholic parents had insisted she leave home when they realised she was pregnant. They knew she had no prospects of marrying the father of her child, so they arranged for her to stay in a mother and baby home in the Midlands, where nobody knew her. Their plan was for her to stay there until the baby was born then, when it was six weeks old, to offer it up for adoption. Then and only then would Anthea be allowed to return and resume her old life and, hopefully, nobody would be any the wiser.

But Anthea had been desperately unhappy in the home. The rest of the girls were unfriendly and had little in common with her. There had seemed little point in endless baby-talk or in knitting matinee coats when she knew that, in the end, the baby was going to be taken away from her. So a few days before the baby was due, she persuaded Davy to help her escape. Caitlin was a bit vague about what happened next. The baby had been born in Exeter Maternity Home a few days later. She thought he'd rented a flat for Anthea in the town but later she and the baby had moved away.

'So she didn't have the baby adopted?' Susan interrupted.

'No. Well she couldn't really part with him,' her aunt replied. 'Nobody would adopt him like that.'

'So where is the boy now? Do you have an address for him? Did Anthea get married?' Susan's head was bursting with questions.

'As you know Anthea is dead. She died two years ago from ovarian cancer, poor thing,' Caitlin replied.

'I know about the cancer,' Susan said. 'That much I found out but I couldn't find out what had happened to the child.'

'Look, I think I need some more tea. All this talking is making me parched. Why don't you put the kettle on while I go and get dressed. Then we'll talk some more,' her aunt suggested. Caitlin looked tired. The animation that had brightened her cheeks earlier had drained away and as she watched her aunt shuffle towards the door, Susan felt that her insistent questioning was probably the cause.

Susan went into the tiny kitchen and refilled the kettle. She could feel her heart racing as she thought how close she was to finding out about her half-brother. At last, after all these years, she would learn what had become of him. But then what? What was she going to do with this information when she had it?

When her aunt returned, she seemed refreshed. She had brushed her wiry white hair so that it swept away from her face in a row of small tight curls, and applied a dusting of powder to her face. She was now dressed in a plain grey dress, with a matching, heavy knit, wool cardigan around her shoulders. She wore lisle stockings and flat leather shoes which had stretched with time to take on the shape of her bunions.

'That's better,' she said with a smile. 'Now pour me a cup of fresh tea, dear and I'll carry on with my story.'

Susan did as she was bid then waited until her aunt was sitting comfortably by the fire, sipping the hot tea before she asked her next question. 'Aunty Kate, what did you mean when you said that Anthea *couldn't* have the baby adopted? Was that a religious objection or something? And why wouldn't anyone adopt him? I don't understand.'

'Say that, did I, my 'andsome?' Sometimes her aunt's Welsh accent resurfaced through the years of Leicestershire brogue. 'Well, because of his condition, of course. Nobody was going to adopt him were they, in his condition.'

'But what was the matter with the baby? Or do you mean because he was illegitimate?' she asked.

'No Susan, of course not. Most of the babies that came up for adoption were illegitimate. No, he was one of those poor little Mongol babies,' her aunt replied, looking surprised that Susan had not been apprised of this fact.

'Mongol babies? Do you mean he had Down's Syndrome?' Susan asked. What ever she had been expecting to hear, it wasn't this. Down's Syndrome. Her brother had Down's Syndrome? There had to be a mistake. She knew of nobody in her family with Down's Syndrome.

'Yes, only in those days they used to call them Mongol babies, because of their slanting eyes,' her aunt continued, oblivious to the shocked look on Susan's face. 'It was a big shock to Davy and Anthea you know. I don't think she wanted to have her baby adopted anyway but of course when she learnt how he was, it was out of the question.'

Susan picked up the photograph of the baby. There was no evidence of Down's Syndrome in his sleeping features. 'You can't tell from this photograph,' she said, holding it out to her aunt. Maybe she was mistaken. She was pretty old, after all. Maybe she was confusing him with someone else.

'No, it's not obvious. Lovely little chap, he was.'

Susan took the second photograph out of her bag. 'Is this Michael, too?'

'Yes, that's him, the little sweetheart,' her aunt replied. 'Where did you find that?'

'With the letters.'

Her aunt peered closely at the photograph. 'Yes, you can see it around the eyes, if you look carefully. Of course it got more pronounced as he got older. Poor Davy, he was distraught when he found out about it.'

'So what did they do?' asked Susan. 'What happened to Anthea?' She began to feel sorry for this poor woman, thrown out by her parents and having to bring up a handicapped child on her own. She couldn't believe her father had been a lot of help to her.

'Well her parents wouldn't have her back to live with them, not with the baby. So for a few years she looked after Michael on her own—they called him Michael you know after her grandfather. Davy used to send her money each week, although I don't know how he managed it without your mother finding out, and Anthea's mother would send her bits and pieces: clothes for the baby, food, sometimes some money. Her father didn't want anything to do with her. He said she'd shamed them and that having a Mongol child was God's punishment to her. He was a cruel man, for all his religious zeal.' She sipped her tea and for a moment said nothing, lost in the past. 'It was a shame. She was a nice girl, well educated. I only met her a few times, but I liked her. She was a lot quieter than your mum, shy almost. Bringing up Michael was very hard for her but she got by. I'll say this for her, she was determined. She wasn't going to give up Michael, no matter what happened.'

'So what did happen to him?'

'Nothing happened to him. He stayed with his mother. There was no real alternative in those days. It was that or he would have ended up in some institution for the mentally handicapped. Neither of them were going to let that happen.' She paused and wiped her eyes with a small, white handkerchief embroidered with cream lace. 'At first the baby was in and out of hospital. He seemed to catch everything that was going. You know these babies often have problems with their hearts. Michael had a tiny lesion in his heart when he was born but they didn't do anything about it. They didn't in those days. They just checked up on him from time to time and I think it must have healed over as he grew older. Nowadays of course they would have operated as soon as he was old enough but not then.' The old lady drank some more tea then continued, 'His biggest problems came when he became old enough to go to school. As you can imagine he was quite a long way behind his peers, his writing was awful and his reading was very slow but he seemed to get there in the end. He had great perseverance—probably got that from his mother—but he needed more time to do things and lots of patience from those around him.'

'And my mother? Did she know about the baby? Did she know he had Down's Syndrome?' She wondered how her mother had reacted to that news. Had it made things worse between her and Susan's father?

'Yes, Davy told her. But it made no difference; she still didn't want him to have anything more to do with them. She knew he sent the child presents but she never knew that he continued to see him.'

'Maybe she did. Maybe that was why they fought so much. And what about the rest of the family?'

'Well everyone knew about your father's affair and that there had been a child, but I'm not sure whether they knew that Michael had Down's Syndrome. I doubt it. Your father never had much to do with your mother's side of the family and your mother certainly didn't tell them.'

She suddenly remembered her parents arguing about money. It had been to do with a school trip to Paris when she was fifteen. A vivid picture of her mother screaming at her father came into her head. She'd accused him of spending all their money on... who? It must have been Michael. Susan had never gone on that school trip. Nor the one the following year.

'So where is Michael now?' Susan at last asked the question she had driven a hundred and fifty miles to ask.

CHAPTER 13

It was almost lunchtime when Susan arrived back at her hotel. She went straight to her room and plugged in her laptop. Her aunt had given her the address and telephone number of the Bramshill Village Trust and said they would tell her where Michael was living now, but Susan wasn't ready to talk to anyone just yet. Her mind was reeling with what she'd just learned from her aunt. Her father had been in a more difficult position than she'd first thought. Not only did he have another family, his baby son was disabled and the mother was homeless. What must he have felt when Anthea told him her father would have nothing to do with her? When had he known that Michael had Down's Syndrome? How had it affected him? He was a kind man at heart. He'd supported his own mother until he left home to get married. He'd been a good husband and father, until he had met Anthea. He wasn't a bad man, she could see that now. So how could he have left Anthea and his son to fend for themselves? Yet in the end that's what he'd done. He had stayed with Susan and her mother, carried on living with them as though the others didn't exist. No wonder he was unhappy. Or was that the real problem? Maybe he didn't leave them. Maybe it was because he kept on seeing them that her mother was crazy with jealousy. Susan began to feel sorry for her father. He'd got himself into an impossible situation. She had never really believed him when he said he loved her mother, how could he when all they did was argue, when their nights were broken with angry rowing? Now she was beginning to realise that she'd never understood him. She had run away from their nightly feuds and made a new life for herself without her parents. She never really knew what went on between them after she left home, only that they continued to live together and that neither of them was happy. How could she have behaved like that? Yes, as a child, her natural instinct was to run away and hide, not to listen to them arguing, but as an adult? Surely she should have tried to find out what was at the bottom of their unhappiness. But she hadn't. She hadn't cared. She'd wanted nothing to do with them and left them to sort out their own miserable lives. Now she felt ashamed that she had been such a poor daughter to them. Her father had been caught up in a web of deceit and lies, it was true, but there was more to it than that. He loved two very different women and he felt a responsibility to them both. It required someone much stronger, much more practical than her father to find a way out of that entanglement.

She typed in the name of the Bramshill Trust and waited to see what came up. She wanted to find out a little about them before contacting Michael. It didn't take her long to learn that the Trust was an independent body, founded in Northumberland in 1940 as a therapeutic community for adults with learning disabilities. Although it was basically a secular organisation, it appeared that a number of Christian societies helped to maintain it. She scanned through the pages and soon located the Bramshill centre nearest to Leicester, in a small hamlet just outside Uppingham. The centre was based in the rural community and ran its own market garden.

Susan stared at the page before her. This was a deciding moment. There was the telephone number in front of her. All she had to do was ring and ask for Michael. But what then? Would he want to see her? Did she *really* want to see him? Or was she just doing this because of a guilty conscience? She suddenly felt angry with her father. Had he known that she would one day find out about Michael? Is this what he'd wanted all along? Is that why he'd left the photographs in the box? He wanted her to find them. He wanted her to find Michael, she was sure of it now. Maybe he expected *her* to take on responsibility for his illegitimate son. She slammed the computer shut. Why couldn't he have talked to her about it? Why couldn't he have told her about Michael? No, it was more his way to let her find out for herself and feel compelled to do something about it. But how could she take care of Michael? He was now a man in his late forties with Down's Syndrome, no longer a baby in a blue bonnet. She paused, contemplating whether she should drive back to Maidenhead before she got in any deeper. She'd never met anyone with Down's Syndrome before. How disabled was he going to be? She knew very little about the condition, only things she had heard, such as: Down's Syndrome babies were born to older mothers, that they looked different to other people and that they were happy, placid children who didn't achieve much academically. She sighed. Somehow she didn't want these stereotypes to be all there was of her brother. Her father understood her too well. He knew she would need to find out more. He knew she would take up his guilt.

There were hundreds of reference sites. The first thing she learnt was that the life expectancy of people with Down's Syndrome had doubled since the 1950s when medical research into the disorder had clarified much of the mystery surrounding it. Although the condition had been identified over a hundred years previously, it was not until a group of geneticists discovered that individuals with Down's Syndrome possessed an additional chromosome, that any real headway was made into understanding the condition. Susan had never been very good at science, so she found much of the material difficult to digest, but she did understand that this extra chromosome occurred at the time of conception and was attached to the 21st chromosome, resulting in what was called chromosomal Trisomy, and that it accounted for ninety-five per cent of all cases of Down's Syndrome. A simple diagram showed her clearly that these people had all their other chromosomes paired perfectly, one from the mother and one from the father, until it came to the 21st, which had three, the extra one normally, but not always, coming from the sperm.

Michael had been born when all this research was new so she felt that it was unlikely that he'd benefited from it. At the time that Anthea became pregnant they didn't scan at fourteen weeks for extra chromosomes, particularly because with a young woman like her, the risk would not have been anticipated. She read on through the causes. There still was nothing definitive; nobody really knew why it occurred. Although people had floated various theories on the detrimental influence of smoking, alcohol consumption and x-rays amongst other things, nothing could be proved. It still remained the case that it was more likely that older women would give birth to a child with Down's Syndrome but, she read with interest, that the disorder could also be passed down through the father. She thought of her own father. Had he known this? His niece Betty had decided not to have any children. Was the propensity for this disorder on his side of the family? Was that why her parents never had any more children? Had he been worried about having another child with Down's Syndrome? Did he explain this to her mother or did he just make a unilateral decision to have no more children? This could well have been another cause of their unhappiness.

She saved the references so that she could print them out when she got home and jotted down some questions for the next day. Her neck and back were aching and a dull headache was forming at the back of her skull, so she packed away her computer and decided to ring the Bramshill Trust before they'd all gone home for the day. A polite young man answered the telephone on the second ring and informed her that Dr Edmundson was out at that moment but offered her an appointment for ten o'clock the next morning. Susan eagerly accepted it. It was done. Tomorrow she would meet her half-brother.

CHAPTER 14

At ten o'clock the next day she found herself outside the gates of Sunny View Farm, a branch of the Bramshill Village Trust. She parked her car and walked up to the front door of an imposing Victorian house built in the vernacular style. Somebody was watching her through one of the Georgian style windows. She rang the bell and waited. Eventually a young woman with Down's Syndrome, and dressed in jeans and a red sweater, opened the door.

'Good morning, I've come to see Dr Edmundson,' Susan said.

'Please come in,' the girl replied, holding the heavy door open so that Susan could pass. She spoke with a slight lisp. 'Do you have an appointment?'

'Yes, for ten o'clock. My name is Susan Masters. I may be a little early,' she added.

Susan was shown into a small office and asked to take a seat. After a few minutes the girl came back and said, 'Dr Edmundson will see you now. Please follow me.'

They walked down a long corridor until they came to a large airy room at the end. An elderly man sat behind a desk that appeared to be too small for him. As he rose to shake her hand, a slow smile spread across his face and she realised he was not as old as she had originally thought. Surprisingly deep blue eyes looked out at her from behind a pair of gold rimmed spectacles and, although his hair was grey, his beard was liberally sprinkled with ginger hairs.

'Good morning Dr Edmundson,' Susan said, trembling slightly as she shook his hand. She was as nervous as a schoolgirl meeting the headmaster for the first time.

'Oh, call me Barry, please. You must be Mrs Masters. Please sit down.' He indicated the chair in front of his desk. 'Now, how can I help you?'

'Well, actually Dr Edmundson, Barry,' she corrected herself hurriedly. 'I'm looking for someone and I thought you might be able to help me.' The doctor continued to smile and waited for her to continue, his hands resting on the desk. 'I'm looking for my half-brother. He has Down's Syndrome and my aunt thought he might be here with you.' The words sounded very lame when said aloud and she could hear the tremor in her voice.

'Your half-brother? Well, we do have some people living here who have Down's Syndrome—this is a centre for people with special needs and we have about two hundred adults and a number of children living here in extended families. He could be one of those. What's his name?'

'Michael David Wright Thomas,' she replied. 'At least I think that's his name. I've never actually met him.'

'Michael. Yes I know Michael well; he first came to us when he was a young lad of no more than twenty. He's a great guy.' The doctor paused then continued, 'So you're looking for Michael. May I ask why, after all these years?'

Susan could feel her heart beating wildly in her chest; this was the part she'd been dreading. 'It's not easy to explain. In fact I don't really know where to begin.' She swallowed and then continued. 'Michael is my half-brother. My parents had a very unhappy marriage and I think Michael's birth had a lot to do with it. To be truthful I think I have known, deep down, for many years that Michael existed but never allowed myself to confront it.'

'So why now?' Dr Edmundson persisted.

'My parents never spoke to me about him, not directly. It was after they'd both died that I came across a photograph of Michael as a baby—it was amongst some old letters of theirs. That was when all the memories came flooding back to me and I had this urge to find out what had happened to him.' Susan went on to explain how she had tracked down her aunt and, through her, learnt that Michael had been born with Down's Syndrome.

The doctor listened patiently then asked her, 'Did you know Michael's mother?'

'No.' For some reason she could feel herself blushing.

'Do you know that she died?'

'Yes, my aunt told me. Is that when Michael came here?' Susan asked.

'In a way, yes, but he's been coming here on a daily basis for many years, long before that. Anthea, his mother was a very caring woman and very religious. She was plagued by a sense of guilt for what she had done and saw Michael's disorder as a kind of punishment. Her father's attitude didn't help either; he was completely unforgiving and never visited her nor his grandson.'

'It all seems very Victorian,' Susan commented, 'especially in the light of today's permissive society.'

'I know, but attitudes were very different in the fifties—unmarried mothers had a hard time,' Dr Edmundson continued. 'Her parents wanted her to put Michael into an institution, but Anthea refused.'

'Is Michael severely handicapped?' Susan asked, feeling her usual composure returning. She had to keep a clear head and not let her emotions run away with her. That was the only way to show Dr Edmundson that she was serious about meeting her half-brother.

'No, I personally wouldn't describe Michael as handicapped at all. He has certain learning difficulties but copes extremely well with them. Maybe it would help if I told you more about him, and people with Down's Syndrome in general,' the doctor offered.

He then explained to Susan how, contrary to their stereotype image, people with Down's Syndrome were as different from each other as anyone else in the world. When they were allowed to integrate with other children in mainstream schools and be part of a wider community, he told her, their personalities and talents developed in much the same way as in any other person. In his opinion the old stereotype image had as much to do with institutionalisation as with Down's Syndrome.

'They're people first and people with Down's Syndrome second. That's why we have fewer residents with that particular disorder nowadays. More and more of them want to live independent lives,' he continued.

'But what about Michael? Does he live independently?' Susan asked.

'As I said, Anthea wouldn't put Michael into an institution. She kept him at home and worked with him every day on his speech, his motor skills and his behaviour. He was very lucky because she helped him a great deal. However, when he was five he had to go to school—it was the law. No mainstream school would accept him, so he was sent to a special school for children with mental disabilities. This upset his mother very much so she insisted that he be allowed to come home every weekend. She used to catch a bus from Uppingham into Leicester every Friday evening to collect him and take him back again on Sunday. I think he enjoyed going to school. He learned to read and write and he made friends with other children and, because of his mother's efforts with him at the weekends, he made more progress than most in his class.'

'She sounds as though she was a very devoted mother,' Susan commented.

'She was but she was also overprotective.' The doctor went on to explain how Michael had first come to Sunny View. 'By the time Michael was twenty he needed to find some work. His mother wouldn't allow him to work in the town, even though attitudes towards employing people with Down's Syndrome were changing by then. She was frightened he would be ridiculed or abused in some way so she came to me and asked if he could work on the farm.'

'And he's been here ever since?' Susan asked.

'Yes.' The doctor stood up. 'Would you like to walk round the farm and see what we do here?' he asked.

'Yes, very much.' She replied, wondering when he was going to let her see Michael.

A door from the room led straight outside to the gardens, where she could see a number of outbuildings and some large greenhouses in the distance.

'We have over two hundred and fifty acres here,' Dr Edmundson said. 'Many years ago it was a refuge for Quakers and some of their ideals still linger on in our work. We promote the concepts of dignity, equality and understanding, and we encourage independence and self-help. Everyone here is encouraged to integrate with the wider community wherever possible.'

He guided her round the farm, showing her the pig pens, the chickens, pointing out the sheep on the nearby hillside and then taking her through the craft workshops. It was all very impressive and a hive of industry, but what most impressed her was the cheerful, independent attitude of the residents.

'Those are some of our residential homes,' the doctor said, pointing to a block of brick maisonettes. 'We have twenty-five in all. There's an extended family living in each one. Michael lives in one over the other side.' He pointed across to somewhere beyond the greenhouses.

'Are we going to see him now?' Susan asked.

'I suggest we talk about that later, in my office, but I'll show you where he works,' Dr Edmundson said, as they left the workshop and walked across to the IT room. 'Besides looking after the residents here, we also provide work and support services for people that live in the town but want to come here during the day. That was what Michael did originally. First of all he came and worked on the farm—he loves animals you know. Then about five years ago, when we opened the IT centre, Michael became interested in the computers. He was very quick and soon learned how to operate them. Now he helps the IT instructor with his classes,' he told her. The doctor stopped outside the Information Technology room. 'We won't go in and disturb them but if you look through here you'll get an idea of the facilities.'

She peered through a glass panel set in the door. The room was light and airy and painted in a light blue, with workstations along three of its walls. On the fourth wall was a white board and a man was writing something on it with a thick felt-tip pen; the students were listening carefully to his instructions. Susan counted fifteen workstations and all but one of them were occupied. When the teacher finished his explanation the students swivelled back to face their computer screens. That was when she noticed a second man standing behind one of the students and pointing out something on the screen.

'That's Michael,' the doctor said. 'The one in the green pullover.'

The man had his back to her so it was hard to see him clearly. He seemed to be about five-feet-six in height and, although he was not fat, he was quite thick-set with a wide neck and shoulders. His hair was brown and curled over his collar—it reminded her of her father's hair when he was young. If only he would turn round. She was desperate to see his face, to see if he looked like her father.

'We won't interrupt them at the moment,' Dr Edmundson continued, turning and walking down the path.

Reluctantly Susan followed him. To be so close to Michael after all these years and not to speak to him, not to even see what he looked like seemed very hard but the doctor showed no sign of stopping. He strode ahead of her and didn't look back until they were once again in the main building. As they went inside the girl with the red jumper came to meet them.

'Beryl, would you mind getting us a couple of cups of coffee?' the doctor asked her, then turned to Susan. 'I'm sure you could do with a coffee after listening to me all this time.'

Susan smiled. 'That would be lovely,' she said.

'Well, did you enjoy the tour?' he asked, sitting opposite her.

'Yes. I found it all very interesting. You seem to have a very happy place here,' Susan replied. She wondered if she should mention how disappointed she felt not to meet Michael. After all that was why she was here.

'Happy? Yes. But more than that I hope. 'Useful' and 'fulfilling' are words I like to think are appropriate.'

'Yes, those too. My impression is that the farm functions very successfully and that the people who live here are happy with what they're doing,' she replied.

This seemed to satisfy the doctor, who leaned back and said, 'Well, and what about Michael?'

What about Michael indeed? She was beginning to realise that she had absolutely no idea where she should go from here. She still felt resentful about the fact that her father had never confided in her about his son. What was she expected to do now that she knew the truth?

'Do you think I could meet him?' she asked. Maybe that would help her to decide.

'Of course you can meet him; he's your brother after all. That is not the question. The question is *should* you meet him?' the doctor replied, regarding her with a serious expression. 'But before you decide, let me tell you a bit more about Michael.'

Susan waited as Dr Edmundson removed his spectacles and polished them carefully. Once replaced, he continued, 'Michael is mentally more active and physically more capable than most of the people here, but he depended on his mother for almost everything. I told you she was overprotective. Well apart from coming here to work, Michael went nowhere without her. She never married and dedicated her life to him, almost to the point of stifling him. Naturally, now he misses her very much, but what is worse he doesn't know how to live an independent life.'

'Is there no-one to care for him?' Susan asked.

'He doesn't really have any family left. There's your aunt. She rang a few times after his mother died but she's never been to visit him. His mother was an only child and any relatives that may be alive probably wouldn't even know that Michael existed.'

'What about my father?' Susan asked. 'Did he visit Michael?'

'Your father would come and see him from time to time; he even came here in the beginning to check that Sunny View was a suitable place for Michael to work. But as he grew older his visits became more infrequent. I think he found the journey rather daunting.' He paused and removed his spectacles once more. 'What I'm trying to say is that Michael is very vulnerable. He desperately wants to belong to a family and would be delighted to know that you were looking for him, but...' He stopped.

Susan finished the sentence for him, 'But once I've met him I might just go away again. Is that what you're thinking?'

'Yes. I can see you understand my dilemma. It wouldn't be fair to Michael. I need to know what you intend to do once you've met him. Is this a genuine concern for him or merely a fanciful notion, a passing interest in a new-found step-brother? A misplaced pity perhaps? Are you prepared to have a genuine relationship with this man? And most importantly, what do your family think about it? Even today not everyone would welcome a person with Down's Syndrome into their family.'

Susan recognised the wisdom in his words but could find no words of her own to answer him. She needed time to think things through more carefully. She realised that she was acting out of character, responding to an emotional need that she hadn't known existed. 'You're right. I shouldn't have come here,' she said, the trembling in her voice betraying her disappointment.

'No, I'm not saying that. Just think about where this is taking you. Don't start a process of events that you will regret, especially if those events lead to Michael being hurt.'

'Give me some time. As you say, I need to talk to my husband and my son about this first. Then maybe we can all come back and meet him together,' she suggested, rather sadly. She felt deflated. How was she going to broach this subject with either of them? Nobody even knew she was here.

The doctor regarded her silently as she replaced her coat and picked up her handbag.

'Do you have a photograph of him?' she asked suddenly.

'Yes, I think I do.' He opened the desk drawer and took out a plastic folder of photographs. 'I collected these together for the local paper. They did a nice little piece on our efforts for the environment last month. I'm sure there's one of Michael.'

She watched him sort through the pile of photographs. 'Yes, here's one of him with Brian, in the IT room,' he said triumphantly, handing her a black and white photo. 'You can keep it if you want.'

Susan took the photograph; the two men were standing side by side, looking directly at the camera, the computers lined up behind them. She knew instantly which one was Michael because, although not pronounced, the facial characteristics of Down's Syndrome were obvious. Another detail in the photograph caught her by surprise. Michael was standing there, his head tilted slightly to one side and his right foot forward, a pose that she had seen her father adopt whenever someone produced a camera. This was her father's son, without a doubt.

'Thank you,' she said, trying to stop herself from shaking as she put the photograph into her handbag. What was Graham going to say about this? And Aidan? Suddenly she was not so sure they would want to drive all the way to Leicester to see someone who had never been part of their lives, no matter what she said to convince them. She could imagine Aidan's comments and even Graham telling her it was best to leave well alone. Whatever her intentions had been—and they were far from clear—maybe she should just walk away and leave her brother to his sheltered, organised existence. The doctor was right; he couldn't allow her to destabilise Michael's life on a personal whim.

CHAPTER 15

As Graham drove into the golf club car park, he was surprised to see that it was almost full. Normally he didn't play golf on a Tuesday but, as Susan was away, he had telephoned Bill, his usual Thursday afternoon partner and had no difficulty in persuading him to change his plans. He backed his 1968 Jaguar Mark 2 into the space, in his usual neat and methodical way. He was very fond of this car. He'd bought it about ten years before, not long after he retired. He lifted his clubs out of the car boot and made his way to the changing rooms. It was good to be away from the house for a bit; a round of golf would clear his head. The burglary had shaken both of them. Even Susan's usual calm posture had cracked under the strain of seeing their lovely home wrecked like that.

*

They'd arrived in Maidenhead with very little. Susan had been at university when he met her and as soon as she had her degree, they'd got married. For him it had been love at first sight, so he saw no advantage in waiting. They sold the tiny flat he owned in Bristol and used the proceeds to buy into a dental practice in Maidenhead. Things were tough for the first few years while he struggled to get his new practice off the ground; they had lived with his parents in a crowded pre-war semi in the north part of the town. It was far from ideal, but it was all they could afford and it was within walking distance of the shopping centre and the local Further Education college—as it was known in those days—where Susan had managed to get a job in the Management Studies Department.

Then, much to their surprise and his delight—he was never sure if Susan really wanted any children— Susan became pregnant. That changed everything and as soon as Aidan was born, he knew they had to buy their own home. One day quite by chance, when they were taking Aidan for a picnic by the river, they saw the house they wanted and had instantly fallen in love with it. It was a large ramshackle building, with high gables, white pebble-dashed walls and a tiled roof, and it was obvious that no one had lived there in a long time. The windows were closed with ill-fitting, blue shutters that needed a coat of paint, and ivy and Virginia creeper grew up the walls, twisting their way around the peeling drainpipes. A few roof tiles had come adrift, blown down in some storm no doubt, and lay smashed on the terrace by the front door. Despite its poor state of repair, they still wouldn't have been able to afford it if two things hadn't happened at the same time: Graham received an unexpected legacy from an uncle's estate and Susan was promoted to Senior Lecturer. With hindsight he could look back now and realise that they had bought in the golden age of property prices, before decimalisation sent the price of houses, along with everything else, on an ever upward spiral. Inflation at twenty-five percent a few years later would certainly have swept that house out of their reach. As it was, it took them many years to get the house into a reasonable state, but that hadn't deterred them. It had been hard work but fun. Even Susan had enjoyed sitting down at night with colour charts, arguing over shades of paint, haggling over the price of guttering with the local builder, wandering from shop to shop to find the cheapest tiles, tracking down timber yards lost in the suburban countryside, then spending their weekends sanding, trimming, rubbing-down, painting, labouring for the bricklayer. 'Yellow Pages' became the best read book in the house, followed closely by 'The Complete DIY Manual.' They were young and in love, and DIY was the fashion. This was their dream home.

Graham couldn't restrain the sigh that escaped his lips as he thought of those halcyon days. They'd been so happy then and so much in love. Susan had been different. Her work hadn't been so challenging and she actually seemed to enjoy spending time at home with him and Aidan. Their life had stretched before them with no end in sight. But people change. He imagined that he too had changed from the fresh-faced young man she had married. Susan certainly changed. It all began when she left the college and joined a management training company. It was no longer just a job of work for her; it was a career. There were more pressures, more travelling, more prestige and more rewards. He had been grateful for the extra money at first, but he soon began to miss her company. She had insisted that Aidan go to a boarding school, even though he'd said they could manage quite well with a child-minder on the days she was away. It had been hard seeing that little chap going off at the start of term and knowing that you wouldn't see him for weeks on end. But Graham's practice was thriving and so Susan was probably right, as usual, because half the time there was no-one at home, anyway.

*

Bill was already in the changing rooms, lacing up his golf shoes, when Graham arrived.

'Hey Bill. Did you get anyone to make up a four?' he asked, sitting down on the bench beside him and removing his shoes.

The style of the men's changing rooms hadn't altered in the thirty years that he had been a member and whenever he entered its dark and gloomy interior he felt at ease. The parquet wood floor was stained dark from years of polish and covered in myriad pinpricks, wounds from the spikes of countless golf shoes over the years. Rows of tall wooden lockers lined the walls, one of which belonged to Bill and its door had swung open to reveal a collection of golf balls, tee pegs, old score cards, an empty water bottle and a battered golf cap. There were few windows in the locker room and the air exuded that familiar warm, fetid smell of cut grass and old socks.

'Yes, Derek's already here and Mike said he was coming. We're due off at 9.30; that way we'll be out of the way of the ladies,' Bill replied, straightening up and closing his locker with an old fashioned iron key.

'Of course. It's Ladies' Day. No wonder the car park's full. I'd forgotten all about that.'

They went out to join Derek, just in time to see him hole a long putt across the putting green. 'Getting in some practice, I see,' said Bill. 'You don't need to bother; we're not playing for money today. Graham's with us.'

Derek looked up and grinned. He was a few years younger than Bill and Graham, but the wide floppy hat he always wore, no matter the weather, and his baggy trousers added to an overall dishevelled and unkempt look that belied his years. Graham never played for money and the others joked that he was too much of a purist to sully his game with side bets. In a way it was true. For him there was enough competition in a normal game and he had no need to look for more. He played the game much the same as he did everything else in life, with precision and care. But he would be the first to admit that he also enjoyed the exercise and especially the companionship.

A hearty shout broke through the tranquility of the golf club scene. 'Hang on, chaps. Wait for me.' There was Mike, puffing and panting as he ran across the putting green, his golf bag slung across his back like a haversack, a golden retriever loping behind him attached to a long length of rope.

'Late as usual, Mike. What's your excuse this time?' Graham asked good-humouredly. 'Hello there Daisy,' and he stooped to pat the dog affectionately.

'Well, it's Tuesday. We don't usually play on Tuesdays, do we? It's bloody Ladies' Day, isn't it. Couldn't find anywhere to park. I've ended up right down by the church, miles away.' Mike was spluttering with indignation.

'Good, you'll be able to call in and say a prayer of thanks when you've finished then, won't you,' said Bill.

'Why are we playing today, anyway? Has someone cried off Thursday?'

'No, nothing like that. Susan's running a training course up in Leicester. She'll be gone for a few days, so I thought I might fit in a bit more golf,' replied Graham.

'Good idea. How are we playing? How about you and me, Bill, against those two?'

*

Later, as the four men sat together in the clubhouse bar drinking pints of the cool local bitter, they talked over the round, retracing shots played and putts missed. Graham felt tired but in a warm, weary way that was not unpleasant; it was a tiredness that came from four hours of gentle exercise in the fresh air. He listened to his friends arguing good-naturedly over the final outcome of a particular hole and smiled to himself. What a pleasant way to spend a day, he thought. Just time for another half and then he would make his way home and see if Susan had left anything in the freezer for him to eat.

'So she's deserted you again, has she?' Mike said, putting two more glasses of beer on the table in front of them.

'It's her job. I'm used to it by now,' Graham said, picking up the beer. It was true he was used to Susan's absences but that didn't mean that he liked them. When he was working it hadn't been so bad, but now he was retired he would have liked to have had more of her company.

'How's the insurance claim going?' Bill asked. 'Are they going to cough up?'

'They sent someone round just after it happened, but since then we haven't heard anything. They were a bit surprised that the alarm didn't go off, but Susan told them that it was obviously faulty and they didn't mention it again.'

'I don't blame them. I wouldn't like to get in an argument with your Susan,' said Mike.

'I'll have to give them a ring to see what's happening, I suppose,' Graham said. It was a shame Susan was away at the moment; she was much better at that sort of thing than he was.

'Yes, you keep on to them. These insurance companies are very good at dragging their heels when it comes to pay-out time,' Bill added.

'Did you hear that old Fred is off to South Africa for the winter? Lucky sod, he'll be playing in shorts while we're freezing our bums off here,' said Derek.

'That sounds nice. Maybe we'll do something like that when Susan gives up work. I like the idea of spending the winters in a warmer climate. This cold weather doesn't do my knee any good.'

'Is she going to retire at last?' Mike asked. 'I don't believe it.'

His friends all knew what a workaholic Susan was. She was not a bit like Mike's wife, who had given up work when she became a mother and never wanted to go back. Mike didn't have to go home to frozen meals, he thought, a little resentfully.

*

Graham was in the kitchen, heating up some beef curry that been left over from the week before, when the telephone rang.

'Six-seven-eight-three-two-one,' he answered in his usual abrupt telephone manner.

'Darling, it's Susan.'

'Susie, how are you? I got your message.'

'I'm fine. The course went well and the reviews were good, so John will be pleased.'

'That's good news. Does that mean you'll be home soon?' he asked, hoping for an affirmative. 'I'm just heating up that beef curry.'

'Beef curry? I thought you had that last night.'

'Yes, I did. I thought I had taken out a Bolognese sauce for tonight, but I didn't have my specs on at the time. So I'm going to have the other pot of curry with spaghetti tonight, for a change,' he explained.

Susan laughed. 'Oh Graham, you're impossible. Good job I'm coming home tomorrow.'

'What sort of time will you arrive?' he asked.

'I'll set off early, so, all being well, I'll be home before lunch,' she replied.

'Don't you have to go to the office first? What about all the training materials and the course reviews? Surely John will want to see them straight away.' Graham knew the usual procedure.

'No, don't worry, Paul will take all of that in his car. He lives in north London anyway. Then I'll go in on Thursday to debrief John. I'd hoped to get away as soon as we finished but, to be quite honest, I'm too tired to drive all that way tonight. My room's booked until tomorrow anyway so I might as well stay. You can do without me for one more night, can't you darling?' she added.

'Yes, of course. I've got Jess to keep me company anyway,' he replied.

'So, how was your golf?'

'Oh, pretty good. I played with Derek, and we beat Bill and Mike three and two. Mike was furious but it was his fault they lost - he was putting very badly. But Bill had some bad news; he's been having some tests done and they've told him he has prostate cancer. He's starting chemo this week. Poor chap, he was quite cheerful about it really.

'Oh, that's awful news. Poor man. I hope they're mistaken.'

Susan had rarely met Graham's friends although he spoke about them frequently. She'd never shown any interest in playing golf even though Graham had tried to encourage her right from the start of their relationship. Fortunately for him, she didn't object to him playing but she said she just couldn't see the point in spending fours hours hitting a little white ball with a stick. In fact, the only sport he ever remembered her playing was a bit of tennis with Aidan and only that because they had their own court and she liked to keep him amused. Graham could understand that she didn't want to play golf, but he would have liked her to have accompanied him to more of the golf club's social occasions. There were the usual annual events: a summer ball, a Christmas dinner and a New Year's Eve party but Susan was never keen to attend them. He knew his friends had formed the impression that she was too stuck-up to socialise with them, but they never said so to his face.

'Well Susan, we're getting to the age when these things start to happen, you know,' he said, rather sadly. He looked at his reflection in the mirror that hung by the telephone; how old he looked. When had that happened? When had he turned into such an old man?

'Now, don't start worrying about things like that. You've got lots of years left yet. Look, I'm going down to the restaurant now to see if I can get something to eat and you get back to your "curry a la Italiana." I'll be home tomorrow. See you then, sweetheart.'

'Okay, Susie. Sleep well. See you tomorrow,' he replied. 'Drive carefully.'

When he had sold his dental practice, just after his sixty-first birthday, he'd hoped that he and Susan would spend more time together, travel perhaps or at least do some of the things that work had prevented over the years. They'd both had demanding jobs for some years and he felt that they deserved to take life a bit easier before they got too old to enjoy it. But when he'd suggested that Susan give up work, or at least work part-time, she'd been horrified, saying she was too young to retire. She loved her job. 'I wouldn't know what to do with myself,' she'd told him. He'd muttered something about more time with the grandchildren and more time at home with him, but the withering look she gave him told him not to press the issue. Now he was an old man with a gammy knee. Ideas he'd had about walking holidays in the Pennines or spending a couple of months in Europe, no longer seemed feasible. He automatically stirred the curry then, on a sudden impulse, he tipped it into Jess's bowl. He would have something down at the pub tonight.

CHAPTER 16

When Susan arrived home the next day, her husband was in the garden, straddling the roots of a large willow tree with the strimmer in his hand, sending a fluttering cloud of debris into the air.

'Hi, Graham. I'm home,' she called from the house.

'Hello Susie. I didn't hear your car,' he said, turning off the strimmer. 'You're early. I wasn't expecting you for another couple of hours at least. And you've brought the sunshine with you.'

The rain of the previous few days had gone, leaving the air clean and fresh; a bright orange sun shone down on them from a cloudless sky. She walked across the lawn to join him. The grass was soft and damp underfoot and her shoes left slight indentations in the newly mown grass. She breathed in deeply, enjoying the dampness that still hung in the air.

'I left straight after breakfast and had a clear run through. No hold ups for once,' she told him.

He removed his plastic goggles and putting his arms around her, kissed her affectionately. 'Well it's nice to have you home,' he said. 'Especially as I've run out of frozen meals.'

Susan laughed. 'I can take a hint. I'll cook you a steak *au poivre* tonight to make it up to you. Okay?' She was pleased to be home with Graham, secure in the circle of his dependability. As she'd driven down the motorway, watching the mileage posts flash by hypnotically, she'd rehearsed what she would say to him, but now that she was here it didn't seem so easy to undo the lies that she had woven. She decided to wait until the evening.

'Did Aidan get in touch with you?' Graham asked.

'Aidan? No. Why should he?'

'Well he phoned on Monday morning for a chat and seemed a bit put out that you weren't here.'

'A chat. Aidan doesn't just phone for a chat; he usually wants something.'

'I was just going out the door so I didn't have time to find out what it was about. I told him to give you a ring on your mobile.'

Susan took her mobile phone out of her jacket pocket and flicked it open. 'No, there're no missed calls here. Maybe he really did just want a chat,' she added, trying to remember the last time she and Aidan had had a chat that hadn't ended up in an argument.

'I expect he'll ring tonight. I told him you would be home today,' her husband said, replacing his goggles and returning to the strimming.

Susan watched him for a few minutes then went back into the house to unpack her bag. Jess followed her, tail wagging excitedly, pleased that her mistress was home again.

*

As she hung up her clothes and put her shoes back in the closet, Susan thought back over the last few days. She had learned a lot. Now she had to put it all into context.

Her father had obviously kept in close touch with his other family—she couldn't help but think of them as a second family now—for longer than she'd thought. What had Dr Edmundson said? Her father even went to check on Michael while he was at Sunny View. He wasn't a child then. He was a young man. So why didn't he tell her about him? It had not been just a case of loving two women at the same time, there had been the children to consider. Here lay the reason behind the open wound that her mother displayed at every available opportunity; her father couldn't have both families but wouldn't choose between them. No wonder her aunt said he was unhappy. Susan knew her father was weak and indecisive but he was a kind man and it must have pained him deeply to be unable to make either woman happy.

She remembered an argument she had with him on returning from university. He had been angry that she didn't want to stay on and take an MSc. 'I can't understand you, Susan. You have had all the advantages. You just don't know how lucky you are,' he'd shouted at her. At the time she'd felt hurt at his words because she knew that whatever advantages she may have had, she'd made for herself. Now she realised that he'd been thinking of Michael when he said it. He must have loved his son yet he never told her about him. She wished her parents were still alive; she wanted to talk to them about Michael. She needed to understand how they felt, what they would advise her to do now.

She heard Graham go into the kitchen and turn on the tap. 'Cup of tea, Susie?' he called up the stairs.

'Please. I'll be right down. Just going to ring Aidan,' she replied.

*

Aidan was getting into his car when his mobile rang. It was his mother. Good. Now he'd find out exactly what she'd been up to.

'Aidan, it's Mum. Your Dad said you phoned while I was away. Did you want me for something?'

'Yes I did, actually. I wanted to know what you were planning to do on this week's holiday that your secretary thinks you're taking.' His mother didn't reply but he knew she was still listening. 'Where have you been Mum? Dad said you were running a course in Leicester. But we know that's not true, don't we? Come on Mum, what's going on?'

'Aidan, I'm sorry you've got involved in this. It's not what you think.'

'What do I think, Mum?'

'Look Aidan, I'll explain it all later, when I see you.'

'Why the secrecy? What's going on?' he repeated. 'Why did you lie to Dad?'

'I've told you. I'll explain later. It's complicated,' she replied. 'You didn't say anything to him, did you?'

'Of course I didn't. But just tell me. Are you having an affair?' he asked.

He heard his mother laugh. 'Don't be ridiculous Aidan. A love affair, at my age,' she replied. 'I don't know whether to be flattered or insulted. And, if you must know, I am still in love with your father.'

'Then why the lies?'

'Look darling, I have to go now. Why don't you come over one evening and we can all talk. I have something I want to tell you, anyway. I'll ring later to arrange it.' His mother rang off before he could ask any more.

He switched off his mobile and put it in his briefcase. He believed his mother when she told him she was not having an affair —it had always seemed unlikely—but the relief at this reassurance was offset by the disappointment he regularly felt after a conversation with her. Once again she held him at arm's length; once again he was excluded from her confidence. Something was going on, that was obvious, but he would be the last to know. He pulled out his diary. He couldn't go over to his parents tonight. It was Wednesday and he always took Zak and Ben to football training. He decided that Thursday would be better; he would leave work early and go straight there. He'd tell Judy when he got home.

*

Susan put the telephone back on its cradle. How like Aidan to ring the office on the one occasion she hadn't gone where she said she was going. Luckily he hadn't mentioned his suspicions to Graham but she knew he would come over to interrogate her at the first opportunity. She decided she'd better talk to Graham as soon as possible; the last thing she wanted was Aidan further complicating an already complicated situation with stories of a non-existent lover.

A lover? The idea made her smile. Her own words came back to her, 'And if you must know, I love your father.' Yes, it was true, she did love Graham. Perhaps not in the way she had when they were young, but in a quieter way. She relied on him. The fact that he was always there, solid, dependable, made her life much easier. Yes, she did love him and she needed him. When had she last told him that? God, she couldn't remember. One New Year's Eve, when she'd had too much to drink?

'Susan, your tea is getting cold,' her husband called.

'Coming, darling,' she replied and went to join him.

Graham was sitting at the kitchen table, reading the local paper. 'There's been another robbery,' he said, 'at The Gables, that big house, further upstream.' He continued reading: 'Last Sunday night. They got away with quite a lot of stuff: cash, jewellery, two televisions, a mobile phone. Hope they were insured.'

Susan picked up her teacup then put it down again. 'Graham,' she said. 'I have something to tell you.' She opened her handbag and removed the photographs.

Her husband put down his paper and looked at her anxiously.

'Graham,' she hesitated. 'I'm not sure how to start. Well, you know that I've never really told you about my childhood, but I'm sure you were aware that my parents weren't very happy,' she began at last. Her nervousness made her voice sound stiff and formal. She could feel her stomach churning with anxiety. How was he going to take the news? It would be a bombshell for him as well.

'Well they were always very civil in front of me but I often felt that something was not quite right with their relationship,' he replied, always the master of the understatement. 'And you were always very vague about your childhood days so I never liked to press you.'

'You know I hadn't really thought much about the past, not for years, until last week when I was clearing out the attic.'

'Oh, that old box of letters. That's what started it, then?' he asked.

'Yes, and this photograph.' She put the photograph of Michael as a baby on the table in front of him.

Her husband picked it up and looked at it carefully. 'Who's this little chap then? I don't recognise the name,' he said.

As Susan took a deep breath and began to explain about Anthea and her father, she prayed that her mother would forgive this betrayal of her long kept secret. She struggled to squash the emotions churning inside her and tried to remain objective, explaining as simply as she could how she had tracked down her father's illegitimate son, fruit of his love affair. Graham listened attentively to all she said. If he was surprised at the news, he didn't show it. Emboldened by his silence, she continued, 'So you see, when my meeting was cancelled and I had some free time, I thought it would be a good opportunity to visit Aunty Kate and see if she could tell me more about what happened to him.' She looked up to see Graham looking at her strangely, as if he'd never seen her before.

At first her husband said nothing then he asked, 'So, the other night when you started talking about your Aunt Kate being at the funeral, you were trying to find out if I had her address? You were already planning to visit her?'

'Well yes, I suppose I was hoping to contact her or something.'

'Why didn't you just ask me for it?' he asked.

Susan didn't reply. She knew she had acted out of character but couldn't explain her actions, even to herself. Graham continued to stare at her. He didn't look angry, just puzzled; he seemed to be trying to take in what she'd said, to make some sense of it.

'Free time? What free time do you mean?' he asked suddenly.

'Well, you see,' she began nervously. Her voice was beginning to fail her. 'My, my meeting with Jim Brady of Beavis's was cancelled …'

'And the training course?' Graham interrupted her.

'There was no training course. I made it up.' As the words came tumbling out she could see them building an instant wall between them, brick by brick.

'And Paul Burton?'

'Paul wasn't there. He doesn't know anything about it. Everyone at work thinks I'm on leave,' she replied.

Her husband continued to stare at her from behind the barrier of her own making. She could not look at him.

'So it was all a pack of lies?'

She nodded, dumb with misery. 'I just needed an excuse to get away and look for Michael,' she admitted. Never had she felt so wretched. She and Graham never kept secrets from each other and here she was admitting to having fabricated the whole thing.

'But why didn't you tell me? I could have gone with you. Why all this subterfuge?'

'Well, darling, I...' she paused. With hindsight she couldn't understand why she hadn't told him. There was no good reason. Graham would have been totally supportive, she knew that. Instead she'd slipped all too easily into the complicity set in motion by her mother. 'I don't know. I suppose I felt a bit silly dredging up the past like that. It might all have come to nothing.' Her justification sounded hollow.

'Susan, I'm your husband. Don't forty-two years of marriage count for anything?'

Graham didn't raise his voice but his anger was evident in the coldness with which he spoke. Susan had never seen her husband so annoyed before; she'd gravely underestimated his reactions and as yet she hadn't told him that she'd found Michael nor mentioned his disorder.

Her husband pushed aside his unfinished cup of tea and stood up. 'Susan, I'm not sure I know you anymore,' he said and turned abruptly and went into the garden.

'Graham, wait,' she said, jumping up in an attempt to detain him, the photographs falling to the floor.

He didn't reply. Susan stood and watched his retreating back but she didn't follow him. Usually so confident, now she was unsure of how to proceed. The high-pitched whine of the strimmer cut through the previous tranquility, in much the same way as her confession had done. How was she ever going to make this up to him?

*

They ate their dinner in silence. Susan had cooked the steak she'd promised, but Graham seemed to have little appetite.

'Here Jess, a little treat for you,' he said to the dog as he fed her slices of fillet steak.

Susan said nothing. It was Graham's strict rule that nobody fed the dog at the dining table.

'Would you like some dessert? I've made an apple pie,' she said.

'No, thank you. I'm not very hungry,' he replied.

Graham had not spoken to her since their talk in the kitchen. He was normally an amiable man and not one given to sulking, so their infrequent quarrels were soon forgotten. Tonight he replied politely to her questions but didn't seem interested in initiating any conversation. She couldn't tell if he was still angry with her but it looked highly unlikely that she would have the opportunity to resume her conversation about Michael that evening.

'I'm quite tired after my journey; I think I'll go to bed,' she said.

Graham didn't look up from his newspaper.

'Good night then darling,' she said, bending down to kiss his forehead.

*

The next morning when Susan awoke, Graham was already showered and dressed.

'You're up early. Are you playing golf today?' she asked.

'Yes, we're teeing off at eight.'

Susan was relieved to see he was more like his usual self. She got out of bed and grabbed her dressing gown off the chair. 'I'll make you some breakfast,' she offered.

'No, don't bother. I'll get something at the club,' he replied. 'I'm going straight out. Maybe you could give Jess a walk today.'

Graham was a man whose life was orderly and regulated; he liked his routine, and this routine included an early morning walk with Jess to collect the daily paper, followed by a substantial breakfast. He never varied it, not even for a game of golf. He couldn't have told her more clearly how let down he felt by her actions.

Susan went down to the kitchen to make herself some coffee. There was a heavy feeling in her chest, and her head ached. She hadn't intended to hurt him, she told herself; she'd only wanted to discover a bit more about her brother first, before telling him and Aidan. As she said it, she realised that it too was a lie—she hadn't considered their feelings for a single moment. As she thought back over the week, she could see that she'd been so absorbed in finding Michael that she'd forgotten that she had her own responsibilities. She was not a twelve-year-old girl anymore; she was a wife and a mother, a grandmother even. Whatever action she finally decided to take about Michael, she couldn't do it alone. They would all have to agree.

She heard her husband's footsteps in the hall and opened the door to see if he was about to leave. He was carrying a brown suitcase and his golf hold-all.

'Where are you going?' she asked, staring at the suitcase.

Graham gave her an icy look and didn't reply.

She watched him pick up his golf clubs and put them over his shoulder. He took his checked cap off the peg by the door, picked up his luggage and opened the front door.

'Are you leaving? Graham. Speak to me. What's the suitcase for?' She watched in amazement as he loaded everything into the boot of his car. 'Graham where are you going?' she called, running after him.

He turned and looked at her coldly. 'Away.'

So that was it? He was leaving her over a few silly lies? She couldn't believe that her quiet, dependable husband was going to leave her. She watched him reverse the car and drive away. Then, with tears streaming down her face, she took her coffee and went back upstairs.

They'd been married a long time—forty-two years. Was it really that long? Surely he wasn't leaving her over something so trivial? After all they were happy or so she'd believed before today.

She'd been happy, but what about Graham? Had she ever thought about his happiness before? Or had she just taken it for granted? Maybe she'd been too wrapped up in her own life to realise that her husband was not as secure in this belief as she was. She turned on the shower, still feeling uneasy about his absence but the warm water drumming on her head and the back of her neck calmed her. He'd be back. Graham wouldn't walk out over something so trivial as a few lies. Or would he? Suddenly she didn't know any more. Her perfectly organised life seemed to be turned upside down and most of it was of her own making. Reluctantly she remembered that she had to be at work, turned off the tap and towelled herself dry. Then she went upstairs to her office to prepare her notes for the day's meeting.

However today she looked at her notes but didn't see them. She thought back to her confession of the previous night and now, as she sat watching a blackbird looking for food in the geranium pots, scattering soil in all directions, she realised how selfish she had been. They'd been married such a long time, so why hadn't she confided in him? Why had she kept it all to herself?   No wonder Graham was angry. She hadn't trusted him enough to tell him what was troubling her, instead she'd concocted a complicated lie that was designed to exclude him and she'd not considered for one moment how he would feel when he eventually found out. Susan thought back to how it had all begun, how a couple of trivial incidents had led to this discovery. Now less than two weeks had passed and yet their lives seemed about to change forever.

CHAPTER 17

When Graham pulled up outside Bill's house, the lights were still on in the kitchen, so he knew he hadn't missed him. He parked his car and walked slowly up to the front door. Bill's house was small but he kept it immaculate: the front door had been recently painted in a muted blue colour and the garden was well cared for. The garden had been his wife's pride and joy and when she'd died, Bill had begun to devote more and more time to it. He joked that he was afraid she'd come back and haunt him if he didn't mow the lawn every week.

'Hello. What are you doing here? We don't have a golf match, do we?' his friend asked, when he opened the door.

'And good morning to you, too,' Graham said, with a good humoured smile. 'No, for once it's not golf. Aren't you going for your chemo this morning?'

'Yes.'

'Well, I thought I'd take you there and give you a bit of company.'

Bill stared at him.

'Aren't you going to ask me in? I'd love a cup of tea—if we've got time that is,' Graham continued.

'The kettle's just boiled. Come in. Come in. I wasn't expecting this,' he said. 'Do you want some bacon and egg? I was just about to cook myself some.'

'Sounds great.'

*

They didn't discuss the ordeal facing Bill, although it was at the forefront of both their minds. What was there to say? It would go well or it wouldn't. There was little either of them could do to alter the outcome.

He dried up the plates and watched as Bill stacked them neatly in the cupboard. The house was no different from when Elsie had been alive—everything in its place. Graham knew how much Bill missed his wife, even though he rarely mentioned her these days. Keeping the house as she would have wanted it was his way of honouring her memory.

'What time's your appointment?' he asked.

'Eleven o'clock.'

'It's the first one, isn't it?'

Bill nodded, carelessly, as though it were no big deal, but Graham knew his friend well enough to tell that he was shit scared. 'You don't need to come. I'll be fine,' he said.

'Well, I'm here now. It's no trouble to run you to Wycombe. Anyway, I wanted to get out of the house.'

'Problems at home?'

'You could say that.'

Bill said nothing, but poured some water into the teapot.

'It's Susan. I just can't believe it,' Graham continued. 'She's been treating me like an idiot, feeding me all sorts of lies. And I am an idiot because I believed her. I don't know what's worse, her lying to me or this feeling that I've been used.'

'Have some more tea,' Bill said.

'God, you sound like my grandmother. Yes, why not. Another cup would be nice,' Graham said, smiling despite his anger with Susan.

'So, are you going to tell me what the lovely Susan has done?' Bill asked.

*

It had helped talking to Bill and he liked to think that his presence at the hospital had helped him a little too. When he saw Graham's suitcase on the back seat of the car, his friend had said that he could stay with him for a few days if he wanted to, but already Graham was regretting his hasty decision. When he'd packed his bag he'd no idea where he was going; he'd just wanted to make a point. He wanted Susan to see that she couldn't take him for granted like that. He felt he'd been a good husband to her over the years. He hadn't stayed out drinking until all hours with his friends; he'd been a good provider and he'd never had any ex-marital affairs, although to be honest, he'd had plenty of opportunities. When he'd suggested that they have another baby and she'd been adamant that one child was enough for them, he hadn't pressed the issue, although he had always fancied a big family. He knew that Susan wasn't really cut out for motherhood. Not that she'd been a bad mother—no, if she had a job to do then she would do it to the best of her ability, whatever it was and this included being a mother. He just thanked the Lord that they had Aidan, although he often wondered if they would have had any children at all if Susan hadn't forgotten her pills that weekend when they went to Paris.

He wasn't a demanding husband. The truth was that he never wanted anyone but Susan and he wanted her to be happy. All night he'd mulled over what Susan had told him and he still couldn't believe it. He felt such an idiot to have been so trusting.

'Pint of the usual?' asked the golf club steward.

'Yes please, Reg.'

'On your own today?'

Graham smiled and nodded. Bill had been feeling a bit rough after his treatment so he had taken him home and left him asleep on the sofa.

He sat down in a chair by the window. Two elderly ladies were putting out on the eighteenth green. If only he could have got Susan interested in golf, but somehow the thought of the elegant Susan marching down the first hole with a woolly hat pulled over her ears was incongruous. He loved his wife but even he could see that she was selfishly bound up in her own life, with little regard for anyone else. He'd been retired for ten years now but despite his protestations Susan continued to work. If only her job wasn't so demanding; she was away at least twice a month, sometimes more, leaving him in that big, empty house on his own.

Aidan was right when he said they rattled around in it. He certainly felt that at times. But he knew people who had down-sized when they retired and then they regretted it because there was nowhere for their grandchildren to stay. He didn't want to sell their house and buy something smaller. That was the house he wanted to die in. It was already written in his will that when he and Susan were both gone, then the house would belong to Aidan. He wanted him to live there with his family, and then leave it to his own children. After all that's what it was, a family house, the sort of house that would pass down through the generations. He smiled to himself. He was being sentimental. That sort of thing didn't happen anymore. A house like theirs could be sold for a vast profit and Aidan's financial worries would be over.

If only Aidan and his family came over more often the house wouldn't feel so empty, but whenever he suggested that they invite them for the weekend, Susan had some reason to put it off. And it was always to do with work. Her job dominated their lives; there were short trips abroad that spilled into their weekends, five-day residential courses, endless meetings, the pre-course planning and the inevitable post-course reviews. She loved it all. But there were times when he hated Coleman's Training with a passion.

Of course it hadn't been so bad when he had the practice, but nowadays when he was on his own, time seemed to hang endlessly in the air. Luckily he had the golf, the garden—and Jess of course —to keep him occupied but when the weather was bad and he was stuck indoors he missed her company. He'd never said anything to her about how he felt nor had he mentioned the fact that he would have liked her to show a little more interest in his hobbies. He felt a twinge of self-pity. She never came near the golf club and most of his friends had never even met her. He often wondered what they thought of her, if they believed him when he told them how smart and funny she was. True he was not very keen on socialising with the golf club crowd—most of them were not really his sort—

but just once in a while it would have been nice if she had met him there for a drink, turned up unexpectedly on a summer evening, dressed in one of her simple but classic dresses. She would turn old Bill's head, for sure. But he knew she saw him as a man of routine, a bit of a stick-in-the-mud, content with his life, and this fitted in perfectly with what she needed from a husband. He made few demands on her and he was always there, at least until now, to support her. Suddenly it seemed all a bit one-sided.

'Here we are.' The barman put his pint on the table. 'Anything to eat?'

'I'll have the special.'

When he finished his lunch he'd go back and see how Bill was feeling. Maybe he would stay overnight with him. He'd certainly appreciate his company more than Susan would.

CHAPTER 18

In the end he decided to stay with Bill, and not just to punish Susan. Bill was very down after the chemo, so they watched the football together, and shared a supper of pork pies and brown ale.

'I think I'll take up your offer of a bed,' he said when it got to eleven o'clock. 'I don't think I ought to drive after all that beer.'

'Fine. The spare bed's already made up. I thought Jim was coming over at the weekend but in the end he had to work.'

Jim was his son. A nice enough lad, but always too busy to spend much time with his father.

'Won't Susan be worried?' Bill asked as he poured Graham another beer.

'Maybe. It'll do her good to be alone for once. She's always leaving me on my own, while she's away working.'

'But you usually know where she is,' Bill commented tactfully.

'Oh, all right. I'll send her a text to say I'm staying here. Okay? Just so she doesn't do anything silly, like ringing the police.'

His friend smiled. 'Thanks for today. I appreciate it,' he said, gruffly. 'I think I'll go up now. It's taken a lot out of me.'

'Okay. I'll see you in the morning then.'

Graham's conscience was beginning to bother him. He didn't like worrying Susan, even though she deserved it. He wrote a quick text to her and then turned off his mobile. The last thing he wanted was to get into a conversation with her at this time of night. He needed time to think about what had happened and whether he could ever trust her again.

*

The next morning he stayed with Bill long enough to ensure that he was feeling all right, then he went home. He knew she'd be at work. It took more than a walk-out on his part to stop Susan from going to work.

Jess was sitting in the kitchen when he got home, her head resting on her crossed paws.

'Hello there, girl. Missed me?'

Jess looked at him with her big, sad eyes and wagged her tail, but she didn't get up.

'I see. I'm in the dog house, am I? Well we can't have that, can we? Come on, I'll take you for a walk.'

He took her lead from the hook behind the door and before he could turn round she was up and waiting at the back door.

It was a lovely morning, cool and clear, with a slight nip in the air. They set off on their usual route, out of the gate and along the tow path. It was barely September, but the trees had already shed some of their leaves and they formed a thick carpet on the ground, browns and yellows that glowed warmly in the early rays of the morning sun. A half-empty pleasure steamer chugged past, heading downstream, its large paddle wheels churning the water into a white foam.

So what was he planning to do? He couldn't stay at Bill's indefinitely. He could go to Aidan's perhaps, but if he did that it would look as though he was intending to leave her. No, he couldn't do that. That would be too upsetting for everyone. He was angry with his wife but he still loved her and he couldn't really imagine living without her. He'd seen what poor old Bill's life had been like since his wife died. He never complained but it was obvious that he was very lonely without her. No, Graham didn't want that sort of life. He just wanted Susan to be a bit more considerate from time to time, and to stop treating him like a doormat.

He felt his mobile vibrate and took it out of his pocket. There were seven missed calls—six from Susan and one from Bill.

He dialled Bill's number. 'Everything all right?' he asked.

'Yes, I'm fine. I just thought I'd tell you that Susan phoned. She's looking for you.'

'What she phoned you? I didn't even know she had your number.'

'She phoned the house. I expect it was easy to find the number. Maybe she rang the club.'

'God, why would she do that?'

'She's worried about you. That's what she said. Wanted to know if you were all right.'

'What did you say?'

'Well, I didn't know what to say. I said you left after breakfast and I didn't know where you were. I thought you might have needed some time on your own.'

'You're right there, Bill. I just needed to think.'

'So what are you going to do?'

'Well, I thought I'd go to the club and have some lunch and a pint. Want to join me?'

*

It was getting dark when he arrived home. Susan's car was in the drive and the lights were on in the house.

'Graham, you're home,' she said when he went into the house. Good game?'

'I haven't been playing,' he answered rather curtly.

'Oh.'

He could see she was dying to ask him where he'd been, but all she said was, 'There's some pasta if you're hungry.'

'I've eaten, thanks,' he said. 'But you can pour me some of that wine.'

He could see she was waiting for him to say where he'd been all day but before he could tell her about Bill, she said, in her usual brisk and straight to the point manner, 'I need to talk to you, Graham.'

'Not now, Susan. I'm tired,' he said, taking the wine from her outstretched hand.

'But it's important. We need to talk. I know you're angry with me but you didn't let me tell you the whole story.'

'The whole story? So there're more lies, are there? Well, I'm sorry, Susan, but I don't want to hear about them. I'm still trying to come to terms with the ones you've already told me. Maybe you should find someone else to confess to. I'm not interested anymore.' It was true. He was tired of all her subterfuge. Why did she have to make life so complicated?

'But Graham, I've said I'm sorry. What more can I do?'

'Sorry? You think that's enough? Susan, it's not just about the lies. It's you. You never consider anyone else, least of all me. A marriage is supposed to be a partnership; it's about sharing. When did that change? When did you stop talking to me, confiding in me? What do you think I am, just someone to look after the garden and walk the dog? If that's all you need, you can hire someone for a few pounds a week. You don't need me.'

'Graham, where is all this coming from? Of course I need you. I love you.'

'No, Susan, you love your job. Work always comes first. Remember when I wanted us to go for a week to the Lake District last Spring and you said you couldn't take any time off because there was a new course coming up. And that cruise I won in the raffle at the golf club—you were working in Scotland at the time and I had to put it back in the draw. It's not just about me. When did your work become more important than your family? We hardly ever see Aidan and the kids, these days. There's always something more important than spending time with your family. I'm tired of it, Susan.'

It was true, every word of it and at last he could see that he had got through to her. She looked shaken and there were tears in her eyes. He was tempted to put his arms around her and tell her all was forgiven, that it didn't matter but the truth was, it did matter. Something was going to have to change.

He drank the wine straight down and said, 'I'll sleep in the spare room tonight.'

'Graham…'
'Go to bed, Susan. We'll talk in the morning.'

CHAPTER 19

The telephone rang dolefully a few times and she was about to hang up when her son answered. 'Aidan, it's Mum,' she said, her heart giving an unexpected skip of pleasure at the sound of his voice.

'Hi, Mum.'

'Everything all right? I haven't called at a bad time have I?'

'What do you want, Mum?'

'Look Aidan, I'm sorry we didn't have a proper conversation yesterday. It was a bit awkward to explain over the telephone. Why don't you and Judy come round for dinner this evening. I'll make your favourite: steak and kidney pie,' she promised.

'It's a bit short notice. We have three kids you know, or had you forgotten?' he said. He'd become very sarcastic lately. Was this her fault? Was Graham right when he accused her of not spending enough time with her family?

'I know darling but maybe you could get a baby sitter. What about that nice girl, Chrissie, who lives downstairs?'

'Well, as it happens, I was planning to come to see you tonight anyway, on my own.'

She'd been right. She knew he wouldn't be able to let it go. Oh well. 'Fine darling, but I would prefer it if Judy could come too. I want to tell you something and I'd like all the family there.' She didn't mention that she wasn't sure if Graham would be home or not; she didn't want to sound any more mysterious than she already did. 'It's just that I need everyone's opinion,' she added, 'and I'll explain about being in Leicester. I promise.'

'Very well. Chrissie will be in school now but I'll give her mother a ring,' he capitulated.

'Thank you, darling.'

'How's Dad? Aidan asked.

'Dad? He's fine. He's playing golf today.'

Graham had returned to his normal routine that morning, walking the dog and collecting the newspaper, before setting off to the golf course. When she said that she was going to invite Aidan and Judy to dinner that evening, he'd just grunted in a non-committal way. He'd been civil but not exactly talkative, so she decided to wait to tell him about Michael until they were all together.

'Okay, look I'll see what we can do. I'll ring Judy at lunchtime and check that she's free tonight. She goes to her dance class a couple of times a week but I don't think Thursday is one of her regular nights.'

'That's wonderful, darling. Ring me when you know. Bye,' she said.

So Aidan had planned to visit them tonight anyway. He was obviously worried about what she was doing. She plugged in her laptop and downloaded the pages she'd collected on Down's Syndrome. While the printer chugged away, spewing out page after page, she made a list of the things she would need to buy for the evening meal.

*

Aidan unwrapped a piece of chewing gum and popped it in his mouth; he would have preferred a cigarette. Judy had not been very pleased when he rang to say that they'd been summoned to his mother's for dinner that night.

'For goodness sake Aidan, we can't go all that way on a week night. Doesn't she realise we both work?'

'I know Judy, but she says she has something important she wants to tell us.'

'Well, you go. You can tell me all about it when you get home. You were planning on going there tonight, any way, weren't you?' Judy's voice had a sharp edge to it.

'I know, but she wants you to be there as well. She wants your opinion,' he explained.

'My opinion? She's never wanted my opinion before or anyone else's for that matter,' she retorted.

'Please Judy. I'll arrange the babysitter for seven. You'll have plenty of time to get ready. You're usually home by four-thirty aren't you?' Aidan knew his wife would ultimately agree once she had made her displeasure clear.

'Okay. But we're not staying late. I've got an early class tomorrow.'

'You're wonderful,' he said.

'I know, especially when you get your own way,' she said but he could hear the smile in her voice.

He opened his electronic address book and found the babysitter's number. Now he just had to convince Mrs Rush.

*

Chrissie arrived at exactly seven o'clock, armed with enough homework to last her all evening. Once they had her settled in and the boys in bed, they set off.

'I don't think we'll risk the M4 tonight; we'll take the 308, there'll be less traffic,' Aidan said when they were at last seated in the car.

'Whatever you think best, darling.'

Judy seemed to have got over her irritation at having to visit her mother-in-law and was smiling contentedly and humming some tune he couldn't quite put a name to. She was wearing a dress that Aidan didn't recognise but, as he felt he probably ought to, he didn't remark on it. Her hair hung loosely from two tortoiseshell combs, a fine golden frame for her heart shaped face. He glanced at her from the corner of his eye. She was lovely woman. He felt the warmth of his love for her; passion yes, but also that comfortable warmth that comes from many years together. He certainly wasn't interested in having an extra marital affair and a pang of irrational jealousy caught him between the ribs at the thought that she might take any other lover than him. He reached across and placed his hand on her knee.

She looked at him and smiled. 'What's got into you?' she asked.

'You don't mind, do you?' he asked. 'Going to Mum's, that is?'

'No, not now. I'm intrigued. Anyway it's nice to have an evening out without the boys for a change, even if we're only going to your parents. Do you have any idea what your mother wants to talk to us about?'

'Not really, but she has been acting a bit strangely lately.'

'Maybe it's something to do with her trip to Leicester. Do you think your Dad knows what she was doing there?'

'Not unless she's told him since I spoke to him. I just can't think what would make her lie to him like that. It's so unlike her.'

'Well you don't actually know that. She could have been deceiving him for some time without anybody knowing. You wouldn't have known if you hadn't phoned to talk to her about that flat,' Judy pointed out.

Aidan said nothing. He didn't like the idea that this was anything more than an isolated incident.

'Anyway, we'll know soon enough,' his wife continued. She switched on the radio and they drove in companionable silence for a while, then she said, 'I've got some news.'

'Mmmn? Good or bad?'

'It depends. I think it's good.'

He looked at her. She was grinning like the Cheshire cat. 'Well, what is it?'

'I'm pregnant.'

'What? How do you know?'

'I went to the doctor's this morning, in my free lesson.'

Pregnant. He was suddenly bombarded with mixed emotions; delight at the prospect of another child collided with fears about how they would cope financially.

'Well. Good news or bad?' she asked, the smile beginning to fade from her face.

'Darling, it's wonderful news. Wonderful. I'm just so shocked. But hey, maybe we'll get lucky and have a little girl this time.'

'I thought you needed another football player?'

'Girls can play football, too.'

They were driving due west and the setting sun had lit up the straggling clouds, turning the sky into a blaze of oranges and reds and tinging the crenellated towers of Windsor Castle a ruddy pink. A baby. Yes, it was wonderful news. Now he would have to do something about finding a larger house for them. Pat's words came back to him. A move away from London was the only answer.

'Shall I ring and say we may be a bit late?' Judy asked. The traffic had slowed to a crawl and she knew how much her parents-in-law liked punctuality, especially Susan.

'No, don't worry. We're only about ten minutes away now. Anyway, it was their idea for us to come over on a weeknight.' He pointed to a breakdown truck with a silver Porsche on the back. The car's front end was smashed and the windscreen broken. 'That looks like the culprit,' he added. 'We'll soon be moving now.'

He was intrigued to know what his mother was going to announce. It had to be important because she never invited them over for a meal during the week, in fact she didn't invite them over very much at all. He ran through the things it could be. A divorce? No, she'd just said she still loved his father. An affair? They had discounted that. Oh, no, maybe his father was having an affair. No, not that. He couldn't imagine it, somehow. A terminal illness? He felt his stomach contract with fear at that one. It had to be something like that. Or maybe they were going to move house after all. Yes, that was probably it. How like his mother to be melodramatic about things, saying she wanted Judy's advice about something, summoning them to dinner in this way, when she could just as easily tell them over the phone. Well now they had some news for his parents too.

CHAPTER 20

It was already seven-thirty and there was no sign of Graham. Susan was feeling distraught. Was he planning on staying out late again? Had he forgotten that she was inviting Aidan and Judy? She'd tried ringing his mobile but he'd switched it to voice mail and when it came to leaving him a message she hadn't known what to say.

The steak and kidney pie was ready to put in the oven, the vegetables were prepared and she had taken a lemon mousse out of the freezer. All she had to do was set the table. But what if Graham didn't come home? What would Aidan say? He would blame her. She sighed. Well, he'd be right. She'd started this mess and now she didn't know how to sort it out. Oh, if only Graham was here. She couldn't make any decision about Michael without him there to help her. She dialled his number again and this time when asked to leave a message, she said, 'I'm so sorry Graham. I never meant to hurt you. I want you to come home, please. Aidan and Judy are coming round tonight. We need you here. Please come home.' Her voice was breaking at the end and before she hung up she whispered, 'I love you, Graham.'

She replaced her mobile in her pocket, wiped her eyes and went into the kitchen to open some wine. She would have to carry on without him. It was too late to tell Aidan not to come; they would be here soon. She unfolded the tablecloth and spread it over the oak dining table. How was she going to tell Aidan about Michael? She had been depending on Graham to back her up, as he always did. Without him there she felt exposed, defenceless. She took out the cutlery and began to set four places then stopped. Tears filled her eyes. She just couldn't do this without Graham.

Suddenly Jess was on her feet, tail wagging; she ran to the front door and began to bark excitedly. Was this Aidan already? Susan ran her fingers through her hair, smoothing it into place. By the time she reached the door, Jess was wild with excitement, jumping up at the door, desperate to be let out.

'Okay, Jess. Just a minute. Give me time to open the door,' she said and let the excited dog run into the drive. Car headlights swept across the front of the house, blinding her. At first she couldn't make out whose car it was, but Jess knew and, as soon as it stopped, she was there to greet him. Her master was home.

*

Her family was sitting in the conservatory, drinking the Frascati that Graham had just poured. Her husband sat in the recliner, recounting his exploits on the golf course to Judy and Aidan, who sat side by side on the William Morris sofa.

'While we're waiting for the pie to cook, I'd like to talk to you,' Susan began.

At the sound of her voice Judy and Aidan turned towards her, but Graham continued to fondle Jess's ears and stared out of the window at the garden. He had said little when he returned, other than to ask what time Aidan and Judy would be arriving. Then he'd gone upstairs to shower and change.

Susan sat down opposite them, her hands in her lap. 'Graham and I have already talked a bit about what I'm going to tell you but he hasn't heard the whole story yet.' She looked at her husband. 'So, if you will bear with me, darling, I will explain.' She stopped and took a deep breath; this was far harder than any training course she had ever had to run. 'First of all, I want to apologise for my behaviour.' She noticed Judy's eyebrows raise. 'I have been very selfish and I have let you all down by being so deceitful. All I can say is that I never meant to hurt anyone and especially not you Graham. I'm truly sorry.' At last she saw Graham turn his face towards her and she continued, 'As you are probably now aware I have been to Leicester for a few days, not to run a training course as I led you to believe, nor to meet a lover, as my son thought,' she saw Graham look at his son in surprise, 'but to look for my half-brother.' Aidan's mouth opened in astonishment and, as he was about to speak, she said, 'Let me explain fully then I'll answer your questions. Actually Aidan, it was you who started this, by encouraging me to clear out the loft.' She took a sip of her Frascati and began to explain about the letters and the photographs. 'When I was going through some things of my parents, I came across this photo of Michael as a baby.' She handed them the photograph. 'As you can see, his name is Michael David Wright Thomas.'

She turned to Judy and explained, 'Thomas was my maiden name—my father's name.' She paused, awaiting a response. No-one spoke, so she continued, 'Well, Michael was born with Down's Syndrome and apart from my aunt Caitlin, who is in her eighties, he has no relatives but us. He is alone in the world.'

She watched the three faces in front of her carefully in the hope she could gauge their reactions as she went on to explain how her search had led her eventually to Leicester, where she'd discovered her brother's whereabouts.

At first no-one said anything, then Aidan asked, 'This Sunny View place, is it a home?'

'In a way, it's a centre for people with learning disabilities but it's also a working farm. Some people just go there during the day and others live there full-time. Their aim is to encourage everyone to be independent,' she explained.

'So he's probably just as well off living there then,' Aidan said.

'Well, I'm not sure. The doctor says he's not nearly as bad as many of the others. He's pretty bright, you know and hasn't any real physical disability. He just has nowhere else to go.'

'But you haven't actually met your brother yet?' Graham interrupted her. 'And how did you find out about the Down's Syndrome?'

She smiled. 'It was Caitlin who told me he had Down's Syndrome. But you're right, I haven't met him but I've seen him. Look, this is a picture of him with the computer teacher—Michael works in the IT department, helping the students.' She handed

Graham the photograph. 'Dr Edmundson, who runs the centre, didn't want me to meet Michael until I was clear about what I intended to say to him. He seems very fond of him. He doesn't want him to get hurt.'

'Well, I can understand that. First of all, he is going to wonder where you've been all these years, isn't he,' her husband said.

'Yes, Mum, that's a good point. How come you knew nothing about him before?' Aidan asked. 'Didn't Gran and Granddad say anything?'

It was becoming difficult for Susan now because she was not used to her family scrutinising her behaviour in this way. She drank some more of her wine before replying.

'It's a long story Aidan, and one that I will willingly tell you some day, but for now, suffice to say that I probably did know that my father had another woman, but not much else. Remember I was only a child myself at the time,' she said trying to excuse herself. 'And I never knew about Michael and the Down's Syndrome until this week.'

Graham was studying the photograph of Michael. 'You can see he has Down's Syndrome but he can't be all that bad if he's working in IT,' he said.

'No, that's just it,' Susan's face brightened as she smiled encouragingly at her husband, 'many people with Down's Syndrome can lead normal lives and have regular jobs.' She pulled out a folder of papers. 'I've downloaded some information about the condition. I hoped you might read it. They know a lot more about it these days.' She felt the need to go carefully with her family.

'We have a chap at work, he's Down's Syndrome. He works in the post room,' said Aidan.

'Oh, Aidan, you mustn't call him that. You have to say a man *with* Down's Syndrome,' his mother corrected him.

'Yet more political correctness?' he asked, tossing his head slightly.

'No, darling, it's not just that. Labels matter. He's a man first and a man with Down's Syndrome second, like anyone else with a health disorder,' she said, paraphrasing Dr Edmundson' words.

'Well, whatever.'

Susan sighed; she knew Aidan didn't like her chastising him, especially in front of Judy. He picked up the sheets she'd printed, glanced at them then tossed them to one side. This was going to be hard.

'This chap has been working with us for about ten years and everyone likes him. He seems a bit simple when you first meet him but actually he knows exactly what he's about. And he's a jolly good worker,' he said.

'Does he live alone?' Susan asked.

'I don't know much about him, really. Never go down to the post myself. I usually leave that to the girl in the office. But I think someone did say that he was married.'

Graham reached across and filled up Susan's glass with white wine. 'So what exactly do you have in mind, Susan?' he asked. Apart from a slight coldness in his voice, her husband appeared to have resumed his usual practical approach to family matters.

'I don't know. It depends so much on all of us. What you all think,' she said, looking at their faces.

'Well, it's obvious to me that you feel the need to do something for this young man. He is your brother after all,' Graham said. 'The question now, is what exactly?'

'But you haven't even met him yet,' interrupted Aidan. 'Don't you think you should meet the man first, before you decide to drag us all into it?'

'Well, it's a Catch 22 situation,' Susan replied. 'They won't let me meet him unless I intend to keep in contact with him afterwards.'

'As I see it, we have three options.' Graham once again tried to focus their attention on a practical way forward.

Susan noted with relief that he used 'we' not 'you.'

'Okay, Dad, what are they?'

'First, we do nothing and Michael continues with his life unaware that we exist.' Susan opened her mouth to protest. 'Just wait a minute, Susan,' he continued. 'You said you wanted to include us all, so give me the opportunity to speak. Second, we find a similar centre closer to us, so that we can see him from time to time. The third option is that he comes to live with us as part of the family.'

At first nobody spoke then Judy, who'd been listening to her husband and her in-laws with some interest, said, 'This is all very well-meaning but nobody seems to have thought of Michael's point of view. From what you've told us, Susan, he already has a job he likes and somewhere to live. You said that he 's been going to the centre for over twenty years and I would think that he has many friends there. Even the doctor, you say, is very fond of him. Have you never thought that he may not want to be uprooted from all that he knows and loves?'

'Yes.' Aidan moved to back up his wife's argument. 'We may be disrupting his life unnecessarily, just to make you feel better, Mum.'

Susan looked at her son. 'Aidan, that's not fair. This is not about me. This is about a man who spent his whole life being cared for and protected by his mother and now she is dead.'

'Yes, but we cannot replace his mother. We're strangers to him,' her son continued.

An insistent beeping intruded on their conversation. 'Oh, God. The pie.' Susan put down her glass and rushed out in the direction of the kitchen.

'Can I help?' Judy called after her.

'No, sit still Judy. Susan has it all under control. You can carry the glasses to the table, though,' Graham suggested.

Sure enough before very long Susan returned carrying two vegetable dishes brimming with home grown carrots, runner beans and squash.

'Are these from your garden, Graham?' Judy asked. 'They look lovely.'

'Yes, and the potatoes,' Graham replied. 'I've put some in a couple of carrier bags for you to take with you when you go. I've left them by the back door.'

'Oh, wonderful. There's nothing like veggies from the garden. Even Ben will eat Granddad's runner beans,' she said.

Susan put the pie in the centre of the table. Gravy bubbled up through the brown pastry crust and dribbled down the side of the dish.

'Gosh Mum, that looks great,' her son said, his attention now on his stomach. 'I hadn't realised how hungry I was until just now.'

While Judy lit the candles that were arrayed at each end of the table, Graham opened a bottle of Chateau Neuf Du Pape. 'I thought I'd open something a little special tonight, as it's a family pow-wow,' he explained.

'Yes, I can't remember the last time we had a big family discussion like this,' Aidan said, swirling the wine around in his glass and holding it to the candle light. 'This looks pretty good.'

'It is. It's the '94,' his father replied.

'I can remember it,' Susan said. 'It was when you and Judy were thinking of emigrating to New Zealand.'

'Gosh, that was years ago,' Judy said. 'I remember, my parents came round as well. I think you cooked steak and kidney pie on that occasion too,' she added.

Susan laughed. 'Well, it is one of my old stand-byes. And it's Aidan's favourite.'

'I think that was the deciding factor for me: your steak and kidney pie,' her son said with a laugh.

Susan felt a flush of pleasure at this although she knew it was not true. Judy was a far better cook than she was but she appreciated Aidan's attempt to flatter her. In the end Aidan and Judy had abandoned their plans to live in the Southern Hemisphere and bought the flat in Wimbledon. Nobody had mentioned it for years. As she looked at her son and her husband, heads close together as they examined their wine like true connoisseurs, she was glad that her son had decided to stay in Britain.

They forgot about Michael for a few moments while the conversation turned to the banalities of passing the salt and refilling wine glasses. Graham asked with interest about his grandsons and laughed when Judy told him that Zak had given up his plans to be a professional footballer and now was going to join the circus and be a trapeze artist.

'That should save you a few bob on school fees, then,' he chuckled.

'Yes, but I was looking forward to being a footballer's father. I was planning to retire as soon as he became a millionaire. I don't think a circus salary will be quite the same,' Aidan said, with mock seriousness.

It was Judy who eventually reintroduced the subject of Michael. 'Look, Graham came up with three options. Surely there is a fourth: we could just leave him where he is and go and visit him from time to time. We could invite him to stay for the odd weekend even and at Christmas, then he'd know he wasn't alone, that he had some family. That wouldn't be so unsettling for him.'

Before Susan could say anything, Graham answered, 'It's a possibility, but he's not someone who is severely disabled nor is he disruptive. As I understand it he is living there because there is nowhere else for him to go. It would be a travesty if we turned our backs on him now.'

'But, Dad, he doesn't even know we exist.'

'No, but we know *he* exists.'

'Aidan, please realise that Michael has only lived at the centre for two years, before that he lived at home with his mother. His life has already been disrupted,' Susan said.

'All the more reason not to disrupt it any more,' her son retorted. The wine was making him a bit aggressive.

Judy stretched across and took his hand. 'We have some news too,' she said. 'We're going to have another baby.'

'That's wonderful, Judy. Congratulations,' Graham said. 'Do the boys know?'

'Not yet. Judy only found out today,' Aidan said. 'We'll tell them at the weekend.'

'I didn't realise you wanted more children,' Susan said. She couldn't believe that this was planned. After all they had three already and Judy was not exactly young.

'We've always wanted a large family,' Aidan said.

'But won't it be a bit crowded in your flat? I mean, what if it's a girl? She'll need a room of her own.'

'We'll get something bigger. We've been thinking for a while about moving out of London,' Aidan said, rather defiantly. She saw Judy look at him in astonishment. 'Maybe we'll move this way.'

'That would be wonderful, son. Then we'd get to see more of the children. I've always thought that London was not the best place to bring up a young family; they need lots of space to run around, especially those three boys of yours.'

'Lemon mousse, anyone?' Susan collected some dishes and retired to the kitchen. She needed a few moments alone. As she stacked the plates into the dishwasher, she considered what had been said. The news about the baby had hi-jacked the conversation, so now she was unsure what their feelings were on Michael. Graham as always was providing a practical structure to their discussion but even so she thought his sympathy for Michael showed through. It was likely that he would suggest that they should help him. Aidan was playing 'devil's advocate' as usual and Judy was being practical. She wasn't related to Michael and she had to consider the impact he might have on their life. What Susan was still unsure about was how much she herself wanted to help him. She couldn't imagine herself in the role of a surrogate mother; there was her job to consider for one thing.

Aidan came into the kitchen. 'Leave those Mum. Come and sit down. We need to explore some more issues and Judy and I can't stay too late because we only have the baby-sitter until eleven,' her son explained, taking her by the arm and gently guiding her back into the dining room.

Judy had already served the lemon mousse and she and Graham were waiting patiently for Susan's return. As soon as his wife sat down, Graham began, 'Look, despite what this Dr Edmundson says, we have to meet Michael before we can make a decision. Judy is right; we need to ask Michael what he wants. I know Susan feels an obligation to do something for him because of her father but it's important that we do the right thing,' he paused, 'for him and for us.'

The three of them had obviously been discussing the situation while she'd been in the kitchen. It didn't bother her. In fact she would be relieved if they took it out of her hands altogether and made the decision for her.

'Yes, I agree with Dad. Michael needs to know you first; he may not even like you. You may not like him. Look, I understand where you're coming from, Mum, and I agree you should do something for Granddad's sake but don't rush into something you may regret later.'

'Judy?' Susan turned to her daughter-in-law.

'Well Susan, I can't help but think you're opening Pandora's box but I'll go along with the others,' she replied.

'So, Susan, what I propose is that you telephone this Dr Edmundson and arrange for you and me to meet Michael. Maybe he can suggest somewhere we can go with him for the day so we can talk to him in a casual, informal manner, get to know him,' Graham said. 'What do you think about that?'

'Well, I can try. But what do I say when he asks about our plans?'

'Tell him the truth. We're neither accepting Michael nor rejecting him out of hand; we just want to get to know him first.'

'But count me out. I'm not traipsing all the way up to—where is it, Leicester?—to see someone I never knew even existed until half-an-hour ago,' said Aidan. 'Some of us have our own lives to lead.'

Susan looked across at Graham for help, but all he said was, 'Well you did bring this on yourself, Susie. It might have been better all round if you'd discussed it with us first, before dashing up there to see him.'

'Yes, Mum. Why was that? Why all the secrecy?'

'All right. All right. We'll go on our own. I just thought you ought to have a say in what happened. I was trying to include you.' She was close to tears now.

'If you and Graham go and see him first, then you can tell us where you want to go from there,' suggested Judy. She put her hand on Susan's arm.

Susan looked at her husband, wondering how he felt about it all.

'Ring him tomorrow and see what he says,' he said. 'But now, I think it's time we put all that to one side and celebrated Judy and Aidan's wonderful news. I have an excellent bottle of Veuve Clicquot that has been waiting for such an occasion.'

CHAPTER 21

Graham was glad to be home. There'd been a point yesterday when he'd thought about booking into a hotel for the night, or taking up Bill's offer to stay with him again, but in the end being in Bill's company had mellowed him. As he thought about what his old friend was facing at the moment, he decided that there were worse things in life than a few silly lies, even though they still rankled him.

It was so typical of Susan. She always jumped straight in and did what she thought was right, with no thought of how it would affect others. She never stopped to consider how he would feel when she told him the ridiculous story about going to Leicester to look for her half-brother. She thought she could feed him a pack of lies then, when it suited her, tell him the truth. And what was he supposed to do? Say, 'Never mind darling, I understand why you felt you couldn't confide in me. Don't give it a moment's thought?' Well no. It was about time she stopped and considered his feelings for once. Maybe walking out on her, albeit for only a couple of days, had made her realise the selfishness of her actions. It had been all a bit childish really, just an act. If he was truthful with himself, he never intended leaving her, certainly not over something as insignificant as this, but it might make her think twice before she treated him in such a cavalier fashion again. He smiled to himself. It had felt quite good, walking out like that. Maybe he should put his foot down more often. He sighed and poured out the last of the red wine. No, he didn't want all the hassle. Susan was right about one thing; he was a man who liked a quiet life.

*

Later that night, as she was getting undressed for bed, Graham said, 'Susan, I understand that this is important to you but you must be careful. Don't go rushing in, in your usual impulsive way. This is a man's life we're dealing with and a vulnerable one too.'

'I won't. I promise you. I'll talk to Dr Edmundson tomorrow and see what he says. I'm just so disappointed with Aidan's reaction. Why does he have to be so negative?'

'It's come as a shock, I expect. You know he always thought he was your father's favourite, that they had a special relationship. I would think that he's very hurt that your father never told him about this man. Not when he was a child, obviously, but later, when he had a family of his own.'

'You know what my parents were like. They didn't tell anybody anything. Aidan doesn't have to feel that he was the only one who was kept in the dark.'

'Maybe you should explain that to him. Anyway, I think it's best that we see Michael together first, just you and I. Then maybe we can persuade Aidan and Judy to come and see him later. We don't want to overwhelm Michael. Remember, he doesn't even know he has a sister, never mind a brother-in-law and a nephew with a family of his own.'

'Yes, you're right. We'll take it more slowly. Oh, Graham, you don't know how much I've regretted not involving you right from the start. I really missed you when I was up there.' She paused and said, 'We could go tomorrow. There's nothing on, is there?'

'There you go, rushing straight in again. I thought you just said we'd take it more slowly? Ring first and find out,' her husband said, patiently, pulling back the bedcovers and climbing into bed. 'Remember this is a big step for everybody.'

He lay facing away from her as Susan got into bed beside him. He didn't stir so she tentatively moved closer to him, until her body lay along the length of his then she put her arm round him. He still didn't move but neither did he pull away, so she kissed the back of his neck softly, letting her tongue slide along the ridges of his spine.

'Darling I'm so sorry about not telling you the truth, really I am,' she whispered to his back. 'You know I love you. I didn't mean to hurt you.'

Her husband turned towards her. 'And so how sorry is that then Susie?' he asked, taking her into his arms, and kissing her.

*

Susan's impatience was palpable the next morning. She had risen early and set the breakfast table before Graham had even come out of the shower. By the time he came into the kitchen, she was drinking her second cup of coffee and reading through the information she'd downloaded from the internet.

'Look, I expect the doctor doesn't start work until nine. Just relax, Susan, and don't drink so much coffee. You know it makes you hyper and you're bad enough as it is,' Graham said, as he put on his coat. 'Where's Jess's lead? I can't find it anywhere.'

Susan went into the hall and returned with the lead in her hand. 'You left it on the hall table,' she said with a smile. 'Bacon and egg for breakfast?'

'Well if you're going to spoil me, yes, that will do nicely.' He reached across and squeezed her hand affectionately. 'I'll get the paper and give Jess her walk first.'

She was pleased to note he was his old self again, slipping back into the usual routine. It had been unsettling to see him act out of character. She hadn't realised until he walked out, just how much she depended on him. He was her rock and it had upset her to have him turn on her.

'Don't forget to pick up the paper,' she said.

'Okay, darling. I won't be long.'

Susan poured herself another cup of coffee and took it into the conservatory where she could sit and look at the river. It was one of those still, glittering mornings that often occur in early autumn, when everything in the garden was still lush and full and the sun had not yet had time to clear the dew that was covering the ground with a carpet of light. It was too early for any river traffic, the only passers-by a lone swan and a pair of grebes.

Susan was beginning to feel apprehensive. Everything seemed to be going her way, but was it really what she wanted? As Graham had reminded her, whatever action they took would affect them all. Her head was spinning with ideas but as soon as she had one plan, a contra argument presented itself. She'd always been very good at seeing both sides of a situation, she told herself—it was nothing more than that. But ultimately it always came back to the same question, a question for which she had no immediate answer. What sort of sister would she be to Michael? After all she'd always kept herself very much to herself—caring and sharing had not really been her thing. That was what happened when you were an only child. She stopped. Only she wasn't an only child and hadn't been for nearly fifty years. She had a brother. She said the words out loud, 'I have a brother.' It made her feel strange. A brother. She didn't want to accept it. She was comfortable being her parents' only child. That was what she was used to. She didn't want siblings, not now. But how would she have felt if she had known about Michael earlier, years ago when she was younger? She couldn't answer that. She didn't know how she felt about him now. The answer was that she had to meet him and soon, before she went completely out of her mind. Susan checked her watch again. It was just after nine o'clock. She drank the dregs of her cold tea and picked up the telephone.

'Good morning Barry. It's Susan Masters. We met the other day and you kindly showed me around the farm.'

'Good morning Mrs Masters. Did you have a good journey home?'

'Yes, thank you.'

'So what can I do for you?'

'Well Barry, I've talked to my family about Michael, as I promised,' she began.

'So soon?'

'Well, yes,' she said, slightly surprised at his comment. 'My son and his wife came to dinner last night so it seemed an appropriate time to tell them,' she replied. 'Anyway, the reason I've rung is because my husband and I would like to come and talk to you together, if you don't mind.'

'No, not at all. When did you have in mind?'

'As soon as possible. This afternoon perhaps? Or tomorrow?' She listened anxiously for any clues to his feelings on the matter. She could hear a soft blowing sound, as though he was thinking about what to say next.

'Well, tomorrow is Saturday. I don't usually come in on a Saturday, unless there's an emergency. Let's see. I have the vet coming this morning to look at a sick pony but this afternoon is quite free,' he said. 'Would that do?'

'Perfect,' she said, barely containing her excitement.

There was a brief silence while he rustled in his desk drawer to find his diary. At last he picked up the telephone again and said, 'Okay, that's fine. I'll expect you both about three. That'll give you plenty of time to get here and avoid the worst of the traffic.'

Susan felt she could detect a lack of enthusiasm in his voice. 'Wonderful, we'll see you then,' she said.

'Goodbye Mrs Masters. I'll see you later,' he replied and hung up.

So that was that. She felt elated at having taken the next step and by tomorrow they would have a clearer idea of where this obsession of hers was leading them.

Susan heard Jess barking excitedly as she chased a squirrel up the drive, so she opened the back door and saw Graham strolling along behind the dog, the newspaper under his arm. She waved to him but he didn't see her; he'd stopped to inspect the roses for greenfly. Would he be pleased to be driving up to Leicester this afternoon? Maybe she should have waited and asked him first.

A few minutes later Graham came into the kitchen. 'Those damn greenfly are back. I shall have to re-spray them this morning before they take hold again,' he said sitting down at the breakfast table and opening the newspaper.

As Susan started to cook his breakfast, she said, as casually as she could, 'While you were out with Jess, I phoned Sunny View and spoke to Dr Edmundson. We have an appointment this afternoon at three.'

'Good God, Susan, slow down a bit. We only discussed it last night,' her husband said, looking at her over the top of his reading glasses. 'Why do you have to rush into things? Everything has always got to be instant with you.'

'I know darling, but there didn't seem much point in waiting.'

'Well, I suppose not,' Graham said, with a sigh. He folded his paper and put it to one side with an air of resignation that spoke of long experience in dealing with his wife's impulsiveness. 'So, this afternoon you say. Today's Friday isn't it?'

'Yes.'

'Well why don't we see if Aidan and the gang can join us there for the weekend,' he suggested.

'Do you think Aidan will agree? He seemed very much against it last night.'

'We can ask him. If he still feels so strongly about it, then we'll come straight home.'

'OK. You ring him. He and I always seem to end up arguing.'

'Well, I'll let him get to work first. Is that all right or did you want me to ring him this very minute?'

She smiled. 'No, of course not. When you've had your breakfast will do.' She poured him a cup of tea and added, 'I think it's a great idea. We could all stay in the Motorway Inn; the kids will love that. They have a big heated swimming pool and a sauna.'

'Yes, that was what I had in mind, somewhere not too expensive. I wonder if it's one of those hotels where children eat free,' he added.

'Well if it is, they won't make much of a profit, not with kids that eat like those three,' Susan replied with a laugh. She was starting to feel a lot more positive now. Graham had that effect on her, despite his reluctance to openly enthuse over the proposed trip.

*

They had eaten the light lunch that Susan had prepared, taken Jess around to their neighbour's house and put a weekend bag in the car. Everything was ready.

'Good hour to leave,' Graham commented. 'We should be there in plenty of time. Might even be able to make a pit stop.'

'Graham, did you have time to read anything about Michael's condition?' Susan asked. 'You know, those papers I printed off the internet.'

'A bit. Why?'

'Well, I did some more reading this morning. It's very interesting to see the progress that's been made in understanding Down's Syndrome,' she began. 'Originally they measured the mental ability of someone with the condition on the basis of their performance in a standard IQ test. Now they realise that the test is inappropriate because it doesn't give any indication how good people are at reading or talking or practical things like preparing a meal.'

'Well I've always thought IQ tests favoured a certain type of person, anyway,' Graham replied.

'Yes, well they now realise that children with Down's Syndrome develop much more slowly in certain areas than other children.'

'Such as?' he asked.

'It seems as though the most frustrating thing for them is that their progress with speech and language lags well behind their ability to reason and communicate.'

'So they know what they want to communicate but have trouble saying it?'

'Yes and researchers now know that these children find it much easier to learn visually than aurally so they're encouraging teachers to use signing and reading to help them. And they're doing it with adults too,' she added.

'With adults? Isn't it too late then?' Graham asked.

'No, that's the interesting thing; their development continues throughout their adult life, just like everyone else, albeit at a slower rate. In the past it was thought that when children with this disorder reached adolescence they stopped learning. Now they know that's not true.'

'I suppose that was another effect of institutionalisation,' Graham said. 'They didn't expect the children to improve so they didn't provide any stimulus and lo and behold they didn't improve. A self fulfilling prophecy. I imagine that's where Michael's mother contributed a lot.'

'Exactly. She had him at home with her every weekend. According to Dr Edmundson she not only helped him with reading and writing but got him to do little jobs around the house.'

'I expect that many people with Down's Syndrome were not so fortunate. They wouldn't have had that opportunity to develop their full potential.'

'Well, worse than that, the people who ran the institutions encouraged certain behaviours from the inmates which has led to there being such a stereotypical view of people with Down's Syndrome.'

'You mean placid and happy, content in their own little world?'

'Yes, exactly.'

Graham switched on the radio. Unlike Susan his car stereo was perpetually tuned to Jazz Radio and he started to hum to an old recording of Ella Fitzgerald singing 'Mack the Knife', his fingers tapping the steering wheel in time to the music. He didn't share Susan's interest in classical music although he usually accompanied her to concerts and even the ballet.

They drove for a while without speaking. Susan listened to the music and watched the junctions flash past with monotonous regularity.

Aidan had agreed to join them in Leicester, although he'd told Graham that it didn't mean he was in full agreement with what they were planning to do. Well at least he would get to meet his new uncle. As for their plans, at the moment they were non-existent. Graham said he'd assured Aidan that this was just a preliminary visit, to meet Michael and work out where to go from there. Nothing had been decided. Susan knew her son; he'd be worried that she would steam-roller him and Judy into doing something they didn't want to.

She noted each motorway sign as they flashed past—120 miles to Leicester. Just over an hour and they would be there and as yet she was still unclear on what she was going to say to Barry.

CHAPTER 22

At five minutes to twelve they drove through the gates and up the long gravel drive to Sunny View Farm.

'Well, that's an imposing house,' said Graham in admiration.

'Do you think we're making a mistake?' she asked him. Now that they'd arrived, she had an overwhelming urge to get back in the car and go home.

Graham looked at her and took her hand in his. 'Now, come on Susie. This isn't like you. Look, we'll go and talk to the doctor and then if you decide it was all a mistake, we can still go home and Michael will be none the wiser.'

Dr Edmundson was not there so, as they sat in the airy hallway and waited, Susan told her husband all that she could remember about her previous visit. She took him to the window. 'Look, that's the IT room over there,' she said pointing to a purpose built rectangular building that was set off to one side. As she spoke, she saw the doctor come out it, carrying a pile of folders. 'And here's Barry now.'

The director of the centre walked purposefully towards the main house. He seemed preoccupied; his mouth was set in a firm line and his ginger eyebrows pulled together in a frown. They watched him approach in silence.

'Ah, good morning Mrs Masters,' he said extending his hand to Susan then turning to Graham, 'and Mr Masters, is it?'

'Yes. Good morning,' Graham replied.

'Please come in. Sit down, won't you.' Dr Edmundson was pleasant and courteous but his frown remained. 'So you would like to talk some more about Michael, I take it?'

'Yes, Dr Edmundson. I took your advice and discussed Michael with my husband. He thought it best if we came and spoke to you together,' she began. She noticed that the doctor was much more formal today and didn't invite her to call him Barry.

'Yes, so I gather.'

Graham spoke next, 'You see Dr Edmundson, until this week my wife didn't know anything about Michael, not that he existed, whether he was alive or dead, where he lived and certainly not that he had Down's Syndrome. Now that she does know, she would like to do something for him. We've spent some time discussing various options, not just between ourselves but with my son as well and the bottom line is that we can't decide what to do until we meet the young man. We believe that he too has to have some say in this matter.' He paused and when the doctor didn't reply, continued, 'However we all realise that this could be very disruptive for him and therefore would be grateful for your advice.'

Graham was being very diplomatic. Thank goodness he'd come with her; she would have been very much more abrupt.

At last the doctor spoke, 'Since I received your call this morning, Mrs Masters, I have been thinking very seriously about the situation. You are, of course, Michael's next-of-kin and have every right to see him and even advise on his future. Indeed I'm sure if you took legal advice you would be able to overrule anything I might say. However I need to be sure that your intentions are genuine and not self-motivated before we take this any further.'

Although she felt a little offended by the suggestion that her motives might be selfish, Susan could see that the doctor was genuinely concerned for Michael's welfare. She took a deep breath. 'Of course, I understand, but the truth is I don't know what to tell you. Are my intentions self-motivated? I don't know. I just know that I'd like Michael to know that we exist, that we're his family and that we'd like the opportunity to get to know him. I can't make you any promises, Dr Edmundson. What happens will depend as much on Michael as it will on us.'

Susan's voice was soft but she spoke clearly and the doctor must have been left in no doubt that she was not going to be dissuaded from seeing her half-brother.

He stood up, seemingly satisfied with her reply. 'Fine. In that case, let's get on with it,' he said. 'I suggest we go over to the IT room now and meet him on his own territory.' He looked at his watch. 'They're due to break for lunch soon, anyway,' he added.

'Does he know we're here?' Graham asked.

'No, I've said nothing to him but I did mention your visit to Brian.'

Graham looked enquiringly at Susan. 'Brian's the IT teacher,' she explained.

They followed the doctor out of his office and down the hall. The clouds that had been gathering all morning began to shed a shower of fine rain which caught them unawares as they crossed the yard. Susan shivered. She wasn't sure if it was from the change in temperature or from nervousness.

As they entered the IT room, the students stopped what they were doing and turned to look at them. Susan recognised one young man from her previous visit; he had been digging the trench near the pig pens.

'Good morning, everyone. Please don't let us interrupt you. Just carry on with what you're doing,' Dr Edmundson said, smiling at them. 'These people have come to see what we do here at Sunny View.'

One or two of the students wished the doctor a good morning and returned to their studies, the others continued to gaze at the newcomers. Susan barely noticed them because her attention was solely on the man in the green sweater. He was looking at them with interest. She searched in vain for signs of her father in his face, but her father's sharp, angular features and distinctive beak-like nose were not in evidence. This man had a square face with rather flattish features and, although his eyes were the same bright blue that she remembered twinkling at her when she was a little girl, they were clearly almond shaped.

'Brian, do you mind if Michael explains to us what the students are doing today?' Dr Edmundson asked.

'Not at all. Michael, you don't mind, do you? Show them what Jimmy has done today. I think he's almost finished anyway.' Brian indicated a student at the end of the row, wearing a set of headphones underneath a blue woolly hat.

'Okay Brian.' Michael said, smiling at Susan and pulling out a chair for her. He indicated that she should sit where she could see the computer screen.

'This is Jimmy,' he said. 'He's been using a new program we've bought. It's to help him with his reading.'

Hello, Dr Barry,' Jimmy said looking up at the doctor.

'Hello Jimmy. How's it going?'

'Cool. This is much more interesting than the other one,' the boy replied, replacing his headphones and continuing with his work.

They looked at Michael for clarification. 'The old ones were a bit young for him,' he said. 'They were really designed for teaching young kids to read. This new package is for adults.'

Susan looked at the screen; it appeared to be displaying a story about two footballers that were up for transfer. 'So how does it work?' she asked.

'The story appears on the screen but, as Jimmy reads it, he can listen through the headphones to someone reading along with him. Then when he thinks he doesn't need any help he can switch off the voice and just read on his own. When he's finished a particular story, Brian comes and listens to him. If he can read that okay he gives him the next one to do. Sometimes I listen to him read too but Brian has to make the final decision,' he added.

'What else do you use the computers for?' Graham asked.

'Lots of things. We have Maths programs and drawing programs. There's one that helps people improve their writing.' Michael pointed to an older woman. 'Maisie's writing has improved a lot since we've had that one,' he said.

Susan could see that the woman held a stylus in her hand, the wire of which was attached to a computer note pad. She gripped the stylus with her thumb and all four fingers and as she wrote on the pad with a wide circular movement, letters appeared on the screen in front of her.

'It's very good for co-ordination,' the doctor commented. He was saying very little, leaving the explanations to Michael.

'And of course we use the internet a lot. We have Broadband,' Michael said proudly. 'So the students can look up information that they need for their other classes, or just for fun. Brian has also set up an internal chat line, so we can send messages to each other.' He tapped Jimmy on the shoulder and said, 'Jimmy, send a message to Alice, please.'

Jimmy smiled, and typed something into his computer.

'Alice is his girlfriend. She's over there.' He pointed to a young girl with Down's Syndrome sitting at the far end of the room.

Jimmy looked across at her and laughed. 'She says she's too shy,' he told them.

Susan looked enquiringly at Michael.

'He just sent her a message to ask her to come over and meet you,' explained Michael.

'Well, I think it's all very impressive,' said Graham. 'These young people make it all look so easy.'

Michael beamed at him.

'Thank you Michael, that was very interesting. We'll let you get back to work now,' Dr Edmundson said, patting him on the shoulder.

'Yes, thank you,' said Susan.

Before they left, the doctor went across to speak briefly to Brian and then led them back to his office. The rain was heavier now and puddles were forming in the yard. Susan picked her way carefully between them, holding her coat tightly around her.

'I've asked Brian to send Michael over to my office when they finish,' Dr Edmundson said, looking at his watch. 'That'll be in about ten minutes. Would you like some tea while we wait?'

'I'd love a cup of coffee, if that's possible,' Susan said, removing her wet coat and hanging it over the back of the chair. She would have preferred something stronger but would have to make do with coffee.

'Yes, that's no problem.' He looked at Graham.

'Tea's fine for me, thanks,' Graham said.

The young woman in the red sweater, whom Susan had seen the first time she visited the centre, came in.

'Some tea and a coffee please, Beryl,' the doctor said, and once she'd gone, he turned straight to Susan. 'Well?' he asked.

She looked at him, quizzically.

'Well, what did you think of Michael?' he asked.

'He seems very capable from what we've seen,' her husband interrupted. He knew Susan found it very hard to make snap judgements. She always needed to weigh up all the angles first. 'It's a fine facility you have here.'

'Yes, we're very proud of it. It's surprising, you know, how some people respond much better to things when they're on the computer. Jimmy for example couldn't read at all before we got the computer. He wouldn't go near a book. Once, when he was younger, he even put all his school books in the dustbin. He was a handful, I can tell you. Drove his teachers mad apparently. But learning to read on the computer, that's much more fun for him.'

Graham nodded. 'It's all a bit beyond me, I'm afraid, but young people seem to respond well to this new technology. And Michael seems to know what he's doing.'

As though on cue, there was a soft knock on the door.

'Come in.'

Michael opened the door then, seeing that the doctor was not alone, stopped. 'Sorry, Dr Edmundson, I didn't know you still had visitors. Brian said to come over.'

'Yes, Michael, come in. Sit down. I want to talk to you.' He waited until Michael was comfortable then said, 'We've just been talking about the computers. They've made quite a difference to us, haven't they?'

Michael nodded. He seemed a little edgy and was trying not to stare at Susan.

'They seem pretty new to me,' said Susan. 'Have you had them long?'

'We've had these computers about three years now but the software is the latest, this year's,' Michael replied, looking directly at her. 'We had computers before that but they weren't very good.'

'They were all donated over the years by various local companies when they were upgrading,' the doctor explained.

'Yes, they were a bit old,' Michael added. 'But that wasn't the real problem; it was because they were all different. It made it very hard for Brian to teach because everyone had a different machine.' The talk about computers was putting Michael at ease.

'It must have cost a lot of money to set up the IT room,' Susan said.

'It did, nearly twenty thousand pounds,' the doctor replied.

'Yes, but we raised most of that money ourselves,' Michael interrupted proudly. 'We had jumble sales, raffles, all sorts of things.'

'That's right, we did. We even had a Christmas dance and sold tickets to the villagers,' the doctor added.

'And the money from the market.'

'Yes. And of course, the local Chamber of Commerce were very generous, too.'

'Did you help with the fundraising, Michael?' Susan asked.

'Yes, we all did. But I designed the tickets and the poster for the dance.'

'You also found the band, didn't you,' Dr Edmundson reminded him.

'Yes, but Beryl helped me a lot with that.'

The doctor picked up the teapot. 'Would you like some tea, Michael? I think it is still warm enough.' He tested the pot with his free hand.

'No thank you, Dr Edmundson.'

'Well, Michael, although these people found the IT room very interesting, it isn't the reason they've come here today. They've actually come to talk to you.'

Susan wasn't sure if Michael looked surprised or frightened; she felt it could be a mixture of both. She hastened to reassure him, 'It's nothing to worry about Michael.' She looked across at the doctor. 'Why don't we introduce ourselves first?'

'Good idea,' Graham said. 'My name is Graham Masters and this is my wife Susan. Dr Edmundson is right, we have actually driven here today from Maidenhead to see you.'

Susan could see that the name Maidenhead meant nothing to Michael, who continued to look at them blankly. She reached forward and took his hand. 'Michael, I knew your father.' She waited to see his reaction.

He was looking at her closely now and let his hand remain in hers. The skin was smooth and warm, the nails wide and carefully trimmed; fine hairs grew on the back of his fingers. She felt surprisingly comfortable holding his hand. At last he spoke. 'You're Susie, aren't you?' he said.

Susan was so surprised that she dropped his hand and sat back. Whatever response she had expected, it was not this. 'Yes, Michael, I'm Susie,' she said at last.

'You're my father's daughter, his other family.' He looked accusingly at her. 'He told me about you.'

It was as though he'd slapped her face. Her father had told Michael about *her* but never thought to mention the boy to Susan, never showed her a photo of him, never suggested she go and meet him. She felt so angry with her father. How could he do that? Michael had known about her all the time and she never knew he existed. Her father's silence had kept them apart for almost all their lives, Yes, it was hard for him, but how could he have done that? She took a deep breath and said, 'Yes, Michael, we had the same father.'

'So, why are you here now?' he asked. 'Where have you been all these years?'

This was the question she had dreaded since her quest began. 'Well, Michael, it was not until last week that I realised that you existed. So I've been looking for you.'

'Yes, but why? What do you want?'

'Why?' She looked down at her hands. They lay in her lap, twisting and gripping each other as if they were an independent life form. 'Because I wanted to see you. Because I wanted to know that you were all right. Because I wanted you to get to know me. Because you're my brother.' She stopped.

Nobody spoke. Then Michael stood up. Susan thought he was going to leave but instead he moved towards her and bending down, put his arms around her. There were tears on his cheeks. 'I knew you'd come one day,' he whispered.

She realised that Dr Edmundson was moving towards the door. 'I'll leave you together for a while,' he said, closing the door behind him.

She remained sitting, her back arched and her head lifted towards Michael, his arms still around her body. She felt a warmth spread through her limbs and slowly reached up to return his embrace. They remained locked in this position for some minutes until Michael broke the silence. He spoke softly. 'My father said he would bring you to see me but he never did. I thought you didn't like me.' Susan couldn't speak; she hugged him tighter. 'Each time he came to see us he said that the next time he would bring you too. But he never did.'

What a bastard her father was. All these years Michael had been waiting for her. She knew then that it didn't matter what they did next, whether he left Sunny View or stayed; the important thing was that she'd come to see him at last. It had never occurred to her that Anthea would tell him about his father's family. Her mother's vow of secrecy had been so powerful that she'd assumed it extended to them as well.

'Michael,' Graham said, putting his hand on the man's shoulder. Michael released his hold on Susan and straightened up. 'Michael, would you like to show us your room? Maybe we could talk in there and let Dr Edmundson have his office back.'

Michael took a paper tissue from his pocket and wiped his eyes. 'Yes, that's a good idea.' He looked out of the window. 'Oh, dear, you'll get wet,' he said, looking at Susan. 'My place is right over the other side.'

'Don't worry, I think it's easing up,' she said, thinking that a short walk in the fresh air was just what she needed right then.

The doctor was in the hall, looking at some papers with Beryl.

'We're going over to my place for a bit, Dr Edmundson. Okay?' Michael said.

'Of course it's okay, Michael.' He looked at Susan. 'We let Michael have a staff flat as he works here. It's part of his salary,' he explained.

'So you don't live with a family then, Michael?' Graham asked.

'No, I live alone. I like it that way.'

She'd been right, the rain was stopping and a watery sun had appeared from behind the clouds. A rainbow curved its way across the sky, disappearing behind a grove of trees in the distance. She walked a few paces behind Graham and Michael, hearing their polite chatter but not listening. Her thoughts were elsewhere, thinking of her father. Had he trusted her so little that he couldn't confide in her? Had he tried to tell her about Michael and she'd refused to hear him? She was confused and angry with him for keeping that part of his life so secret. He'd given her no clue. Only her mother had provided the clues and Susan had refused to pick up on them. She knew she was also to blame. She'd shut herself off from him and his life; she hadn't wanted to know what was happening. Now she was finding it hard to reconcile the father of her childhood with the father of Michael's childhood. They seemed like two different people.

'This is it,' said Michael, stopping and looking at her. They were outside a small apartment block, two storeys high and rendered with white pebble dash. 'I'm on the first floor,' he said, opening the door and standing to one side to let them enter.

It was very small but appeared to contain everything that a single man might need, even a small washing machine was plumbed into the bathroom, next to the shower. The walls were all painted white and some blue and white curtains hung at the windows. It was clean and tidy—Susan felt a bit too tidy. There was little evidence of anyone living there, no magazines strewn around, no clothes on the back of the armchair, no CDs open on the coffee table. Susan couldn't help comparing it to the time she'd visited Aidan's bachelor pad, as he called it then. Despite his voluble protests she'd insisted on tidying up even though it had taken her three hours to make any impression on the chaos. This flat lacked the feel of a home; it was as if the occupant was not planning to stay for long.

'It's lovely Michael. You keep it very nice,' she said. 'Very tidy.'

'We can sit in here,' he said, taking them into the kitchen.

Once they were all seated, Susan asked,'Did my, *our* father come and see you very often, Michael?'

'At first, when I was little, he came every weekend but then, when I went away to school, he started coming once a month. He always brought me a present and sometimes something for my mother but he never stayed long. Sometimes in the summer we would go to the park and once we went to the zoo.' The man smiled to himself at the memory.

'So you didn't think it strange that your father didn't live with your mother?' Susan was puzzled to know what the child had made of this arrangement.

'Not really. I didn't know any different, I suppose. I didn't go to the local school, you know. They wouldn't have me. So most of my friends didn't live with their families anyway,' he explained.

'Where did you go to school then?' she asked.

'In Leicester. It was a special school for people who needed extra help. My mother said it would be better for me to go to a school where they could give me extra help,' he continued.

Susan listened as he told her how unhappy he'd been at first until he realised that his mother wasn't abandoning him there for ever. 'She was always there waiting for me at four o'clock on a Friday afternoon to take me home. I used to spend all week waiting for Fridays to come.'

'It sounds as though she loved you very much, Michael,' Susan said.

'Yes, she did but it must have been hard for her at first. When I was born and the doctors told her I had Down's Syndrome, they said I would always remain a child and be totally dependent on her.' He looked at Susan and smiled. 'Now look at me. I live on my own. I do my own shopping and cooking. I wash my own clothes and I have my own bank account. How wrong they were.' He beamed at her—his independence obviously pleased him.

'She would be very proud of you, Michael,' Susan said. 'They both would.'

Perhaps the mention of household chores reminded Michael that it was lunchtime, because he said, 'You must be hungry. Can I make you a sandwich?' He smiled at them and pushed the hair back from his face in a way that reminded her instantly of her father. She felt her throat tighten with emotion. This *was* her brother.

'That would be nice. I'm quite peckish,' Graham replied. 'The gurgling in my stomach tells me that it's been a long time since breakfast.'

Michael walked over to the small refrigerator that was tucked under the work surface. 'What would you like? I have cheese and, oh dear, just cheese.' He looked at them both and a wide smile lit up his face. He was enjoying having visitors in his home. 'Would cheddar be all right?'

'Cheddar would be fine,' Susan said, although she had never felt less like eating. 'Can I help?'

'No, thank you. I can do it,' he said and began preparing their lunch.

'So have you always known about your father's other family?' Susan asked. 'I mean, when did your mother explain to you that he was already married?'

'I can't remember. I must have been older, I suppose.' He stopped to think for a moment. 'I remember once, when I was about ten, being very upset by the two boys that lived next door; they were always shouting at me and calling me nasty names. I ran inside crying and told my mother I wanted a big brother to look after me, to stop people being so horrid to me. Then the next weekend, when my dad came to see us, he showed me a photo of you and said that you were my big sister.'

Susan felt a prickly sensation behind her eyes. She blinked hard. 'Well, Michael, I haven't been much of a sister to you, have I? Maybe I'll be able to make up for that now.'

'That's okay, Susie. It was nice to know I had a sister. I told everyone at school about you. I said you were grown up and one day you were going to come and look after me.'

He handed her the sandwich which he had cut into four equal triangles and arranged neatly on a blue plate. 'Here, Susie, I hope you like it,' he said. 'Now I'll do yours Graham.'

'Michael, have you always known you had Down's Syndrome?' she asked.

'Yes, I think so. I can't remember when I didn't know about it. My mother used to say I was both lucky and unlucky. Unlucky because I was born with it but lucky because I had her to help me. She was right. When I went to the special school, the other children had to live there all the time. Sometimes their parents would come and visit them but they hardly ever got to go home. My mother took me home every weekend and all through the holidays. She told me that having Down's Syndrome meant that I would have to work harder than the other children and sometimes it would take me a long time to do things but that I must never give up.'

'That sounds like good advice,' Susan said. She was beginning to change her opinion of Anthea—this didn't sound   like the heartless harpy that her mother had so often maligned.

'Yes, I know but sometimes I wanted to give up. But she wouldn't let me. She said I must be patient and keep trying.' A tear rolled down his cheek as he thought of his mother. 'I miss her, you know.'

'Of course you do. That's only natural. I miss my mother and father too,' Susan said, but she knew it wasn't the same.

'She was very ill. They had to take her into hospital because she was in a lot of pain. That was when I started living here.' Michael waved his hand to indicate the space around them. Susan didn't say anything and waited while he wiped his eyes with a paper serviette. 'We had a cat you know. Mr Jiggs I called him. He was very old. When my mother went into hospital we had to send him to the cat's home. I expect he's dead now, too.'

Nobody spoke. The atmosphere was becoming rather heavy so Graham, to change the subject, asked, 'Well, Michael, how do you do your shopping? Do you have a car?'

'No, I can't drive but I have a bicycle. There's a shop in the village, Mrs Earnshaw's, and I usually cycle there once a week to get what I need. Sometimes if Dr Edmundson is going into Uppingham, he invites me to go with him. That's when I go to the bank or buy things I can't get at Mrs Earnshaw's,' he explained.

'So you're pretty well organised then,' Graham said with an approving nod of his head. He took the proffered sandwich from Michael's outstretched hand. 'Thanks, this looks good.'

They sat in the tiny kitchen, chatting and eating their sandwiches until Michael said, 'I'm sorry, but I have to go back to work now.'

Susan looked at her husband for guidance. 'Of course Michael, we understand. Do you have to work tomorrow? It's Saturday.' Graham asked.

'No, not on Saturdays nor on Sundays.'

'Well, would you like to come out for the day with us tomorrow?' Graham asked.

Michael looked first at Graham and then at Susan. 'I would like that very much,' he replied.

'What time shall we come over then?'

'Well, on a Saturday I have to wash my clothes and do my shopping. But I can get up early. Would eleven o'clock be all right?' he asked, counting on his fingers as he calculated the time he needed to do his chores.

'Perfect. Maybe Dr Edmundson can tell us somewhere nice to have lunch.'

At this Michael stopped smiling.

'What's the matter Michael?' Susan asked.

'I haven't been to a restaurant since my mother died,' he said. 'I'm not used to restaurants.'

'That's no problem,' Susan replied. 'We're very used to restaurants and Graham is going to pay.' She punched her husband's arm, playfully. 'Aren't you darling?'

'Don't I always,' he replied with a laugh.

Their light heartedness seemed to make Michael relax and the smile they were now becoming accustomed to, returned to his face.

'I'll show you the way back to Dr Edmundson's office,' he said.

CHAPTER 23

Judy leaned across and slotted the buckle of Ben's seat belt into place. She straightened up and regarded her three sons gravely.

'Right. Now, have we got everything?' she asked. It was as much effort getting them ready for a weekend break as it was for a fortnight's holiday; the car boot was already loaded to overcapacity.

'Did you pack my swimming costume?'

'Ben, that's the third time you've asked that.' Aidan's voice had that cracking note to it that said he was about to lose patience.

'Mummy, what about the football?'

'Yes Zak, the football is in the back. But I don't know whether you'll have the opportunity to play with it,' she warned. Zak just grinned at her; he was very adept at finding places to play football. His look said: 'No problem.'

Jason had Buzz Lightyear on one knee and Woody on the other. He was holding a discussion with them in a low voice. Judy thought she heard something about 'holidays'.

'We're not going on holiday, Jason. We're just going to stay with Nan and Grandpa in a hotel for the weekend,' she explained.

'But that's a holiday isn't it?' the little boy asked. Hotels meant holidays to him.

'Well, I suppose so, but a very short one. You have to be back at school on Monday, and Daddy and I have to be back at work.'

'Will we have a room to ourselves?'

'Yes, right next door to ours, so Mummy and I can keep an eye on you,' Aidan said.

'Where will Buzz and Woody sleep?' Jason asked anxiously.

'They're not sleeping in our bed,' his two brothers chorused together.

'I'm sure there'll be lots of room for them. We'll have a look when we arrive?' she assured him.

'Will there be a telly?' Zak asked.

'Yes.'

Judy knew the questions would last for most of the journey. They were so excited they could hardly keep still. She hoped they wouldn't be disappointed.

'Are we going to stop at a motorway service station?' This question came from Ben, who clearly remembered the arcade games they'd played in one once.

'Depends. We'll see.'

'On what? Depends on what?' he insisted.

'On whether we have time to stop,' Aidan replied, trying to keep the exasperation from his voice.

'Why are we going to visit Nan and Grandpa in a hotel? Why can't we go to their house? There's lots of room to play football there.' Zak had just realised the illogicality of their actions.

'Well, we're actually going to meet someone else as well. Your Nan's brother, my uncle,' Aidan explained.

'But Nan hasn't got a brother,' said Ben and Zak together. This news surprised the two elder boys while Jason appeared to be more interested in the opinion of the toys on his knee.

'Well actually it seems she has. She's only just found out about him.'

'How can you not know you've got a brother,' Ben said, shaking his head in bewilderment. 'Didn't he live with her?'

'Did his mummy lose him?' Zak asked.

'I hope I don't get lost,' said Jason, who'd obviously been listening all along. 'You won't forget you've got a brother if I get lost, will you Ben?'

'Nobody's going to get lost and nobody could ever forget *you* Jason,' Aidan said, with a smile. 'I'm sorry boys, I can't tell you very much. All I know about him is that his name is Michael,' he explained. 'I expect your Nan will tell us more when we see her.'

This seemed to satisfy the children for the moment, but Judy could see that Aidan was already having doubts as to the wisdom of this trip. 'You'll meet him soon enough,' he added.

Judy put on her seat belt. 'At last, I think that's everything. Shall we go? It'll be lunchtime before we set off at this rate.'

'Okay. Have they all been to the loo?' Aidan whispered to her, reluctant to start an exodus back to the bathroom.

'Yes, that's all done.'

'Right it is folks, off we go.'

The first half-hour of the journey passed peacefully enough; the older boys played a car spotting game which ended abruptly with a screech from Zak when Ben thumped him for allegedly cheating. Jason had fallen asleep.

'Here play with these for a bit and don't wake your brother,' Judy said, handing over two Sony Tablets.

'Oh cool.'

Judy strictly limited the time that they were allowed to play with electronic toys, so this was a treat.

'Have you heard anything from your mother?' she asked Aidan.

Apart from the monotonous beeping of their toys, it was now quiet in the back of the car.

'No, not since she telephoned with the address of the hotel. Dad's going to pay for everything, by the way.'

'Oh, that's generous of him.'

'Yes, I'm pleased about that because we have the MOT at the end of the month and I think we may need some new tyres. Another reason for changing the car—the tyres on the Shogun are very expensive.'

Judy ignored the comment about buying a new car and said, 'So you don't know how they got on yesterday?'

'No. You're as bad as the boys. We'll just have to wait until we meet him. Mum said we should ring her mobile once we arrive.' He signalled and turned off down the slip road to the M1. 'I just hope she's doing the right thing. I have this awful feeling that she will expect us to be the ones to take care of him. We have enough on our plates at the moment as it is, with the boys and our jobs, and now the new baby. I really don't want us to get involved.'

Judy said nothing.

'What is it?' he asked her.

'I thought you were quite relaxed about this? We're only going to visit him, you know. We're not bringing him home with us,' she said. 'Let's try to enjoy the weekend, for the boys' sake. There's plenty of time to discuss the future later on.'

'It's just that I can't see my mother giving up her job and staying at home to look after her brother. Can you? After all, she's never even suggested she take the children for the weekend while we have a break. She's always too busy.'

'It probably won't come to that. She's already told us he's very independent. He won't need looking after.'

'But what if he does? People with Down's Syndrome are more susceptible to illness than other people and I know who she'll expect to step in and look after him. Us.'

'So what do you want to do? You could turn the car round and we can go back home. Then you can ring them later and say that we don't want to get involved. Is that what you want to do?'

'No, of course not.'

She knew he was worried. She'd been thinking something similar. Taking a new member into their family would affect all their lives.

'It was a nice evening at your parents' house, wasn't it?' she said, hoping to change the tone of the conversation. 'Your mother certainly knows how to get round you, doesn't she. Steak and kidney pie, indeed.' Judy kicked something with her feet. 'What are these?' she asked, pulling up a yellow folder.

'Oh, nothing. They're just the brochures from the estate agents. I had planned to show them to Mum but then after her bombshell it seemed inappropriate,' he explained.

'Bombshell is right,' she said, opening the folder and flicking through it.

'I wonder if she knows what she's doing. It's so unlike my mother; she never does anything without working out all the pros and cons first. Anyway I can't see them wanting to down-size now, so we might as well throw those away. Maybe it's the menopause, making her act irrationally,' he suggested.

His wife looked at him and burst out laughing. 'Don't be ridiculous Aidan, she went through all that years ago. No, this is something else. It's been a shock for her too, remember. It must have been hard for her to suddenly learn that her father had kept his son a secret, even from her. I imagine she feels quite hurt.'

'I know, it's strange. I can't really believe that granddad would do that.'

'People do strange things when they're in love.'

'But afterwards? Why didn't he tell us about his son?'

'I don't know. You'll have to ask your mother,' she said.

'I really don't think she realises how this whim of hers is going to affect us,' Aidan continued. 'Suppose they do bring him to live with them.'

'I can't see that happening, Aidan. But you're right, it's not your Mum's thing, is it? She isn't going to give up her career, and even she can't expect your Dad to look after him while she's off running courses,' she said.

'Well, let's suppose they do. What if one of them dies or becomes very sick, who will look after Michael then? I told you: us,' he repeated.

'Well, I must admit I'm not very keen on that idea, Aidan. I have my own mother to think about, remember; she'll be eighty next year.'

'I know. And it's not as if Michael has always been around. We really don't know anything about him, do we?'

She put her hand on Aidan's arm. He was going over the same ground time and again. She could see he felt confused. He loved his mother, despite their frequent disagreements and he wanted her to be happy but she knew he was also thinking about his family.

'Look, sweetheart, there's no point worrying. We'll go and see her brother and then we'll all have a clearer picture of what's entailed. After all, it may not be that complicated; this Dr Edmundson seems to think there's not much wrong with Michael. Maybe he will be able to live an independent life, and we won't have to get involved,' she said.

'You're right. Let's wait and see what happens,' he replied and smiled at her.

Judy could understand his anxiety. She too had her doubts about where Susan was going with this and she didn't altogether trust her mother-in-law to leave them out of her plans. But she had a greater worry, one that she hadn't spelled out to Aidan. What if this new baby had Down's Syndrome? She had booked a doctor's appointment for next week and was going to talk to him about it. She was at the vulnerable age for having a child, coming up to forty. She had read the information that Susan had given them. The statistics said it was usually older women who had babies with Down's Syndrome— and she fell into that category now. Knowing about Aidan's uncle made the risk all the more real. She'd been offered the screening test each time she'd been pregnant but always declined it. They couldn't guarantee a definitive result, which was why she decided not to bother, but this time it was different. She felt she should take the test. If the baby had Down's Syndrome there was nothing she could do about it, but at least if the test was negative, she would sleep easier at night.

*

As they walked into the hotel, Aidan's mobile rang. It was his mother.

'Hi. We've just arrived. We're actually checking in right now,' he said. 'Where are you?'

'Good, you're early. Look we're on our way to collect Michael now. Why don't you get the kids sorted out and then come over and meet us for lunch?'

'Fine. Where and when?'

'There's a small village near Beacon Hill, called Bradley. It's not far from Swithland, just off the M1. Dr Edmundson recommended a pub there called The Robin Hood. It's got a play area and the food is good.'

'The Robin Hood? The kids will like that. Okay, Bradley near Swithland, you say. I'll put it in the sat nav and see what comes up. If we have a problem I'll ring you.'

'All right darling. See you all about one o'clock?' His mother hung up.

'Good morning,' the receptionist said, smiling at them. She was a very pretty girl; she looked Spanish with her dark skin and long black hair tied back with a ribbon that matched her uniform.

'We have a reservation in the name of Masters.'

'Ah, yes. Three rooms? Your friends have already checked in.'

'My parents,' he said, automatically.

'They are in room 322, and you have rooms 324 and 326.'

He signed the form that the receptionist pushed towards him. 'How long will it take us to get to Beacon Hill?' he asked her.

'On a Saturday? Not very long, probably about forty minutes,' she replied, handing him two key cards. 'There you are sir. Have a nice stay.' Her smile was dazzling and her accent made him think of blue skies and golden beaches.

'Daddy, can we go to the swimming pool now?' Ben was tugging at his arm.

Aidan looked at his watch; it was only eleven o'clock. 'Sure, we have time for a quick swim. But let's take your bags up first.'

He smiled as he watched his three sons head in the direction of the lift, struggling with an assortment of cases, coats, toys and of course the football. He couldn't imagine his life without the boys. What must it have been like for his grandfather to know he had a son and not be able to see him, never acknowledge him openly, never tell his daughter that she had a brother or take her to visit him?

'Are you sure there's time for a swim?' Judy asked. 'When did your mother say to meet them?'

'One o'clock. Yes there's plenty of time and anyway it will be good for the boys to use up some energy after sitting in the car all morning.'

'Okay, but I don't want to upset your mother by arriving late. You know what she's like about punctuality.'

'Don't worry.' Aidan kissed his wife, and put his arm around her. 'We won't be late.'

*

The strong smell of chlorine and the hollow sound of their voices reminded Aidan of his own childhood and of Friday evenings at the municipal pool, learning to swim. It was usually his grandfather who took him. He liked going with his grandfather because he always let him buy sweets from the vending machines and when his swimming class was over they would go up to the top terrace and have hot chocolate and sit and watch the other swimmers.

He still couldn't understand why his grandfather had told him nothing about Michael. He'd confided everything to his grandfather, things he never told his father. He told him how he was caned for smoking in the toilets at school, when he knew he could never tell his mother because she would have caused a fuss. He told him all about his first girlfriend and how he was hopelessly in love. He told him when he stole some chocolate from the school tuck shop and nobody knew it was him. They shared secrets. They were all so petty now: staying up late on the nights when Granddad baby-sat, a pen-knife that his mother said he was too young to own and even the bicycle lessons were a secret at first. Yes, his grandfather liked secrets. He would often tell him something and add, 'Don't tell your grandmother.' But he never told him about Michael. The most important secret of all was withheld from him. There had been opportunities when he could have mentioned him —the time when he gave him the bike, for instance. That bike must have belonged to Michael. Why else would his grandfather have had a boy's bicycle hidden in his shed? He remembered how annoyed his grandmother was when she saw him riding it. And there had been other occasions when he could have told him, when he was a grown man, watching the football together, and the time when he went hurrying round to tell his grandfather that Judy was expecting a baby boy—he'd wanted him to be the first to know. Granddad could have mentioned something then. But he'd said nothing. It made Aidan sad to realise that his grandfather hadn't trusted him with such an important secret. Not only that—and this he found hardest of all—he'd told them nothing about the Down's Syndrome. He knew that he and Judy were planning to have more children and he'd never mentioned it. It probably would have made no difference to their decision but he felt he should have known. He was beginning to feel that he'd never really known his grandfather after all.

He dangled his feet gingerly in the tepid water. Jason was already splashing about in his armbands and the older two were poised ready to launch themselves into the pool. He knew they were waiting for him to get in first so that they could then jump in and splash him. 'No jumping, you two. It's not allowed,' he called and pointed to the sign at the far end of the pool where the watchful attendant stood. Then, not waiting to look at their disappointed faces, he slipped smoothly into the pool and pulled away in a strong breaststroke. It felt good. As he glided effortlessly through the water, he realised how much he needed the exercise. He spent too many hours behind a desk or sitting in his car. It was time he took himself in hand; he was becoming flabby. He had noticed Judy looking at his stomach lately; she never commented but he knew he was putting on weight. He reached the far end and, in a single movement, turned and struck out again. When he got home he would renew his membership at the gym; he'd not been there since Jason was born. He changed to the crawl. The muscles in his shoulders were aching but it was a good feeling. He swam another ten lengths before stopping and pulling himself up onto the pool edge. His head felt clearer now. He looked across at his children; they were having swimming races across the width of the pool and Ben seemed to be winning.

Aidan looked at his watch; it was almost twelve o'clock. 'Two more minutes, boys and then it's time to go. Nan and Grandpa will be waiting.'

'Yeah, lunch.'

'I'm starving.'

'Right then, into the shower first then back to your rooms. We've got to leave by half-past-twelve.'

'Will Nan's brother be there?' Ben asked. 'Is he having lunch with us?'

'Yes, he will and yes, he is.'

'So we'll see him then?' asked Zak. 'Does he play football?'

'I don't know. You'll be able to ask him yourself, soon.'

He felt his stomach contract, whether from hunger or from apprehension about the coming meeting, he couldn't be sure. He tried to remind himself that he was a grown man now and there was nothing to be nervous about.

CHAPTER 24

Saturday morning, when they went down to breakfast, Graham was in very good spirits; he seemed to have forgiven Susan her earlier deception.

'What's the plan with Aidan and his gang?' he asked as they sat down at a table by the window.

'He's going to ring when they get here,' she said.

'So we'll just go ahead and meet Michael as promised or do you want to wait?'

'No. I think we'll go and pick up Michael anyway then, if they haven't phoned, I'll ring them to see where they are.'

'Sounds the best idea. We don't really want to leave him hanging about while we wait for that lot to get themselves organised.' They both knew what a military operation it was to get their grandsons ready.

Susan was pleased to see that her husband had entered into the venture so wholeheartedly but so far he hadn't given her any indication about how he thought they should proceed.

The dining room looked different today; the tables set for one had been rearranged. There were no businessmen, no computers but lots of families with small children and people who looked like hikers, with thick roll-neck sweaters and walking boots.

'Do you want some orange juice?' Graham asked, getting up and heading for the buffet.

Susan shook her head; she still didn't have much appetite. The emotional events of the last few days had upset her digestion. She poured herself some coffee and waited for Graham to sit down again.

'Where do you think we're going to go from here, Graham?' she asked, at last.

'How do you mean, Susie? I thought we were going up to the Charnwood Forest, as the good doctor recommended.'

Dr Edmundson had been very helpful the previous day, suggesting some pleasant walks and giving them the names of a number of pubs that sold good food and real ale. His attitude to them had warmed somewhat and Susan felt she could take that as a sign of his approval. He hadn't asked them about Michael and nobody had mentioned the future. But she knew she had to face up to it sooner or later.

'No. I mean with Michael? What are we going to say to him?' Anxiety was making her voice quiver.

'What do you want to say to him?' Graham asked, helping himself to some toast and spreading it liberally with butter.

'That's just it, I don't know. I feel even more confused than ever. I wish my father had told me about him. I just can't believe that he kept it secret all those years.'

'I know it's been a shock. You've gone from thinking you were an only child for almost sixty years and now you have a brother. Of course you're confused.'

'It's not just that. It's the fact that his son had Down's Syndrome and we were never told. Even at the time I was expecting Aidan I was given the choice of checking for Down's Syndrome and asked if anyone in the family had ever had it. But my father never said anything. And neither did my mother.'

She saw her husband looking at her strangely. 'No, I wouldn't have used it as an excuse to have an abortion. Of course not. I love my son. But we should have known.'

'I understand. It's hard to believe they kept it to themselves all those years. But that was then and now we know about Michael and his condition. So let's move on from there.'

She nodded. Thank goodness Graham was here with her.

'Let's look at what we've learned so far,' her husband continued. 'One: he already knew about you.'

'Yes,' she interrupted, 'that was a shock. I never knew my father had told them about me.'

'It shouldn't have been that much of a surprise, Susie. Don't you think Michael's mother would have wanted to tell her son something about his father?'

'Yes, but why did nobody tell *me* about him?' This was the part that hurt her the most. Did her parents think she'd be upset? Or did they just not consider it her business?

'I don't know. Your parents were very private people; they never spoke of their own lives, not to me anyway. So, if I may continue. Two: Michael seems to be a very nice man. Three: he likes his independence. Four: he has a job. And five: he likes you.'

'Yes, that's all true but maybe living in the centre is distorting his sense of independence. Maybe he wouldn't feel so secure away from Sunny View and the people who care about him.'

'Maybe. We don't know yet. Look Susie, we only met him yesterday. I know it's very emotional for you but you have to give it time.'

Susan had pulled out her compact and was attempting to stop the tears that were forming from ruining her make-up.

'One thing I do know,' he continued, 'is that we're not whisking that man away from Sunny View and everything he knows this weekend. So relax. And eat something, for God's sake.' He got up and went to the buffet, returning a moment later with a croissant and a glass of orange juice.

'Here, this is better for you than all that coffee,' he said, putting the food in front of her.

She smiled. Another of Graham's theories was that you couldn't think logically on an empty stomach, so she dutifully ate.

*

When they arrived at Sunny View, Michael was standing by the gate.

'Hello, Michael. I hope you haven't been waiting long?' Graham smiled and extended his hand to him.

'No. I finished early so I thought I would wait for you here,' he replied, evidently greatly relieved to see them.

'Hello, Michael. You look very smart, today,' Susan said, kissing him on the cheek. He was wearing a pair of brown cord trousers and a fawn jumper; his shoes were sturdy and had thick soles, and he carried a leather jacket over his shoulder. 'Do we need to speak to Dr Edmundson or someone before we go?'

'No. He's not here today. Brian is on duty but he knows I'm going out with you.'

'Fine, let's get going then.' Susan sat in the back and indicated that Michael should sit at the front with Graham.

'We're going out to Beacon Hill,' she explained. 'Dr Edmundson said that there were marvellous views from up there, right over Charnwood Forest.'

'Do you know the way?' Michael asked.

'More or less,' Graham replied. 'And anyway Susie has this electronic gadget that should get us there okay.' He pointed to the GPS that Susan had switched on for him.

'Oh, a navigation system. That's good,' Michael said approvingly. 'I have a small one I use when I go out on my bicycle.'

'Well in that case you can make sure that Graham follows the instructions properly. He likes to do his own thing sometimes,' Susan said. 'Then we end up going round and round in circles.' She thought she sounded rather patronising, speaking to him as though he were a child but Michael didn't seem to notice. Instead he twisted round in his seat to look at her, unsure if she was joking or not, then said, 'Okay, I'll help you Graham.'

As they drove Susan listened to Graham chatting to Michael about his life at the centre and took the opportunity to lean back and just enjoy the view. Inevitably her thoughts returned again to her father. It was all so strange. Why hadn't he ever told her about Michael? If he hadn't wanted to say anything when her mother was alive, he could have told her after she died. Maybe he just wanted to take his secrets to the grave with him. There were so many unanswered questions. Had he known that Anthea had cancer? Had he visited her? And whom had he loved, her mother or his mistress or maybe he *had* loved them both? Her aunt seemed to think that he was in love with both women but she might just be making excuses for him; she had adored her brother after all and didn't want anyone to think ill of him now he was dead. Susan was never going to know for sure; all the people who could tell her the truth were dead now. But as she sat there in the back of the car, listening to Michael and Graham chatting away like old friends, her concerns began to slip away. Perhaps it wouldn't be so difficult after all for Michael to become part of their family.

They drove up to Beacon Hill first and parked in the car park. Michael was eager to get out and look around. The view stretched before them, a panorama of patchwork fields in one direction and the vast canopy of the forest in the other, with the ribbon of the motorway cutting its way between them. The drone of the traffic surfaced every so often on the wind.

'Dr Edmondson was right. It's wonderful up here,' she said, pulling her coat tightly around her and facing into the wind that whipped up the escarpment tugging at her hair.

Up there on the hill, where the wind was strong and gusting, people were taking advantage of it to fly kites. She turned to see Michael watching a young boy struggle with a box kite.

'Have you ever flown a kite, Michael?' Susan asked, looking at her brother. His face was sad.

'Yes, but not for a long time. My father bought me a kite when I was little but we only ever went to the park with it. I wasn't very good and one day I let go of it and it flew away.'

'That was a shame.'

'Yes, but my father wasn't cross. He said that maybe we should wait until I was older and then he would buy me another one. He was always so kind to me.'

'And did he buy you another one?' she asked.

'No. We didn't remember about it.'

That sounded familiar. Her father had been someone who loved to make promises but rarely kept them. She remembered many a time when he'd promised to take her out somewhere or meet her from school, but in the end he'd forgotten and she'd been left angry and disappointed.

They walked along the ridge for a while, comfortable in the silence. Then Graham said, 'I think we'll head for the Old Man of the Beacon.' He and Michael headed up the steep slope towards where the autumn sunshine cast long shadows across the rocks, giving the illusion of a man's head.

'Not for me. I'll stay here,' Susan called after them and was rewarded with a wave of Graham's hand. She spotted a wooden bench and made towards it.

*

'Well? Good view from up there?' she asked as the men returned and slumped down beside her.

'It was very windy,' Michael said. The wind had stung his face, turning it a rosy pink and he looked decidedly cold, but he was laughing. 'And I was the winner.'

'You were indeed. He was up there five minutes before me.' Graham clapped him on the back. 'I'm absolutely whacked. That wind made it very hard going,' he said, standing up. 'But I think we should make our way back now or we won't get any lunch.'

'Graham likes his food, Michael,' Susan said with a laugh.

'Yes, you're quite right, as usual, but it's not just that. What we haven't told you yet Michael, is that our son Aidan and his family are going to join us for lunch. We're meeting them in the pub at one o'clock.'

'Your son?' Michael asked. He stopped and stared at them.

'We haven't had time to tell you about our family yet, have we. We have just one son, Aidan. He's married to Judy and they have three little boys, our grandsons,' Susan explained.

Michael looked at his watch and didn't reply. He seemed taken aback by the news.

'You'll love the boys,' she added, trying to alleviate his discomfiture.

'How old are they?' Michael asked politely. He was no longer smiling.

'Oh well, Ben is about ten, Zak is …' She hesitated.

'Ben is nine, Zak is seven and Jason is six,' interrupted Graham. 'Don't you remember we were at Jason's birthday only the other day?'

'Oh, yes, of course. Sorry I just can't keep track of the children's ages—they grow up so quickly.'

'Do you like children?' Graham asked Michael.

'I haven't had much to do with children really. There are a couple of families with children at Sunny View but I don't see them very often,' he replied.

'I'm sure you'll like our boys. They're looking forward to meeting their great-uncle,' Graham said.

'Great-uncle?' Michael seemed bemused by the idea.

'Yes, that's the great thing about families; you can have so many roles. Now you're a brother, a brother-in-law, an uncle and a great-uncle. All in one day,' Graham said.

But you're not a son, thought Susan. She suddenly felt a twinge of guilt. What would her mother think about all this? After all he wasn't really her brother, only her step-brother. Her father had betrayed her mother with Michael's mother. Poor Michael had been the unwitting cause of so much unhappiness in her family. If only her mother had had the capacity to forgive her husband or even to let him go. How different Michaels' life would have been. How different all their lives would have been.

They continued down the track and entered a wooded area. In this part of the park the soil was thin and poor, rock stuck up from the earth like carelessly thrown boulders, and bracken and ferns grew in abundance. Birch trees stretched their slender, silver trunks upward, their delicate canopy shading the forest floor. Susan blinked; her eyes needed a moment to accustom themselves to a dim light that was broken only by the sunshine glittering on the moving leaves. Despite the cars in the car park, there was nobody to be seen in this part of the forest. She could no longer hear the sounds of the motorway, nor the buffeting wind; there was only a restful silence, broken intermittently by the persistent tapping of a woodpecker.

She wondered how many opportunities Michael had had to walk in the woods. His mother had to work to support them; she wouldn't have had that much time for walking in the woods. How often had Susan's father come over and taken the boy out? Once a week? Once a month? Maybe even less.

Susan watched Graham and Michael walk ahead of her. Even from behind, the two men looked very different; Graham's tall thin frame was inclined slightly towards the stockier figure of his younger companion. She could hear him talking about forest life, pointing out the habitat of some creature or other, indicating the spore it had left behind. Occasionally they would stop and examine a clump of fungi or pick up a fallen leaf. She enjoyed seeing them together, two men who both believed in happy families.

The path led them through a clearing that had been laid out as a picnic area with wooden tables and benches made from rough hewn wood. Here the trail forked offering a a path to the right leading to another lookout spot—a walk of ten miles—or alternatively a path to the left, towards the car park.

'This way it is, then,' Graham said, guiding them down towards the carpark.

*

When they arrived at The Robin Hood, they saw Aidan's Shogun pulling into a space near the entrance.

'Well, how's that for good timing? There they are,' said Graham.

Michael didn't reply; he was busy studying the small people that were clambering down from the car. They'd seen their grandmother's VW Golf arrive and were waving, frantically. Zak ran over to see them.

'Hi Nan. Hi Grandpa,' he shouted. 'Where's the Jag?'

Graham got out of the car and gave his grandson a hug. 'I didn't want to get it dirty on the motorway,' he told him.

The boy laughed and went round to Susan's side of the car. 'Hi Nan. We've been swimming,' he said.

'So I see,' Susan said, patting his wet hair. 'You'll catch cold if you don't dry that hair my boy.' She kissed his damp skin. 'You're freezing.'

The other two boys waited with their mother while Aidan locked the car. Jason was hanging onto Judy's skirt and watching them curiously. As Susan walked across to greet them, she heard Ben say: 'We've got one of them in our school.' He was looking at Michael. She saw Aidan speak to him sharply and although she couldn't hear what he said, whatever it was caused Ben to blush.

'Hi everyone. You found it okay then?'

'No problem Mum.' Aidan kissed his mother on the cheek.

'Hi boys. Hello Judy.' Susan kissed them all in turn. 'Come on, I want you to meet Michael.' She indicated, with a slight movement of the head, the spot where Michael was waiting next to the car. She noticed with an enormous feeling of relief that Zak was already talking to him about something.

'It looks as though Zak has lost no time in introducing himself,' Judy said.

Once all the introductions had been made they went into the pub, Graham leading the way and Zak following, holding Michael's hand. The others trooped behind and Susan brought up the rear.

The Robin Hood was a typical English pub, with wooden pillars and cross-beams and tiny mullioned windows that let in very little daylight. The interior was warm and cosy, the walls, decorated with horse brasses and plates, while heavy brass jugs, once used for measuring perfumes, stood in the alcove of the fireplace and numerous other brass knick-knacks added to the warm gleam that they cast around the room. A second, larger room led off the bar and Susan could see tables set for lunch, with white tablecloths and small posies of flowers.

'Well this is nice, all the family together,' Graham said, once they had all sat down. He beamed at his wife across the table. He'd engineered the seating so that he sat to Michael's left, Zak sat on his right and Susan was opposite. Aidan sat next to his mother— Graham knew the danger of seating mother and son opposite each other. And, just as Judy had predicted, any awkward silence was quickly dispersed by the excited chatter of the boys. They as usual commanded all the attention.

'Grandpa, you are going to come swimming with us when we get back to the hotel, aren't you?' asked Ben.

'Yes, Grandpa. It's cool. You can dive as well; there's a big diving board.'

'Please Grandpa.' Jason adopted his most appealing expression.

'Well, I was thinking of having a sleep when we got back.' Graham was trying hard to look serious.

'Noooo,' the boys chorused. 'You can sleep later. Come swimming with us.'

'I suppose you won't stop until I agree, so all right then. What about you Michael? Would you like to have a swim with us?'

'Yes Michael, you come too,' Zak cried.

'That would be nice Graham but I ought to get back to Sunny View.' He noticed the disappointment on Zak's face then added, 'Perhaps another time, Zak.'

Michael seemed at ease but Susan noticed that he was watching everyone carefully. She tried to bring him into the conversation more. 'So, what sort of things do you usually do at the weekends, Michael?' she asked.

'Sometimes if it's a nice day, I cycle into the village or I take the bus into Uppingham and look around the shops. Mostly I stay at home.'

'Do you like to cycle?' Aidan asked.

'Yes, very much. I've had a bicycle for as long as I can remember. It's very useful, and good exercise,' he added.

Aidan didn't reply; he seemed deep in thought.

'All our boys have bikes. Aidan taught them all to ride. They love it but where we live the roads are too busy for them to go out on their bikes alone. Sometimes at the weekend Aidan takes them on the Common where there're miles of cycle tracks,' Judy explained. 'They love it.'

'My father taught me to ride. He bought me a bicycle when I was seven then when I got too big for that he bought me another one,' Michael said. 'He said it was good for my coordination. Usually we just went to the park but sometimes we cycled along country roads.' He took another mouthful of his food and chewed it slowly. 'Did Graham teach you to ride?' he asked, looking at Aidan.

'Dad? No, he didn't actually. It was my grandfather who taught me to ride, your father in fact, Michael,' Aidan replied.

'He taught us both to ride, then?' Michael seemed pleased at the thought.

'Yes, it looks that way,' said Aidan.

Ben as usual managed to turn the conversation to football and for a while he and Zak discussed the merits and demerits of their teams with Aidan. Michael listened at first then   joined in the discussion; he too had been initiated into the mysteries of football by his father. Now he regularly watched matches on the television.

As Susan listened to her son and Michael talking, she realised that her father'd had, over many years, a similar relationship with both boys. They had in fact, enjoyed more of his company than she had. A sense of loss enveloped her. There had been so much she hadn't known, so much she'd missed.

The waitress came over with a small blackboard to show them the dessert menu. Someone had chalked on it: Blackberry Crumble, Toffee Pudding, Jam Roly-Poly, Upside Down Cake and Banoffi Pie.

'My, they look good,' Aidan said and read them aloud for the pure satisfaction of hearing the sound of such tempting puddings.

Jason was giggling and trying to stand on his head. 'I want Upside Down Cake,' he said.

'You'll get nothing if you don't sit down and behave,' his mother admonished him.

The waiter stood patiently by, his notepad at the ready.

'Toffee Pudding, for me,' Graham said. 'And what about you Michael? They have Blackberry Crumble.'

'No, thanks. No pudding for me. I don't eat puddings.'

'You don't eat puddings!' Zak said, his eyes, so like his father's, opening even wider in astonishment.

'No. I'm diabetic, you see, so I have to be careful not to eat too much sugar,' he explained to the boy.

'Why, what would happen to you?' Ben asked.

'I don't know really. I suppose I would become ill.'

'How long have you been diabetic, Michael?' Susan asked, wondering how many more things this man had to endure.

'Only about three years. I started getting very tired and I was always thirsty, so Dr Edmundson sent me for some tests. People with Down's Syndrome often get diabetes when they get older,' he explained.

It was the first time anyone had mentioned his condition. Susan realised that it wasn't because they were avoiding the subject, it just hadn't come up in the general flow of conversation.

While the adults waited for the bill and drank their coffee, the boys played outside on the grassy area behind the pub that passed for a garden. The lunch had gone well, Susan reflected but she was anxious to get Aidan alone to ask him what he thought of Michael. In the meantime Michael was explaining to Aidan about his work in the IT department; he seemed fairly knowledgeable, Susan thought, as she listened to her son's technical questions.

'You should come and see the IT centre one day, Aidan. It's very interesting and Dr Edmundson is a really nice man. He has been so kind to me since my mother died.'

'I'd like that Michael. It sounds a nice place.'

'We ought to make a move, folks,' Graham said. He'd paid the bill and, while he was deliberating on how much tip to leave their patient waiter, Judy went through the side door to collect her sons.

'We're off now boys. Come and say goodbye.'

The children came rushing up to the waiting adults, their faces rosy and damp from their exertions. Perspiration had flattened Jason's curls against his head.

'Jason, look at the state of you. Your trousers are covered in mud,' Susan said, bending down and kissing her youngest grandson.

'Don't worry Nan. My Mum will wash them.'

'Bye Michael. Will we see you tomorrow?' Zak asked.

Susan looked at Aidan. 'What do you think?'

But it was Judy who answered. 'Shall we pop round to see you tomorrow, Michael, before we leave? Would that be all right?'

'Yes, I'd like that and I can show you the IT room. I have my own key.'

'Okay then, that's settled; we'll call in on our way home. It won't be too early, probably about half-past-eleven. Is that all right?'

'That's fine. Goodbye Judy, goodbye Aidan.'

They waited until Aidan had his family settled in the car and was driving off before returning to their own car.

'I feel exhausted after a couple of hours with those boys. Just looking at them makes me tired,' Graham said, as he buckled his seatbelt.

'Yes, they do seem to have limitless energy,' Susan replied. 'What did you think of them, Michael?'

'I like them a lot, especially Zak. He's very friendly. I think Jason is a little nervous of me, but he's nice. Ben asks a lot of questions. He seems a very clever little boy.'

'Yes, you're spot on. Ben's the brains, Zak loves everyone and Jason is still a baby.'

'Michael, would you turn on the GPS. I think I remember the way back, but we might as well be sure,' Graham said and started the car.

*

Sunny View seemed deserted when they arrived back. They parked by the main building.

'Are you sure you won't come over for a swim?' Graham asked. 'I'll bring you back afterwards.'

'No, thank you Graham. I'm a bit tired. I think I shall just put the TV on and watch the football.'

'Okay, then. We'll see you tomorrow before we go.'

'Yes, I'd like that. Thank you for lunch. I have enjoyed myself.' He shook Graham by the hand and, turning to Susan, continued, 'It was nice to meet your family, Susan. They are very nice people.'

'Yes, they are, aren't they. But they're your family too, remember.' She gave him a hug. 'We'll see you tomorrow, Michael. Bye for now.'

As they drove back to the hotel, Susan felt a heaviness come over her body. She was exhausted. It had been a successful day so far but she was no nearer to knowing how Aidan felt.

'He's a very pleasant man, you know and so keen to learn,' Graham said. 'And, what's more, he seems to have his life pretty well organised.'

'Yes, I wonder what Aidan and Judy think of him,' she said, closing her eyes.

CHAPTER 25

Once they were back in their hotel room, Susan showered, changed then lay on the bed, waiting for Graham to get ready. They'd arranged to meet Aidan and Judy for an early dinner in the hotel restaurant. The food wasn't much to her taste but it was convenient and the boys liked it. Despite the shower she still felt tired; it was if her body didn't want to do anything, as if all the energy had leaked out of her like a faulty battery. She lay there, staring at the pale blue ceiling. Her legs felt like lead and there was a dull throbbing above her eyes. The emotions of earlier in the day had now transformed into a deep lassitude that paralysed her. She knew some important decisions had to be made but, at that moment, she felt incapable of making them.

'Are you all right? You look a little pale,' Graham said, emerging from the bathroom in a cloud of warm steam.

'I'm just tired.'

'Is that all?'

'Oh Graham, I don't think I can do it,' she said, wiping a tear from her eye. 'What if I mess up his nice, comfortable life? What if the others don't want to have anything to do with him? You know how stubborn and uncompromising Aidan can be at times.'

She saw her husband raise his eyebrows and stifle a smile. 'I wonder where he gets that from?' he murmured.

'The point is that we may have raised his expectations and maybe we've got nothing to offer him.'

Her husband sat on the bed next to her and took her hand. 'Come on Susan, this is not like you. You're the positive one in this family. You're the one who always finds the solution.'

'I know but this is different. It's like Aidan said, this is someone's life we're playing with.'

'Don't be silly. We're not playing with anyone's life. You found out you had a brother and, quite understandably, you wanted to meet him. What's more, he obviously wanted to meet you too. If nothing else happens I don't think any damage has been done. He will go on with his life and we will go on with ours.'

'No, you're wrong. I don't think I can go on with my life as before, not knowing that he lives here. I feel a responsibility for him.'

'Well I think you're getting upset over nothing. Didn't we say that we would decide what to do once we'd all met him. As I said before, there are a number of avenues we can explore. We're not going to walk away and never see him again. Anyway, buck yourself up; we said we'd be down in the bar at seven-thirty.' He took his jacket off the hanger and slipped it on.

'Okay. I'll just freshen up my make-up and I'll be ready,' Susan said, forcing herself to sit up. This wasn't going to be easy. She had no idea how Aidan was going to react. He had seemed fine at lunch but then he would. He wouldn't embarrass anyone, least of all Michael, by revealing his true feelings. No, one thing she could say for her son was that he was considerate of other's feelings—well, everyone's except hers.

*

'Oh, there you are,' Graham said, as Judy and Aidan came into the hotel bar. 'Boys in bed?'

'Yes, and asleep I hope.'

'Have they eaten?' Susan asked, moving over to let Judy sit down next to her.

'Yes, we took them in as soon as the restaurant opened at six-thirty but, to be quite honest, they were so tired after being in the swimming pool that they didn't eat much. I don't think we'll hear anything from them until the morning,' Judy said.

'And not too early, I hope,' Aidan added. 'Two gin and tonics, please.' He addressed this last remark to the barman.

Susan looked at her son; he would soon be forty and a few grey hairs were appearing in his thick brown hair. She was wondering what she could say about Michael that would not arouse a negative reaction from him when Graham, as usual, came to her rescue.

'Well then Aidan, what did you think of Michael?'

'He's okay. Quite a pleasant chap, in fact. Seemed a bit strange, him talking about his father all the time and it's actually Granddad he's talking about.'

'It's difficult isn't it,' Susan said. 'It's the same for me. It's like there are two men and they are both my father but I only know one of them. I must admit, Aidan, I'm finding it hard to come to terms with it.' She put her hand on his and said, 'I know how much you loved your Granddad. It must be hard for you, as well.'

Her son didn't reply.

'So what about you, Graham? You seemed to be getting on famously with him,' Judy asked.

'Yes, he's a nice young man. I like him.'

'Don't keep calling him a young man, Dad. He's nearly fifty. He's a good ten years older than me,' snapped Aidan.

'Well, he doesn't look it, does he?' Judy interceded.

'No, he doesn't and he's so innocent of the world that I can't help but think of him as a young man. But then again, everyone is young compared to me, these days,' Graham added, with a smile.

The barman returned with the drinks and Susan took the opportunity to order a second glass of wine.

'You remember when Granddad taught me to ride a bike?' Aidan said.

'Yes, you were about eight or nine,' Susan replied.

'Seven, actually. He had that bike hidden in the tool shed. I don't know if Gran knew it was there but I remember her being very cross when she saw me riding it.'

'Really? I never knew that.'

'Seems there were a lot of things you didn't know, Mum. I think it belonged to Michael.'

'Well it's quite possible,' said Graham.

'I can't believe Granddad never mentioned anything about him. Not then, of course, but later when I was grown-up. We spent a lot of time together; you'd have thought he'd have said something, wouldn't you?' He looked at his mother for an explanation.

'Not really, Aidan. I would imagine that by then he'd become so used to keeping the two halves of his life separate that it would never have occurred to him to tell you anything.'

'But what about Gran? Why didn't she say anything?'

Susan realised that her son's antagonism had more to do with the failure of his grandparents to confide in him than the existence of an illegitimate uncle.

'I think your Gran's heart had been broken and she lived in a permanent state of denial. She never told me anything about Michael either,' Susan said and then began to explain to her son a little of her childhood and her parents' marriage.

'I never realised you had an unhappy childhood, Mum. You never said anything,' Aidan said, looking accusingly at her.

'What could I say? I had plenty to eat. I went to a good school. Both my parents loved me and cared for me. And I loved my parents. What could I tell you? That I felt caught in the middle? That I couldn't side with either of them, so I sided with neither, that I shut my feelings in a box and tried to ignore their pain?'

'God, the skeletons are coming out of the cupboard today,' he said, drinking down the remains of his gin and tonic in a single gulp. He lifted his hand to catch the waiter's attention.

Susan hoped he wasn't going to drink too much; it would be impossible to talk rationally to him if he did.

'Another gin and tonic, please,' he asked the barman. 'What about you Judy? Dad?'

'I haven't finished this one yet,' his wife replied. She leaned towards him. 'Slow down, will you. We've all evening to go,' she whispered.

'I'll have another glass of the house wine, thanks Aidan,' his father replied.

'Look Aidan, it's not that I've deliberately kept things from you. I've kept them from myself as well. This is as much a voyage of discovery for me as it is for you.' Susan stretched out to take his hand again but he snatched it away.

'And now that you do know about Michael, I suppose you're hoping to include all of us in your plans. Well, we have our own lives to lead, Mum. You've never wanted much from us before, so why now?' The gin was beginning to loosen his tongue.

'Aidan.' Judy put a restraining hand on his knee. Some other residents had entered the bar and were looking at the evening's menu. 'Let's talk sensibly about this,' she said.

'That's unfair, Aidan,' Susan replied. The conversation was not going as she'd hoped. 'I just felt it was important for you to meet him. And,' she added, 'I thought it was time that all of this was out in the open.'

'Look, Aidan. Let me tell you how I see it developing,' Graham interjected. He leaned across and exchanged his empty wine glass for the full one that the waiter was holding out to him. 'Thank you.' He put a twenty pound note on the tray.

'Okay Dad, how do you see it developing?'

'First of all, there's no going back. We may not know exactly how we'll proceed, but proceed we will. I suggest that we invite Michael to stay with us at Lock End next weekend; it's an easy journey up here to collect him. Then we'll be able to see how he copes away from that safe environment that you referred to earlier.' He looked at Susan as he made this last remark.

She smiled at him weakly.

'That's fine Dad but what is this all leading up to? Are we going to adopt him or something?' He made Michael sound like a homeless puppy.

Susan started to feel angry with her son. 'Aidan, what is the problem? We, that is, your Dad and I, want to help Michael in some way. At the moment, it's too soon to say what sort of help would be most appropriate. It's as simple as that.'

'I understand, Susan. I think what's worrying Aidan, and me to some extent, is what will happen in the future,' Judy tried to explain.

'In the future?'

'Well, suppose that Michael comes to live with you then, if something were to happen to you, who would look after Michael? Oh, I'm sorry. I'm not making myself very clear.'

'You're making yourself perfectly clear. What you want to know is, if we die, will you have to look after Michael? Is that it?'

'Well, something like that.'

'For goodness sake, Judy, don't be such a pessimist. Who knows what will happen tomorrow? We could all be killed in a motorway pile-up on our way home. We could live to be ninety. Who knows?'

'Susan, I'm just trying to be realistic. You were the one who said we needed a family consensus on this. All I'm saying is that we have some concerns.'

'Well, in that case, being realistic,' Susan barely kept the sarcasm from her voice, 'Graham and I are both in good health so we have no plans to pop off and leave you just yet.'

'Also,' Graham interrupted, 'according to all those articles on the internet that Susan has been reading endlessly, people with Down's Syndrome have, on average, a lower life expectancy than most. Michael may outlive me but probably not Susan.'

Susan was not happy with this turn to the conversation; it seemed cruel to view Michael in this clinical way.

'Look, let's take this more slowly. I like Graham's suggestion about bringing Michael down to Lock End next weekend and, if you're not busy, perhaps you and the children could come over,' she suggested.

Neither Judy nor Aidan replied.

'Judy, I understand that you're worried about taking on more commitments. After all, you have your mother to consider and three young sons, and now there's another one on the way. But as Susie says, who knows what the future has in store for us.

However I will promise you this: if Michael does come to live with us, I will make some provision in my will for him. He will never be a burden, financial or otherwise, to you and Aidan.'

Aidan looked at his father but didn't reply.

'Okay, as you say, let's take it step by step,' Judy said, eventually. She turned to her husband, who was gazing intently at the bottom of his empty glass. 'Are you going to football next weekend, Aidan?'

'What? No, it's the following one. Oh, okay Mum, you win as usual. We'll come over.'

'Good. Why not come on Saturday and stay overnight? As you keep reminding me, Aidan, we've plenty of room.'

'Fine, whatever.' Aidan was intent on finding the barman again.

'Shall we go and eat?' Judy asked.

Susan could see she was anxious that her husband didn't have any more gin and tonics on an empty stomach.

'Good idea,' she replied, getting up and heading in the direction of the dining room. There was a week for Aidan to get used to the idea. Maybe he'd see things differently by the following weekend.

CHAPTER 26

Michael felt confused and tired. The wine made his head ache. He wasn't used to drinking wine. There were lots of things he wasn't used to. He wished it wasn't Saturday. He wanted to talk to Dr Edmundson or to Brian but they were at home so now he would have to wait until Monday.

He filled the kettle and switched it on. A cup of tea would help him think. His mother always said there was nothing like a nice cup of tea. She drank a lot of tea: dark brown tea, with lots of sugar and a dash of milk. A tear trickled down his cheek. He missed his mother. She would have told him what he should do. They would have sat together, drinking tea and he would have told her about Graham and Susan and about the pub and the children. If she was here he wouldn't feel so lonely.

He heard the kettle switch itself off and hurriedly put two teabags in the teapot. He poured the boiling water on the tea bags and watched them stain the water brown. It was important to use boiling water, his mother always said. She wouldn't have approved of the teabags. She always used loose tea but Michael didn't like the mess it made. He covered the teapot with a tea cosy that one of his friends had knitted for him. It was red and white, his team's colours. Seeing the tea cosy reminded him of the football match and he switched on the television. The match was almost over but he knew he would be able to watch another one later, in 'Match of the Day'. That was his favourite TV programme.

He sat on the sofa and sipped his tea. He liked Susan. She was tall and her mouth went up at one side when she smiled. He was happy that she had come to see him at last. He thought he would be angry with her because she hadn't come to see him before, but she was so nice he couldn't be angry. He didn't want her to go away again. She said that she didn't know where he was and that was why she hadn't come before. This surprised him. Why hadn't his father told her about him and where he lived? Why hadn't they come together? Then when his father was too old to visit him, she could have come on her own. And she could have met his mother. His mother would have liked Susan. And he liked Graham too. Graham knew lots of things about the countryside. Michael's mother had taught him about the countryside, even before he had come to Sunny View. She had told him the names of trees and plants and lots of birds. He liked the countryside. He had enjoyed walking in the woods today with Graham. Graham had told him about his dog, how he took his dog for walks by the river. He said that Michael could visit them in Maidenhead and he would take him for a walk by the river. That sounded nice but he was not sure how he would get there. Graham said there was a train but he'd never been on a train. He usually went everywhere on his bicycle or sometimes by bus.

He'd felt very nervous of the children. He'd seen the older boy staring at him. He knew he looked different to other people but he thought it was very rude of Ben to stare at him. His mother had always told him to walk away if people were horrid to him but he couldn't walk away today, not there, in the pub. Luckily the boy Zak was nice to him. He asked him lots of questions and was very interested in the farm. He would like to show Zak the animals on the farm. Perhaps when they came to say goodbye to him tomorrow, he would offer to show him the piglets but that would have to be after he had taken Aidan round the IT room. He was looking forward to seeing them all tomorrow but he felt a bit nervous. He hoped Susan and Graham would be there when Aidan arrived. He wasn't sure if Aidan liked him. After all he was Susan's son and now Susan had a brother that he knew nothing about. He had seen Aidan look at him when he thought he wasn't looking. At first he seemed cross but then later he had talked to him about football and smiled at him.

It was true what his mother said: the tea did make him feel better. He poured himself a second cup. Tomorrow he would see them all again.

*

The children had slept well but by seven o'clock they were wide awake. Aidan could hear them bouncing on their bed in the next room. He pulled the pillow over his head and tried to ignore them while Judy slept peacefully beside him. Well, they couldn't have it both ways; at least they didn't wake up during the night any more —although that would soon change with the new baby on the way. He was delighted that Judy was pregnant but he didn't really fancy going back to the sleepless nights and getting up to make bottles at two o'clock in the morning.

Aidan got up and put on his dressing gown. His head was hurting. He fumbled in the dark for his swimming trunks, trying not to wake his wife, then went in to see to his sons.

'Right boys. Who's for a swim?'

It took no more than two minutes for them to pull on their swimming trunks and grab their towels and then they were out of the room and running down the corridor to the lift.

'Keep the noise down. People are still trying to sleep,' he called in a loud whisper.

The swimming pool was empty save for the attendant who could not suppress the smile that rose to his lips when he saw Aidan, bleary eyed and unshaven, a dutiful father escorting his excited sons.

The pool wasn't so inviting today. The fluorescent lights were bright and hurt his eyes and his head was still pounding. The exuberant cries of his sons seemed louder and shriller than the day before and it was all he could do not to snap at them. Perhaps part of his new regime should be to drink less or, at the very least, stay off the gin.

'Right guys, diving lesson number two. But first of all, let's see what you've remembered from yesterday.'

The boys lined up on the edge of the pool and crouched forward as he had instructed then, at his signal, dropped into the water.

'Excellent. Let's take you on to the next stage now.'

He showed them what to do then sat down on the edge of the pool to watch. They were lucky; there were hardly any other people in the pool at that hour. An elderly woman wearing a purple bathing cap swam elegantly up and down in the far lane and there was a harassed father trying to teach a little girl wearing arms bands not to be frightened of the water. From time to time he glared across at Aidan's children when he thought they might come too close and splash his precious daughter.

So his mother was thinking of bringing Michael to live with them. That was so typical of her, only considering herself. And why was she making all this fuss about her new brother when she rarely had time for her own grandchildren? Well the news had certainly been a shock; even now he couldn't come to terms with the fact that Michael's father and his grandfather were one and the same man. He felt let down although he knew it was ridiculous to feel that way. After all why would his grandfather confide to a young boy that he was having an extra-marital affair? Would he have done so if he'd been in that situation? No, of course not. But how would Aidan have felt if he'd known about Michael then? Curious? Jealous perhaps, that there was a rival for his grandfather's affection? But that was then. He was not a boy anymore and his grandfather was dead. He suddenly felt ashamed of his behaviour the previous night. Judy had not said anything to him when they went to bed but he knew she was angry with him and rightly so. He had behaved like a prat. He wasn't convinced that his mother was doing the right thing nor that she was doing it for the right reasons but nevertheless he resolved to take a more objective stance the next time they spoke of it.

The clock on the end wall said nine o'clock.

'Time to wake Mummy, boys. Then we'll have some breakfast.'

'Yeah, breakfast.'

'Will they have Cheerios?'

'Pancakes? I'm having pancakes.'

'I expect they'll have everything. Now come along, into the showers.'

*

Michael was already waiting for them when they arrived at Sunny View; Aidan could see him sitting on a bench not far from the main house and as soon as he saw their car he came over to meet them.

'Hello, Aidan. Hello Judy,' he said, with a big smile of welcome. 'You've come then.'

'Hi, Michael.'

It was Zak who was out of the car first and rushing up to his new uncle. 'You should have come for a swim, Michael. The pool was brill,' he said, 'and Daddy is teaching us to dive. I was the best, wasn't I Dad?'

'Well you all have a long way to go yet but you're getting there,' his father replied. 'And how are you Michael? Are you going to give us a guided tour, this morning?'

'Yes, I've got the key to the IT room,' he said, producing a Yale key from his pocket and showing it to Aidan. 'Follow me. We'll look in there first then I'll take you to see the animals.'

At the mention of animals the three children became more interested and started up an unceasing train of questions which Michael did his best to answer. Aidan listened to him patiently explain to them which animals they had and why they kept them. He seemed to know a lot about the workings of the farm but then he had been there for quite a few years.

'Have my parents been to say goodbye?' Aidan asked, catching up to the excited group in front.

'Yes, they were here about half an hour ago but they couldn't stay. Graham said it was a long way to go and he didn't want to get home too late,' Michael explained, unlocking the door to his place of work. 'Here we are. This is the IT room, where I work. Would you like me to tell you about the computers?'

'That would be nice,' said Judy, smiling at him.

Michael grinned back at her, delighted at her interest.

The next fifteen minutes were spent admiring the new computers and testing out some of the programs that Michael thought the children would enjoy.

'Well Michael, that was very interesting. I am very impressed with what you do here,' Aidan said when they'd finished. At least he seemed to know what he was talking about.

'Look Dad, this is easy,' called Jason. 'I can read it all. But if you make a mistake the computer corrects you and then makes you do it again.' His youngest son was using the reading program that Michael had set up for him. Michael beamed. He seemed very happy that they'd come to see him.

'Now we'll go and see the pigs,' he said, looking at the children.

'Oh, piiigs,' squealed Zak. 'I love pigs.'

'But I want to do the next level,' Jason complained.

'You can do that next time you come,' Michael said. 'I have to switch the computers off now or Brian will be cross with me.'

'And then, I'm afraid, we must be on our way, too,' Judy said. 'I don't want to get the boys home too late because they've all got school tomorrow and I think Ben still has some homework to finish.'

'I understand Judy. It's very important that they do their homework. My mother used to give me homework,' he said, confidingly.

Aidan watched him walk around, switching off all the machines and leaving everything just as it had been when they arrived.

'Follow me. It's not far to the piggery,' he said as he locked the door behind him.

'I think I'll wait in the car,' Aidan said. 'I've got a dreadful headache. You go.' He watched his family troop off behind Michael and once they were out of sight he pulled out a packet of cigarettes. As he lit one he thought again about his grandfather. That was another of their secrets: that Granddad smoked. 'Don't tell your Nan.' He could hear the familiar words drifting back from the past and mingling with the smoke of his own cigarette. Yes, his grandfather was a man who liked to keep secrets. But the trouble with secrets was that they didn't remain hidden for ever. One day they resurfaced and then people got hurt. Slowly he wandered back to the Shogun.

*

Michael stood watching their car disappear into the distance and a feeling of sadness descended on him. He liked the children, especially Zak because Zak always spoke to him first, before he had time to say anything. And today when they went into the pig-pen Jason had held his hand. He liked the feel of that little hand in his. It was nice having nephews. No, not nephews. What had Susie said? Great-nephews. He was their great-uncle. And he liked Judy. She was kind but strict, just like his mother had been. And Aidan had said he was impressed with the IT room. He would tell Brian that tomorrow. Brian would be pleased.

A girl from the computer classes, came out of one of the flats. 'Hello Michael. What are you doing?'

'Hi Anne. I've just been saying goodbye to my family. They have to get back to London. It's a long way to drive and they're going on the motorway.'

He felt a special warmth as he said 'My family.' It made him feel good, less strange and less alone. It was nice to have a family again.

'Oh, that's nice. Do you want to come over to the recreation hall and play table tennis?'

'Yes, okay. I'll catch you up.'

He walked back to his flat to get his table tennis bat. What a lot had happened in such a short time. He found it rather hard to take it all in. He was not used to so many people taking an interest in him. He needed to think carefully about it all. He was beginning to realise that he had become too dependent, first on his mother, then when she died, on Dr Edmundson. He never did anything on his own except go to the local shop. Maybe now was the time to change all that. He felt a flutter of excitement at the prospect of going to visit Susan and Graham.

*

Graham was in a hurry to get home; he never really liked leaving Jess behind, even though she was perfectly well looked after. If there were no hold-ups on the M25 he would be able to give her an evening walk as usual. He looked across at Susan; she seemed deep in thought. Well she had a lot to think about. She had suggested they stop at a pub for lunch but when she saw he was reluctant to do so, she didn't mention it again. Perhaps he would suggest taking her to that nice Italian place in Maidenhead tonight, instead.

'Aidan seemed in a better mood this morning,' she said, as they entered the southbound lane of the M1.

'Yes. But I wish he wouldn't drink so much. It makes him bad tempered and quite unreasonable.'

'I know. I haven't seen him like that for years, not since before he was married.'

'Well, it's all been a bit of a shock for him, I suppose.' He didn't mention his own feelings on the matter. He'd been shocked to learn that David had had a second family. Graham had come across plenty of men who'd cheated on their wives, some who'd ended up divorced, others who'd somehow managed to juggle the demands of both wife and mistress. But David? He would never have thought it of him. You could never tell what went on in someone's marriage.

'It was a shock for all of us,' his wife added.

'Maybe we shouldn't try so hard to include them,' he suggested. 'I'm sure Judy sees it as manipulation on our part, not really a search for consensus at all.'

'Perhaps you're right. I won't make a big issue of the weekend. I'll just wait for them to phone me. If they want to come over, fine; if not …' She didn't finish.

'Do they know it's definitely on then?'

'Yes, I told them this morning when I rang to see if they'd left.'

'What did Aidan say?' he asked.

'Nothing really, I just asked if we'd see them on Saturday and he said okay.'

'Well, it doesn't sound as though there's a problem, then.'

'No, I suppose not. Did you tell Michael we would come and collect him?'

'Yes but he said not to bother. He reckons he can get a bus. On Monday he's going to ask that Dr Edmundson which bus he should take.'

'That's good. I'm sure he could get a bus to Reading if there isn't one straight to Maidenhead, then we could run over and pick him up.'

'Well it would certainly be a lot easier than driving up here again,' Graham said. The traffic was heavier now and they were stuck behind a slow-moving car in the outside lane. 'Bloody Sunday drivers. About time too,' he added as the offending car pulled over to the inside lane.

Graham didn't like driving in heavy traffic; it stretched his normal placid nature to breaking point but, unlike his wife, he never leaned on the horn or flashed his lights at the offending driver.

'Would you like me to drive for a bit?' Susan asked. Graham just looked at her so she smiled back at him. She knew it was a waste of time asking; he didn't like to be the passenger. 'Suit yourself,' she said, switching on the radio. 'I think I'll ring Aunty Kate later and let her know how we got on.'

'Yes, good idea.'

His wife lay back in the seat and closed her eyes but he knew she wouldn't sleep. She would be going over the events of the weekend, replaying the conversations in her head. The fingers of her right hand began tapping out the beat to the music. Suddenly she sat up and said, 'I think it's time Aidan and I had a talk.'

'A talk? What about?'

'Everything. I think I've kept him in the dark for too long. I need to talk to him about his grandparents, so that he can understand why his grandfather behaved as he did.'

'Is that a good idea, Susie? Your talks with Aidan usually end up with one of you storming off in a rage.'

'You're exaggerating. I know we argue a lot but he is my son and there are things I need to tell him.'

'Fine. But don't say I didn't warn you.

The traffic was moving at a steady pace now so he slipped the car into cruise control and removed his foot from the accelerator. Well Susan had opened a can of worms this time. He just hoped that they would be able to resolve it without Michael getting hurt. He liked the man; he was pleasant and polite and obviously trying to cope in a world that had not always been kind to him. He would like to do something to help him, but what? Judy was right when she said that neither he nor Susan were getting any younger. Whatever they decided to do they had to take that into account. They couldn't take away Michael's safety net and then leave him stranded if one or other of them died. Aidan and Judy were right to be concerned; the responsibility would fall on them. But Graham knew his son. No matter what he said when he'd had too much to drink, he was a man who would not abandon his responsibilities. He sighed. Were they making a mistake putting their son and daughter-in-law under such an obligation, when they had their own children to worry about?

'What's wrong?' Susan asked.

'Nothing. I was just thinking about Michael and wondering where this will all end.'

She smiled at him and reached across and stroked the back of his neck. 'It'll all work out, you see,' she said.

Well at least Susan had regained her optimism. If there was one thing he knew about his wife, it was that when she set her mind on something she never gave up.

CHAPTER 27

Judy rode through the main gate of the school, swerved to the right to avoid a group of teenage girls practising a dance routine and headed for the bicycle shed. She padlocked her bike to the stand, unloaded her bag and made her way to the domestic science building. Her first lesson of the week was with the Second Years and it was a practical one, pastry making. She liked the practical classes; they were so much easier than the theory. Most of the children in her class were interested in cooking but, inevitably, there were a few troublemakers amongst them who could be disruptive, especially during the theory sessions. There were three boys in particular. It wasn't really their fault; one poor kid had an awful home environment and the other two could barely read and write. She was amazed that they had got so far through the system and were still semi-illiterate. But all that changed when they had practical lessons, especially cookery; even the most disruptive of them enjoyed the challenge of turning a collection of disparate ingredients into something delicious to eat. Today it was going to be apple pie.

She dumped her bag on the work surface and took out the apples she'd brought with her. She always had some extra ingredients in case a pupil had forgotten theirs or, as often happened, had no money to buy them. There were still fifteen minutes before the bell for Assembly so she had time for a quick coffee in the staff room.

As usual, the tiny room was packed with her chattering colleagues. She edged her way over to the coffee machine and took her cup off the shelf.

'Hi Judy. You're early this morning,' said a man with a thick ginger beard who was holding a half-empty coffee cup in one hand and a bundle of exam papers in the other.

'Andy, hi. Yes, I couldn't sleep last night.'

'Something bothering you?'

She filled her cup from the coffee machine and squeezed in next to him. 'There is actually. We spent the weekend in Leicester with my parents-in-law.'

'What, with the Ice Maiden? No wonder you couldn't sleep.'

She laughed. Andy had met Susan at one of their summer parties and had instantly christened her the Ice Maiden. 'Yes. You won't believe this but she's just found out that her father had an illegitimate son. The boy, or should I say man, is in his fifties now.'

'Wow, that must have been a bit of a shock for her.'

'It was a shock for all of us. But that's not all. This guy, he's called Michael, lives in   sheltered accommodation. He's got Down's Syndrome.'

'And she never knew anything about him?'

'Well she says not. None of us had met him until Saturday.'

'So what's the problem? Why the sleepless night?'

'Oh Andy, she's talking about looking after him, doing something for him. She feels she should make it up to him. I'm probably just being selfish but I can't help feeling that, in the end, it will be us looking after him, not her. My father-in-law is in his seventies and Susan isn't that much younger. What will happen to Michael if they die?'

'So he's pretty handicapped then?'

'Well no. Actually he's quite independent; he works at the centre and he has his own flat.'

'But he's in sheltered accommodation, you said?'

'Yes but they're talking of bringing him to live with them. If anything happens to them, how can we send him back to his flat in Leicester? And that's assuming that the centre would take him back. I get the feeling that the man running the place only took Michael in as a favour, when his mother died. So what would happen to him then? I'm just not ready to take on more responsibility, not with the kids, work and my own mum. I don't think I'd be able to cope. I'm pretty exhausted most of the time these days, as it is.' She didn't mention that the tiredness was probably due to her pregnancy. It was too soon to mention that at work. She'd wait until she'd had the first screening test before saying anything.

Andy nodded his head and eventually said, 'Look Judy, don't you think you're worrying too much about this? After all you've only just met this guy. Take it step by step. You may find it will sort itself out.'

'You're right, but I know what will happen. Susan will get her way, as always, and Aidan won't stand up to her. He's the one who's been saying that it's not a good idea to move this guy, but I know him, in the end, he'll give in. He always does where his mother is concerned.'

'If you feel so strongly about it, you should tell her.'

'I know. But it's not easy telling Susan anything.'

Before he could give her any more advice the sound of the bell announced that the school day had begun.

'Thanks, Andy. See you later,' she said, quickly rinsing her cup in the sink and putting it back on the shelf.

The Ice Maiden indeed, well she had seen a crack in Susan's icy exterior yesterday that made her realise that her mother-in-law did have a softer side to her, after all. Maybe Andy was right; maybe things would work themselves out. She oughtn't let her own fears affect Michael's chances of being reunited with his family; that would be selfish.

CHAPTER 28

Susan was at her desk early on Monday morning; she needed time to reassemble her thoughts before anyone else arrived. There was nothing else to be done about Michael until later in the week, so she could concentrate on work. She pulled out the notes she had made for the Foreign Office proposal and began to read them. The ideas started to flow and soon she was busy sketching the outlines for four one-day, tailored courses. It was all very familiar work, courses that she'd run before, just adapted to suit the new client. She never used the same material twice but it was usually a variation on a theme. She believed that was why she always had a fresh approach to both the training and the delegates; her motto was that if she wasn't bored then neither would they be.

A beep from her computer told her she had an incoming email. She clicked on her mailbox. The email was from John: *'Susan would you mind coming into my office please. I need to speak to you.'* Unbelievable. She could see the shape of her boss's head through the frosted glass door. Why the hell didn't he just get up and tell her in person? She wanted to barge straight in but politeness made her knock lightly on his door and wait for the usual grunt that meant she was allowed to enter.

'Ah, Susan. Come in, sit down.' He was seated, his hands linked behind his head and his feet on the desk, looking very pleased with himself. A man of about thirty, wearing a grey suit, was sitting opposite him. 'This is Mark Stephenson. Mark, Susan. Susan, Mark.' He gave her the oily smile he usually saved for new clients.

Susan could feel her irritation rising and wondered why she had continued to work for this obnoxious man for such a long time. 'Good morning, Mark. Nice to meet you,' she said, remaining standing.

The young man rose and shook her hand politely. Now that she could see his face, she thought he could be no more than twenty-eight; he had a very thin neck which protruded from an overlarge, stiff collar and, as he swallowed nervously, his Adam's apple bobbed up and down. There were traces of acne on his face and he'd shaved badly that morning. She was not impressed.

'Mark is joining us,' John said, beaming at her.

'That's nice,' she said, her tone giving no hint of her feelings on this matter.

'He used to be with Training Times. Our big rival.' For one awful moment she thought he was going to wink at her. Instead he turned to Mark and said, 'Now he's joined the opposition.' John laughed and rubbed his hands together in pleasure, evidently delighted with his new acquisition.

'Were you with them long?' Susan asked, politely.

'About two years.'

'And before that?'

'Oh, I wasn't in training before that. I was an accountant.'

'Now, Susan, that's enough of the third degree. Leave the man alone. He comes highly recommended.' The smile was fading. John didn't approve of her questioning his new protégé. He slid his feet off the desk and sat up. 'I've called you in because I want you to take Mark through the Foreign Office tender.'

'The Foreign Office tender? I don't understand.'

'The new tender for the training courses that the FO want. We discussed it just the other day. Have you forgotten?'

'Of course I haven't forgotten. But why do you want me to take Mark through it?'

'Because I thought it would be a good project for him to start on. Something to get his teeth into. They want one-day courses and he has experience of one-day courses. Good match.'

'But John, we don't really know what they want yet. You said yourself they're looking for us to guide them.' She tried to keep her voice as calm as possible.

'Well, in that case, this would be just up Mark's street. Something interesting to get him started and show us what he's made of,' he added, beaming once more at the young man. 'And I'd like you to give him a hand.'

'But what about Paul? Do you want all three of us to work on it?' She could hear the shrillness in her tone.

'No, Paul is busy with the McMillan's training. This will be Mark's baby.'

Mark was looking even more uncomfortable; his Adam's apple continued to bob, repetitively. Susan had difficulty averting her eyes. She almost felt sorry for him. It was so ridiculous. He'd only just walked in the door and John was handing him the plum training tender. What did that say about his opinion of her?

'What do you mean Mark's baby? He hasn't even started working for us yet.' She couldn't stop the words from coming out.

John looked as though he would explode. 'Just get me the tender,' he said, his voice icy.

'Very well,' she said. Experience told her there was no point arguing with her boss, certainly not in front of Mark. It would get her nowhere.

'Good, and while you're doing that, I'll tell Mark a little about the company.'

'Oh, by the way,' she said, stopping in the doorway. 'Have you decided where Mark will sit?' She knew there were no spare rooms and not even a spare desk. Was she supposed to give up her office as well?

'Perhaps he could share with you for a bit, especially as you'll be working so closely together,' John said with that oily smile.

She turned and closed the door firmly behind her, barely resisting the urge to slam it. What was John trying to do? He knew she wouldn't like him bringing in someone else to work on the tender. Was he trying to get rid of her? It would suit him if she retired or better still resigned. There had already been a few hints about retirement—nothing overt but he had said a few times how important it was to retire while one was still young enough to enjoy life. His other heavy hint had been along the lines of how important it was to have a young and vibrant team of trainers, with the emphasis on young. In his eyes she no longer qualified as young. Soon she would be sixty but she had never once considered retiring; she just intended to carry on working as long as she could. Was this what it was about? Was John trying to push her towards retirement? He could hardly sack her and he'd never make her redundant—it would cost him too much. What was he up to? She sat down at her desk and stared at the empty screen.

After a while the two men came out of John's office. Susan watched her boss lead Mark over to introduce him to Anne and the other staff. She knew she ought to speak to John alone, to find out what else he expected her to share with this newcomer, but reason told her it would be sensible to wait until after lunch when he was always more amenable.

She pulled out the folder containing the Foreign Office letter but she was finding it harder and harder to concentrate. The more she thought through the implications of what had just happened, the more agitated she became. When she saw John return to his office alone, having left Mark to discuss the eccentricities of the photocopier with Anne, she knew she had to speak to him right away. Without waiting to reconsider, she walked straight into his office and this time she didn't bother to knock. She pushed the door shut behind her and stood looking down at him. He was sitting at his desk, the telephone in his hand. 'Susan?' he said, a look of surprise on his face.

What a weed he was. He'd never have kept that job if it hadn't been for the fact that his wife was the Chairman's daughter. For some reason the thought of adding nepotism to his other failings incensed her so much that she bellowed at him, 'John, what the hell do you think you're playing at?'

'I beg your pardon?' he said, icily and replaced the receiver.

She ignored him and continued, 'How on earth can you bring in this boy and give him such an important tender as the Foreign Office? We'd discussed it before I went on leave. Or don't you remember? I was under the opinion that I was handling it and Paul was going to assist me. That's what we agreed. You know it's complete nonsense to risk losing such a prestigious contract by giving it to someone so inexperienced.' She could feel her adrenalin rising and without waiting for him to reply, she went on, 'You've done this to me before, John. And not just once. But it's always been with someone who was just as well qualified as I was and when there wasn't so much at stake. But this is ridiculous, and you know it.'

'Now, calm down Susan. You'll still be working on the proposal. I just wanted him to get his feet wet on something worthwhile,' her boss started to explain.

'You have no idea, do you? Not only do you give the project to a pimply youth, who is younger than my own son, but you expect me to hold his hand,' she interrupted.

'There's no need to take that attitude, Susan. And don't raise your voice.'

She could see that John was beginning to get annoyed with her, but she didn't care. 'I'll raise my voice if I want to, John. And actually I'm a little tired of your attitude towards me. I've worked here for fifteen years and I've made a lot of money for this company during that time and still you treat me like a junior. Without any consultation you've decided to give him my project, put him in my office and I wouldn't be at all surprised if you haven't given him my secretary as well.'

John blushed. 'It's only until he gets settled. The man has to have somewhere to work and he can't do all his own typing, now can he?'

'Great. I knew it. You really know how to motivate people, John.' She couldn't believe he could treat her like this.

'Look, Susan, you're making too much of this. We're a team here, after all. Mark is just one of the team. I really would appreciate it if you could make him feel welcome.' He was trying to appeal to her better nature now, but Susan was not in the mood to compromise. Any weakness on her part now would mean that he would continue to walk all over her. She had to make a stand.

'John. That is only part of the issue.' She spoke slowly, as though to a retarded child. 'If we win this tender, it will mean a contract for five years. The Foreign Office do a lot of training. They could invite us to bid for other tenders. They're a government department. They share information with other government departments.There are dozens of government departments and they all have training needs. Do you understand? We can't afford to cock this up.' She could see that John didn't appreciate her speaking to him in that way but by then she was past caring.

'I don't think there is any point in discussing this further, Susan. I am sure, when you start working with Mark, you will see that I have made a wise choice,' John said, his tone brooking no dissent.

'On the contrary, John. You're making a big mistake.' She was determined to have the last word.

As she left John's office she noticed Anne and Mark still standing next to the photocopying machine; they looked at her but didn't speak. She went into her office and slammed the door. As she sat down she realised she was trembling. She had given so much of her time to this damned company and this was how he treated her. She wanted to scream and throw things across the office but what good would it do? They would just say it was female hysterics; you'd never get a man behaving like that. She could hear his patronising voice. No, she couldn't win in this sexist, ageist company.

She took a deep breath. This was ridiculous; fancy letting John get to her like that. She turned back to the computer where the blank screen continued to stare back at her, offering no comfort, no words of encouragement. It was no use; she couldn't work in these conditions. Suddenly she saw her future stretching before her. This scenario would repeat itself over and over as John found more ways to cut costs. That was what it came down to, a cost cutting exercise; Mark would be paid half what she received. Experience didn't seem to count for anything. Young and vibrant was what John wanted—and cheap. He would continue to make her feel old and out-of-date until she was obliged to leave. She switched off the computer and picking up the Foreign Office file, she headed towards the photocopying machine.

'Mark, look I'm rather busy this afternoon, why don't you have a look at these papers and we'll go through them together tomorrow?' she said to the nervous looking youth. 'And Anne, I'm going out. I'll see you tomorrow. You can get me on my mobile if anything urgent crops up.' She wasn't going to give them the satisfaction of seeing how upset she was.

*

Graham was still out walking the dog when she arrived home. It was already six-thirty, so she went straight to the kitchen to prepare the evening meal. The row with John had left her feeling drained and calm but the anger remained, simmering below the surface. As she stood at the sink, peeling the potatoes, she tried to analyse why she had reacted so strongly to his actions. It was stupid really but she had felt insulted; Mark was not much more than a child. She'd thought for a long time now that John considered her too old for the job; she was the oldest on his staff by about fifteen years. Philip Smith, who ran the accountancy courses was the nearest to her in age and he was only in his forties. They were a very young team and Mark would surely fit in well. But she had the experience, she told herself once again. She also knew that many clients didn't like to have someone their own age, or even younger, telling them how they should manage their staff; they often had more respect for an older person. She sighed and rinsed the potatoes under the tap. John and she had never got on well and now, after her outburst, the situation would be worse. She should have left Colman's Training years ago, while she was still a marketable commodity. There was too much ageism about now, nobody wanted to employ you if you were over fifty and this despite the fact that the state retirement age had been increased.

'Hello, darling. Had a good day?' Graham came into the kitchen. He hung the dog lead on the hook behind the kitchen door.

'Not really. I've had a row with John.'

'Not again. What's it about this time?'

'Oh, it's a long story. I'll tell you later, once I've got this meal in the oven.'

'Okay, darling. I'll go and sit in the conservatory and read the paper. Want a drink?'

'Yes, please, a big one.'

'Oh, by the way, Aidan phoned. They can't make it this weekend, after all,' he said.

'What?' That was all she needed. She'd been relying on Aidan and the children being there. It would make things so much easier for Michael to have the children to talk to, instead of just her and Graham. 'Did he say why?'

'No, but I have the feeling he just didn't want to come.'

'I'll ring him. Tell him we need them to be here.'

'Is that wise? We shouldn't push them into something they don't want to do. They have their own lives to lead. It will only lead to resentment, Susie. Better to let them get used to the idea.'

'I need to talk to him.'

'Well not on the phone. Go round and see him. You said you wanted to talk to him about your father, you can start there.'

'I'll go now.'

'But I've just poured you out a glass of wine.'

'You drink it.'

'And dinner? No, Susie, slow down. It's only Monday. You can go and see him another evening. You've had a long day—and a difficult one by the sound of it. Here, take your wine and sit down. Maybe *we* should talk first. Tell me more about your childhood, for a start. I still can't get my head round the fact that your kind, charming father had a second family.'

Susan took the glass from her husband and sat down at the kitchen table. He was right. She shouldn't go rushing into this. She needed to have Aidan and Judy on her side. She'd ring her son tomorrow and ask when she could pop in to see him.

'Well, I suppose I first knew something was wrong when I was about twelve and the rows started,' she began. 'At first I didn't know why everything had changed, but as the rows became a nightly occurrence I realised that it was something more than the fact that my father had come home late from the pub. This was something serious.'

She took a gulp of her wine and tried to continue but the memories were crowding in on her. They were becoming too much for her to bear. She was once again a twelve-year-old child, burrowing her head under the pillows to blot out the noise of her parents' rowing.

'Maybe tomorrow, darling. I don't think I can talk about it right now,' she said.

CHAPTER 29

Michael heard a slight sound behind him. He glanced up from his early morning task of switching on the workstations and laying out the morning's lesson plan, to see Dr Edmundson standing in the doorway.

'Morning Michael,' he said. 'All alone?'

'Good morning Dr Edmundson. Yes, Brian isn't here yet. The class doesn't start until nine o'clock.'

'That's okay. I just wanted to know how you got on at the weekend. Did you have a nice time?'

'Very nice, thank you,' Michael replied. He put down the pile of worksheets and proceeded to tell his employer about his trip to Beacon Hill.

'Well, it sounds as though you had a really good time. What did you think of Susan?' he asked.

Michael beamed at him. 'I think she is very kind. She and Graham have invited me to visit them next weekend,' he replied. He was pleased that Dr Edmundson was interested in Susan.

'Oh, and what do you think about that?'

'Well, Graham wanted to come and collect me but I don't want to put them to so much trouble. I thought,' he hesitated. 'I thought if you would help me, I would go on the bus.'

'Are you sure about this Michael? You've never been further than Uppingham on your own before. And where is it they live?' The doctor was frowning slightly—he did that when he was worried. Then he removed his glasses and polished them with his pocket handkerchief.

'They live in Maidenhead,' Michael replied. 'But Graham said I could probably get a bus to Reading. That's not very far away from them.'

'Then what? Will they come to collect you from the bus station?'

'I don't know. I suppose so.' He hadn't considered that part of the journey.

'Well you think about it for a few days. If you're sure you want to go on the bus, I'm going into Uppingham on Thursday, you can come with me and buy your ticket. If you change your mind, we'll ring them and let them know.'

'I promised I would telephone them to say when I would arrive,' Michael said, anxiously. He hoped this wasn't going to be too complicated.

'Yes, well don't worry about it. We'll telephone them anyway and let them know what's happening. Although, having met your sister, I expect she'll be ringing me anyway.' He patted Michael on the shoulder. 'And now I think you'd better get on with your work; the students are here.'

The door opened again and three men and a young girl came in and took their places at their computers.

'Oh that group are always early,' Michael said. 'We've still got five minutes to go yet.'

'Well I have to get back to work. Let me know what you decide, Michael,' said Dr Edmundson. 'Good morning Brian.'

'Good morning Barry,' Brian said, coming in and throwing his books on the desk. He looked at the retreating back of his boss and said, 'What did Dr Edmundson want?'

'He wanted to ask me about my day out,' Michael replied.

'Oh yes, how did it go?'

'Very well, thank you. I enjoyed it.'

'Good. Are you going to see them again?'

Michael nodded. He would have liked to have told Brian all about it but by now the rest of the class had arrived and Brian was busy. He would speak to him later.

*

When the lesson was over he decided he would walk over to the craft centre. Helen worked in the craft centre; she embroidered tablecloths. Helen had been his girlfriend once.

He had met her not long after he first came to Sunny View and they became good friends. What a long time ago that was. His mother had brought him to Sunny View to meet Dr Edmundson. She told him that Michael was a good worker and that he would not be sorry if he employed him. She told him that they had tried to get him a job in the town but there was no work for him. Dr Edmundson had listened very carefully, nodding and smiling at her and then he promised to ring her if he could find a job for him.

Michael thought that Dr Edmundson wouldn't telephone them but the very next week, just when they were about to sit down to their tea, the telephone rang and it was him. He wanted them to go back to Sunny View the next day at nine o'clock. He had found a job for Michael working on the farm. Michael had been very nervous but his mother told him that everything would be all right and it had been. It had been better than all right. It had been fine. Dr Edmundson had introduced him to a man called Bob. Bob was in charge of building the new pig pens and Michael was to help him. He dug ditches and mixed cement. Then when the pens were finished and the pigs arrived it was his job to feed them and clean out the sties. He liked that better than digging ditches; he liked the pigs a lot. They were very young and ran around squealing all the time, especially when they were hungry. He gave them all names. He tried to remember all the names: Bessie, Mary, Jimmy, Spot, Freddy, Blacky and there was one he called Susie, after his sister. His mother used to laugh at him because he got so dirty. She said he smelt like a proper farmer since the pigs had arrived.

Helen was not his girlfriend straight away. It was not until he started working with Brian in the IT department that she became his girlfriend. It had been Brian's idea. Brian said they should invite her to go to the cinema with them one evening. That had been nice. They'd sat next to each other and she had held his hand.

The next week he bought her some chocolates and Brian had laughed and said that Michael never bought him chocolates. He hadn't told his mother at first but when he did she smiled and said 'That's nice, dear.'

When his mother died he stopped going to the cinema with Helen. He didn't really know why; maybe it was because he was so sad. Well now he would go and talk to her and tell her all about Susan and Graham and the boys. She would like that. Maybe she could go with him to visit them one day. But not yet. Later, when he knew them better.

*

He could barely wait until Saturday; he was so excited. He had his ticket and clear instructions of what to do. Dr Edmundson had talked to the man at the bus station and asked him if the bus stopped anywhere on the way. He had written it all down for him. He didn't have to change buses because that bus went straight to Reading. When it stopped so that the people on the bus could go to the toilet or have a cup of tea, he was to keep close to the other passengers and not wander away, in case the bus left without him. But he wouldn't do that anyway. He wasn't a child. He knew Dr Edmundson was concerned about him but it wasn't necessary. He would be fine. Susan and Graham were going to meet him at the bus station and he had their address and telephone number in his notebook, just in case. His mother always used to say that: 'Michael take this, just in case.'

Brian had offered to take him to the bus station on Saturday morning. He thought that was very kind of Brian because that Saturday was Brian's day off and he usually went fishing with his friends. He was going to collect him in his car. He liked Brian's car; it was a Mini Cooper, and went very fast. He would like to have a car then he wouldn't have to travel on the bus all the time but he knew it was impossible. Still he had his bike; he liked his bike.

Although it was only Thursday evening, Michael decided to pack his suitcase for the weekend. It was the suitcase he had when he arrived at Sunny View, two years before, after his mother died. Each time he looked at the suitcase it reminded him of her and he wanted to cry.

He remembered going to the hospital to visit his mother. Irene, the lady who lived next door, was a friend of his mother's and she'd taken him to see her. The hospital smelled of disinfectant and there were lots of doctors in white coats. His mother lay in a big, white bed and there were tubes sticking out of her arm. She'd smiled when she saw him and told him not to cry. She said he must be a man now and try to look after himself, just like she'd taught him. But he couldn't stop crying because she looked so thin and her eyes were sunk into her head. He asked her if it hurt but she said no, she was fine. She said the medicine helped stop the pain. Then Irene'd said they should leave because his mother was very tired and needed to sleep. It was true, his mother's eyes kept closing and sometimes she didn't know he was there. He had laid his head on the pillow next to hers and stroked her hair. When he whispered in her ear that he loved her, she opened her eyes and smiled at him and then she put her arm around him. 'You have to be a man now, Michael,' she repeated. 'And always remember that I love you.'

The next day Irene had come round to tell him that his mother had died in the night. She said his mother was in heaven now. Michael didn't know if there was a heaven but he knew that if there was, his mother would be there.

He wiped his eyes with the back of his hand and took some clean pyjamas out of the drawer. He carefully went through all his shirts and jumpers and selected two of the newest; he would pack his trousers later. He didn't want them to get creased. Then he pulled out a large cardboard box filled with photographs; he would take a few photographs to show Susan. He selected some of himself as a child, some with his father, and one of his mother before she was taken ill and put them all carefully at the bottom of the suitcase. He placed his bus ticket and directions on the top and closed the case. He would finish packing on Friday evening because he had to be up early on Saturday as Brian was coming for him at seven.

His mother would have been so happy to know that he had met Susan at last. She had always said that his big sister would come and see him one day. And she had been right. It had taken Susan a long time but that was because she didn't know where he was. But now she had found him. And now he was going to her house to stay with her. And he was going on his own. His mother would have been so proud of him.

CHAPTER 30

Aidan expected his mother to telephone and do her usual review of how the weekend had gone but he'd heard nothing from her. He picked at the salmon cutlet on his plate; Judy liked them all to have fish at least once a week but it was not his favourite. His youngest son didn't like fish either and was pushing it around his plate in an attempt to make it seem as though he had eaten some.

'Jason, if you don't eat that fish, I'll give it to the cat.' The sound of his wife's voice broke through his reverie.

'But we don't have a cat, Mummy,' Jason responded delightedly.

'Well, I'll give it to someone else's cat.'

Aidan put a forkful of the salmon into his mouth; he had to set an example. 'Yes, come on Jason; it's really delicious,' he said encouragingly.

'Don't like it,' the boy complained, pushing his plate away.

'Have you heard from your parents about the weekend yet?' Judy asked, ignoring her youngest son.

'I said we couldn't go. I rang Dad.'

'You said we couldn't go? But why?'

'It's too soon. We don't know anything about him.'

'Well how are we going to get to know him if we don't spend some time with him? Look Aidan, I'm as worried as you are about where this is going, but we ought to give the guy a chance. He's your mother's brother. He's family whether you like it or not.'

'Jason, stop messing about and eat your dinner, right now,' Aidan snapped.

The boy looked up at his father in surprise and quickly put a forkful of fish in his mouth.

'Don't take it out on the kids,' Judy said. 'I know what this is all about and it's nothing to do with Michael. It's your mother again.'

'Okay. You're right. Michael's a good chap. He can't help the way he is,' Aidan said.

'And he didn't ask to be born,' added Judy.

'Can you ask to be born?' Zak asked. 'I thought you just grew in your mummy's tummy. How can you ask if you aren't here? It doesn't make sense.'

'Mummy's tummy. Mummy's tummy,' chanted Jason.

'I'm going to get cross with you, Jason, if you don't get on with your meal,' Judy said, sounding exasperated. Aidan wasn't sure if Jason was the cause of Judy's irritation or he was.

'I thought you got on all right with Michael. I thought you liked him. You were chatting away to him when he showed us around the IT room,' she continued. 'He is your uncle, after all.'

'Half-uncle. Look, I said he's all right. I don't dislike him. It's just I feel that we're being bullied into something before we've had time to take it all in.'

'It's this perennial battle between you and your mother again. It's time you sorted it out. It's not fair to exclude Michael just because you and Susan don't get on.'

The shrill warble of their house phone interrupted them. 'Ben, get the phone for me, will you?' Judy said. 'You ought to get involved, Aidan. Whether you like it or not, if they decided to bring Michael to live with them, we'll all be caught up in it.'

'It's Nan,' said Ben, brandishing the phone. 'She wants to speak to Dad.' Aidan shook his head violently. 'He's here, Nan. He's just finished his dinner.'

'Mum?' Aidan said, scowling at his son.

'Aidan, I wondered if we could meet up for a chat tomorrow?'

'Why doesn't Daddy want to talk to Nan?' Jason's piercing voice asked. God, now his mother would know he didn't want to speak to her.

'What do you want to chat about, Mum?' he asked, aware from her silence that she had heard her grandson.

'I'm not interrupting anything, am I?' she asked.

'Of course not.'

'Well, you keep saying that I never tell you anything, so I thought maybe we should spend some time together and talk. Do you think that's a good idea?'

'It would make a change, I suppose.'

'Shall we meet tomorrow at that wine bar near where you work? "Rumours?" Or will it be busy?'

'No, that sounds fine. I'll leave work early. Say five o'clock? It doesn't fill up until after six.'

'Good. How's Judy?'

'She's fine. Do you want to speak to her?' He heard his mother hesitate and then she said, 'Yes, I'd love to.'

'See you tomorrow then,' he said, handing the telephone to his wife. 'Here, Judy, it's Mum.'

Judy chatted for a few moments to his mother and then said goodbye. She turned to Aidan and asked, 'You're seeing your mother tomorrow?'

'Yes. She wants to talk. Bully me into going at the weekend, no doubt.'

'Well, do you want us to go or don't you?' she asked.

'What do you want to do, Judy?'

'Me? I'm easy. They're your parents. As far as I am concerned, it would be another weekend with no cooking to do and you know the boys always love going there.'

'Are we going to Nan and Grandpa's?' Zak interrupted.

'Maybe. Would you like to?'

'Yeah, cool,' Jason said. He saw his mother direct a meaningful look at his salmon and started eating it hurriedly.

'Jason, it's yes not yeah,' Aidan said, for what seemed like the thousandth time that week.

'Will that retard be there?' Ben asked.

'Ben!' His mother looked at him in surprise. 'Ben, don't ever let me hear you say that again. It's cruel, unnecessary and untrue. Michael is your great-uncle. You will treat him with respect. Go to your room until I say you can come out.'

'But Mum, I haven't finished my dinner,' he wailed.

'I don't care. Go to your room, now.' When Judy was angry her eyes flashed dangerously and the children did not disobey.

Ben stood up, pushing his chair back so that it fell on the hard floor with a clatter. He scowled at his mother and left the room.

Aidan looked at his wife; her face had flushed an angry red and her hand trembled slightly as she cut Jason's remaining salmon into smaller pieces. He wondered if she spoke to her pupils like that.

'Well if you're keen for us to go, we'll go,' he said.

'I told you, I'm easy either way. Why don't you wait and see what your mother says tomorrow. And find out if she wants us to stay overnight.'

'All right. I suppose that would be nice, not having to drive straight back on Saturday. You know I can't remember the last time she invited us to stay overnight.'

'Neither can I. She's usually in a hurry to see the back of us.'

'Can we take Grandpa's boat out on the river?' asked Zak, who'd been listening intently.

'If the weather's nice, I don't see why not,' Judy said.

'We don't know for sure that we're going yet,' Aidan said. They should have waited until they were alone before talking about it. Now the boys would keep on and on about it until they had a clear assurance that they were going.

'So will Michael be there?' Zak asked, finishing the remains of his meal and helping himself to some potatoes from Ben's plate.

'That was the plan. I'm seeing your Nan tomorrow and I'll know more then about what's happening.'

'Maybe Michael can go in the boat, too,' Zak said.

Judy began to clear the table; her anger, as always, had subsided quickly. The boys still sat there, their heads almost touching, Jason's blond curls resting against Zak's dark straight hair; they were making their own plans for the weekend.

He decided it was time to talk to his eldest son and find out why he was so hostile to Michael. He'd been quite shocked at Ben's outburst. When they'd visited Sunny View, Ben had seemed quite impressed by Michael's guided tour of the computer department. He overheard him saying to his brothers that their computers were much better than those they had at school. Aidan had to admit that he too had been surprised that Michael was so knowledgeable about the technology. He obviously enjoyed his work and, if it were true what he said, the teacher relied on him a lot. Maybe he should read the information his mother had given him. There seemed to be more to Down's Syndrome than he'd realised.

He tapped on his son's bedroom door and went in. Ben was lying on his bed, face down. He didn't move. 'Ben,' Adrian said. The boy grunted something but remained where he was. 'Ben, sit up. I want to talk to you.' His son turned over and sat up; his eyes were red from crying.

'Now, Ben, what's the problem?' Aidan softened his voice as he spoke but there was no reply, so Aidan continued, 'Now, you know we have always brought you up to be respectful of other people, especially those more unfortunate than yourself.' He paused, looking for some reaction from Ben but none came, so he continued, 'I'm very surprised at your behaviour today and, frankly, disappointed.'

This time there was a reaction. Ben was a very kind-hearted boy and Aidan could see that his words hurt him. Two large tear drops made their way slowly down the boy's cheeks.

'There's no need to cry,' Aidan said, handing him a paper tissue. 'Just tell me why you feel this way about Michael.' He waited a moment, while Ben regained his composure then continued, 'It's not his fault, you know. He was born with Down's Syndrome. It could happen to anyone.'

At these words, Ben began to cry again and muttered something inaudible.

'What's that? What did you say?'

'He looks funny,' he spluttered.

'Yes, I admit he doesn't look the same as we do but he's just the same as us inside.'

'People, people will ...' Ben was having difficulty articulating what he wanted to say.

'People will what?' Aidan encouraged him.

Ben took a deep breath. 'People will say that I'm retarded too when they know he's my uncle,' he blurted out at last.

Aidan put his arm around his son. 'Look, Ben, you know there are horrid people in this world, people who say and do unkind things. We don't listen to those people, do we? They're not worth listening to. You have to find friends who respect you and don't say unkind things. Just imagine what poor Michael had to go through when he was a boy; it must have been much harder for him.'

Ben wiped his eyes again. His nose was running so Aidan gave him another tissue and then continued, 'But Ben, it's very unkind to call Michael a retard. You saw how clever he was with the computers. Because of his disorder it has been much more difficult for him to learn to read and write and do other things, but he's done them anyway. That shows you he's a very brave person.'

'And he perseveres,' Ben added. This was a word that had started to appear in Ben's report lately.

'Yes, he perseveres. So Ben, please try to be nice when we see Michael next. You don't have to be his friend, if you don't want to. I can't make you like someone but, even if you don't like him, you can at least be polite to him. Okay? And no more name calling.' Ben was sitting with his head down. 'Okay son?'

Ben looked at his father, and sniffed. 'Okay Dad. I'm sorry.'

*

That night as Aidan lay alongside Judy in their king size bed and listened to the owls hooting somewhere out on the Common, he thought back to his talk with Ben. It was curious how that conversation had clarified some of his own feelings about Michael. Prejudice was such a powerful emotion; it adhered itself to the stupid and the intelligent alike. Educated people liked to believe they were without prejudice but usually it was just better hidden, wrapped up in rational arguments and justifications. Then it was even more insidious than the blatant prejudice of the bigots and zealots of the world because it denied its own existence.

He realised his reactions to Michael had stemmed from his own preconceived ideas. What he had pretended was a concern for the future and an unwillingness to take on more responsibility was nothing more than prejudice. His real objection, his real fear, was very similar to Ben's, that anyone would associate him, or his family, with someone with Down's Syndrome. He didn't want his friends or the people at work to know about Michael.

He'd read that evening that Down's Syndrome was the most common genetic condition. For mothers over the age of forty, the incidence was one in thirty-five but, as he now realised, younger women could give birth to children with the condition too. It could have happened to them but they were the lucky ones; they had three sons who were all sound and healthy. He hoped this new baby would be the same.

His mother had been right, as usual, when she said that the future could take care of itself. He wouldn't stand in her way if she wanted Michael to live with them and he would no longer nag them about moving house. It was their life and it was up to them what they did with it. He was looking forward to seeing her tomorrow. There'd been a warmth in her voice when he spoke to her that he hadn't heard for a while.

*

As he stood in the train, hanging from the overhead strap and squashed up against a corpulent man in a pin-stripe suit with a bad case of BO, he thought about how his meeting—he could no longer

266

think of it as a chat— with his mother had gone. He wondered if he'd be able to convey to Judy just how very different she had been today, open, expansive and surprisingly affectionate. She looked the same, her voice was the same but the way she spoke to him was quite unlike her usual cold manner. She had let him buy her a gin and tonic and then she'd started to tell him about her childhood and her relationship with her parents—his grandparents. Now, as he swayed to and fro with the motion of the train, he still had trouble equating the parents of her childhood, angry, unhappy and secretive, with the grandparents he had known and loved. They'd kept their unhappiness masked from the world. Now he understood why his mother had always been so cold towards everyone. She had forgotten how to show her emotions because she'd spent so many years keeping them hidden, even from her own family. It had been a different world then, where adultery and illegitimate children were taboo—nobody spoke about them—where having a child with Down's Syndrome was something to be ashamed of, where a father would throw his daughter out of the house because she was pregnant. What a screwed up world it had been. No wonder he'd had trouble understanding his mother at times. The train screeched to a halt and people stumbled out onto the platform. He was pleased to see the man in the pin-stripe suit go with them. This leg of the journey was always quieter. He spotted a vacant seat in the corner and made for it.

When he'd asked her why she'd packed him off to boarding school, she'd been honest and said she didn't really know. It was the thing to do then, if you could afford it. They had wanted him to have a good education. But she also admitted that she had allowed her work to take over her life and now she regretted it. For the first time she talked to him about her own problems, how she felt that her boss was trying to force her to leave, how she had struggled to succeed in a male-dominated world and now, when women were at last getting an equal share in the work-place, ageism was rife. She said she felt as though she'd spent all her life battling to succeed. For the first time he felt he understood his mother; what he'd always taken for coldness was merely her reluctance to let down her guard.

She didn't mention the weekend, so in the end, he'd said that they were able to make it after all. The smile on her face told him that he'd done the right thing. He couldn't turn his back on Michael, just as he couldn't turn his back on his parents. Family was important to Aidan and, as Judy had reminded him, Michael was now part of that family.

CHAPTER 31

When they arrived at Lock End on Saturday, Graham was already showing Michael around the garden and Susan was in the kitchen preparing the lunch.

'Hi there,' she called when she saw them.

'Michael got here okay, I see,' Aidan said, looking through the kitchen window at his father expounding to Michael on the importance of good rich mulch for the garden. 'And I see Dad has an attentive audience.'

'Yes, we were already waiting at the bus stop when he arrived so there was no problem. I think he enjoyed the journey; some old lady had taken him under her wing. She even got off the bus to check that someone was meeting him.'

'That was kind of her,' Judy said. She lifted the lid of a saucepan. 'Oh lovely. Broccoli. Is it from Graham's vegetable patch?'

'Yes, of course. He won't allow me to buy vegetables in the supermarket unless I really have to. He is becoming quite an organic veggie snob.'

Judy laughed. 'Can I help?'

'Well, you could peel some potatoes if you like. Aidan, why don't you check that the boys are okay. I can hear them shouting something about the boat. I don't think they have time to go out before lunch; it will be ready in about forty minutes,' she explained.

'Okay Mum. I'll tell them we'll take it out after lunch,' her son replied.

The children had surrounded their grandfather and were dragging him in the direction of the jetty. Michael followed behind with Jess. Aidan could hear his father's faint protests.

'It's not big enough for all of us. We'll have to take it in turns.'

'Okay, Grandpa. We'll do a rota,' said Zak. This was his favourite word at the moment ever since they had introduced a monitor rota at his school. 'How many people can fit in it at one go?' he asked his grandfather.

'Four maximum or it will sink.'

'What about Jess?'

'Including Jess. But I don't think Jess will want to go, anyway. She's a land lubber.'

'Okay, then I'll go with Michael and Jason and you. Then Dad can go with Ben and Jason and Mummy.'

'That means Jason goes twice,' Ben pointed out. 'Why don't we let Michael go twice because he hasn't been in Grandpa's boat before?'

'That's a good idea, Ben.' Zak turned delightedly to Michael. 'That okay Michael?'

Michael smiled and nodded his head.

'Hang on boys. It's a good plan but it will have to wait. Lunch is in half an hour and your Nan says that you can't go in the boat until after lunch,' Aidan interrupted. Groans escaped in unison from three little throats.

'That means we will have to eat *all* our lunch or it will be no boat,' complained Jason, imitating his grandmother's voice as he said it.

Judy came across the lawn towards them. 'Hello Michael,' she said, giving him a quick kiss on the cheek. 'Susan asked me to show you your room. We can take your case up if you like.'

'Hello Judy. Yes, I'll get it.' The man followed her into the house. He retrieved his suitcase from where he'd left it in the hallway and they went up the stairs, together.

'Don't forget, Michael,' called Aidan, 'Lunch is in half an hour.'

*

Judy returned to the kitchen just as Susan was telling her son the latest in her dispute with John.

'So what are you going to do?' Aidan asked.

'I don't know. I just don't have the stomach for all this arguing any more. I sometimes feel I've had to fight every step of the way in that company. It wasn't much better when Conrad was the director.'

Conrad had been her previous boss and, when he had retired five years earlier, everyone had expected her to get his job. Instead they had advertised nationally and appointed John as the new Director of Training. Susan had been angry and disappointed at being passed over but she'd swallowed her pride and got on with her job. Now she wasn't sure she wanted to continue working there anymore.

'How long do you have to go until retirement?' Judy asked, sipping her wine.

'Well, under the new legislation, I really should continue until I'm sixty-seven but I can take my private pension at sixty. And that day is almost here.' She grimaced as she said it.

'Well, why not just tell them to stuff their job and retire,' suggested Aidan. 'It's not as though you need the money, is it?'

'Straight to the point as usual, Aidan, but you're right,' his mother said, turning down the gas under the potatoes. 'The thing is I'm not sure I'm ready to retire. What would I do all day?'

'Well, Dad's retired.'

'Yes but your Dad has his golf and his garden and Jess. Apart from looking after the house, all I have is my work.'

'Oh Susan, you'll find masses of things to do once you're retired: holidays, art classes, museums, amateur dramatics,' Judy said.

Susan was not convinced; she pulled a face at her daughter-in-law, 'Amateur dramatics?'

'You could even take up golf,' her son suggested.

'I don't think so,' she laughed. 'I've tried that stupid game. I'm useless. I can't even make contact with the ball. No, it would have to be something less physical.'

They were still trying to invent new pastimes for Susan when Graham returned with his three grandsons.

'Dad, I've been thinking,' said Ben.

'What about?'

'Well, you know what we were talking about,' he hesitated.

'Give me a clue.'

'About Michael.'

'Mmnn.'

Susan glanced across at them. Where was this leading? Her grandson was looking very serious.

'Well, next term we have to do a project on people who are worse off than ourselves.'

'Yes?'

'That sounds interesting,' Susan said, liberally topping up her son's glass.

'I was going to do something on African babies not having enough food but I wondered...' Ben stopped.

'Yes?'

'I wondered if I could write something about Michael and what it's like to have Down's Syndrome. Do you think that would be all right?'

'I think that's a great idea,' they all said together.

'Do you think Michael would mind talking to me about it?'

Aidan looked at his wife. 'No, darling, I'm sure he won't mind,' Judy said. 'Maybe you could ask him the next time he comes to visit, when he knows us all a little better. Now come along you three; let's get those hands washed before lunch.'

'So where is Michael?' Graham asked.

'He's unpacking. I gave him the room at the back,' Susan explained. 'You're in the room next to us, Aidan, and I've put the boys all together in the big, blue room.'

'I'll take their things up, now, before lunch is ready,' Aidan said. 'Come on Ben, you can help me.'

'I think I'll just go and see if Michael's okay,' Graham said.

'Well don't be long,' Susan said, as she took the chicken out of the oven. 'Half an hour for this to rest and then I'm dishing up.'

*

Michael was looking out of the bedroom window when Graham knocked on the door.

'Yes?' he said, nervously.

This was such a big house. He'd never been in a house like this before. And the garden. It was like a park. Susan and Graham were very nice to him but he still felt awkward. It had been easier to talk to them when they had come to his flat.

'Everything all right?' Graham asked.

'Yes thank you, Graham. This is a very nice room. I've been watching some squirrels over there in the wood.'

Graham went to the window. An ancient oak, its trunk gnarled and twisted with age, had formed a wide canopy across the far corner of the garden and underneath it were the squirrels.

'Oh yes. Grey squirrels. We get a lot of them; they especially like that oak tree. Mind you, they can be a bit of a nuisance at times.'

'You have a lovely house, Graham. It's very big.'

The driveway to the house wound its way through a thick copse of beech and hawthorn; the haws had already started to ripen and their reddish hue had attracted a pair of hungry thrushes who were squabbling noisily over the fruit.

'Yes, we like it. We've lived here a long time. But Aidan thinks it's too big for just the two of us. He thinks we need something smaller and easier to manage.'

'It's good for visitors,' Michael said. 'And for when Aidan and his family come to stay. It's just like a hotel.'

Graham laughed at this comment.

'You're absolutely right. The house is ideal for the grandchildren. I just wish they came over to stay more often, but Susan is always very busy with her work.'

'Does she enjoy her job?' asked Michael.

'Well you know, I'm not sure. She used to love it but lately I think there have been a lot of problems.'

'Perhaps she will become retired, like you Graham. Then you can do things together and see more of your grandchildren.'

'Maybe. That would be nice, wouldn't it.'

'Yes, it would.'

'Well Michael, you know that you can come and stay with us here any time you want, don't you? Now that you've seen how easy it is to get here by bus, you must come again.'

'I would like that, Graham.'

'Shall we go down for lunch now? It must be almost ready.'

*

It was good to have all the family there. Graham enjoyed seeing the boys, although he found it hard to keep up with them; they had so much energy.

He'd noticed a distinct thawing between Susan and Aidan today. She'd been right to go and talk to him. After all that had been part of the problem with her parents; nobody ever talked about anything. There had been too many secrets and too many lies. Poor David. It had been a problem of his own making but Graham still felt sorry for him. His father-in-law had been trapped between his two families, struggling to support them and unable to make either happy. Maybe now they could at least do something for his son; give him back the family that he'd lost.

*

Susan had pulled out the extra leaves of the table in the conservatory. It was an ideal setting for a family lunch, not too formal and with a lovely view of the garden.

'Everything all right Michael? Have you unpacked?' she asked. 'Would you like to sit over there, between Graham and Zak?'

He nodded and looked about anxiously. Was he nervous? It must be a bit overwhelming for him to be here with people he hardly knew.

'Can I get you something to drink?' Graham asked him.

'Some water please.'

'There's coke if you want it? Granddad always buys coke for us,' said Ben.

'No thank you, Ben. Water is fine.'

'Right, well now we're all here, let's dig in. No need to stand on ceremony in this house,' Graham said with a smile.

'You always say that Granddad,' said Jason, reaching for the roast potatoes.

'Not you, boys. You wait until I serve you,' added Judy as she began dishing out her sons' food.

Once all the plates were full and the children had received permission to start, the atmosphere lightened and Michael began to relax. 'This is very nice, Susan,' he said.

'Thank you.'

'Roast chicken is my favourite. My mother used to cook it every Sunday.'

'It's my favourite too,' chirped Jason, chewing enthusiastically on a drumstick.

'Tell us a little about your life at Sunny View, Michael. Do you have many friends there?' asked Aidan, pouring some wine into his mother's glass and then topping up his own.

'Yes. Brian is my friend and so is Jimmy. Sometimes I play table tennis with Anne. She's my friend too.' He hesitated then continued, 'And I have a girlfriend.'

'A girlfriend? That's nice. What's her name?' asked Susan. She tried to keep the surprise out of her voice.

'Ben's got a girlfriend, too,' cried Zak.

Susan looked at her eldest grandson; his face was scarlet.

'Ben's got a girlfriend. Ben's got a girlfriend. Ben's got a girlfriend,' Zak and Jason began to sing.

'That's enough of that,' their mother said. 'Any more and there'll be no boat trip.' The boys fell silent and looked at their mother; this was no bluff.

'Brian says that you can have friends that are girls and girlfriends. Maybe Ben's friend is a friend who is a girl,' Michael said, quietly.

Susan saw Ben flash a look of gratitude at his great-uncle. 'She's not a girlfriend,' he said. 'She's just a girl in my class.'

'So what's your girlfriend's name, Michael?' asked Graham.

'Helen.'

'That's a pretty name.'

'She works at Sunny View but she doesn't live there. She lives in Uppingham with her mother and father. Her father brings her to work each day in his car. It's not far, only ten minutes.'

'Is she pretty?' asked Zak.

Michael blushed. 'Yes, I think she's pretty.'

'Well maybe one day you can bring her to visit us,' suggested Graham.

'That would be nice.'

*

After lunch Susan took her half finished glass of wine and sat on the bench on the terrace. It was a warm afternoon and she felt tempted to remove her cardigan. Despite the aggravations of the week she felt relaxed and at ease. As she watched Graham and Aidan explaining to Michael how to steer the boat, she was reminded of the outings they used to have with Aidan when he was a child. When had she stopped doing things with her son? Was it when he went off to university? Or before, when he was in the sixth form? Now he had a family of his own but she rarely saw them. She was always too busy—that was what she told herself— her work took up too much of her time. That was true but did it need to be that way? Other women had full time jobs and still had time for their families. No time for her own grandchildren? She felt guilty.

She looked at them, waiting patiently to get in the boat. They were nice little boys but she didn't really know them and that was her fault. She knew that Graham loved to see them and would be happy for them to come over more often. They came sometimes for a day during the school holidays and he'd play football with them and cook them beef burgers on the barbecue—usually when she was at work. She also knew that Graham would have liked to have had more than one child—he loved big families—but it had been her who'd said they couldn't afford it, that she needed to work. Rubbish. Looking back she could see how selfish she'd been. Well maybe now she had the chance to make it up to all of them, including Michael.

Her father's affair had ruined her childhood, had devastated her mother and, in the end, had made him very unhappy. All this was true but Graham was right when he said it was a long time ago. There was no need for her to harbour her childhood resentment; it was time to let it go. It had been their marriage and their problem, not hers. Now she had the opportunity to do something for the innocent outcome of all that passion and rage; she would become the sister that Michael had longed for. She would become the mother that Aidan wanted.

The sun shimmered on the water, catching the eddies and swirls in the river and painting them silver. It was as though the shadows of the past were lifting and she could see everything more clearly now. Her parents weren't bad people and neither was Anthea; she'd fallen in love and become pregnant, a terrible transgression in those days unless you were married. She was a good woman who'd loved her son and done all she could to bring him up to lead a normal life. She could see that her father had tried to be a good parent to the boy but having two families had not been easy. He must have struggled financially—she remembered the regular rows her parents had over money—and it must have pained him to be able to do so little for the child. For the first time she felt a pang of pity for her father; he had just been unable to chose between the two women he loved. It suddenly occurred to her that maybe he had stayed with her mother for Susan's sake. Maybe he just couldn't abandon his daughter for a new child, even though that child had Down's Syndrome. And her mother had been torn apart with jealousy, unable to forgive him and unable to forget. If only she'd had the strength to break away. If only Susan had not turned her back on her mother's unhappiness. But it was all too late now. They were all dead. Only she and Michael survived.

Susan watched her husband rowing away from the bank, Michael and Jason at the back of the boat and Ben next to his grandfather. The others stood on the jetty watching them. There they were: her husband, her son, her grandsons and Michael, six men at different stages of their lives. She loved them all.

Zak came running towards her.

'Nan, guess what. Dad's taking us to see Chelsea on Saturday. He's got tickets for us all and Michael is coming too.'

The excited boy carried on past her, looking for his mother so that he could tell her his news. Susan sipped her wine. Maybe it would sort itself out after all; all she had to do was wait and see what the future would bring.

POSTSCRIPT

Susan poured herself another cup of coffee. It still seemed strange sitting in the conservatory, drinking coffee at ten o'clock on a Monday morning. She turned the radio on. She would just listen to the news headlines then she would get on with the chores she had planned for the day. Mondays and Thursdays were Graham's golf days so she was free to spend the time as she wished. It was funny but she didn't really miss going to work. It was surprising how quickly she'd become used to her new freedom.

She watched Jess dash across the lawn to greet the new gardener. The garden was quite bare at the moment but already she could make out the green shoots of the crocuses pushing their way up through the frozen earth. Another new year. They seemed to come round with relentless monotony these days. Such a lot had happened since last January that sometimes she felt as though her life had been turned upside down.

As expected, John had been quite amenable about her taking early retirement. She had offered to stay on until the middle of December to see the tender process through to its conclusion and had been gratified that he'd been quick to accept her help. After that it had all been fairly straightforward. Mark turned out to be quite a nice chap after all, quick-witted and eager to learn. The company hadn't reduced her pension because she wanted to leave a year early and had paid her a substantial lump sum—which, in the end, she and Graham decided to give to Aidan so that he could buy a bigger house. So, all in all, it had turned out for the best. She had her freedom, John had his young, vibrant training team and Aidan's financial problems were eased.

She turned up the radio. 'The current mild, sunny weather we are experiencing in the south of England is set to stay with us for at least another week,' the weather announcer said. 'Temperatures for January have reached an unseasonal high.'

Maybe she would invite Aidan and his family over for lunch on Sunday, while the weather held. She flicked open her mobile and dialled his number.

'Hi Mum,' the familiar voice replied.

'Hello Aidan. I wondered if you were free for lunch on Sunday? The weather's so lovely, we could take the kids for a walk in the woods.'

'Nice idea Mum but I don't think we can make it. I think Judy wants to go house-hunting this weekend and it's football on Saturday.'

'Oh, okay.' She tried not to sound disappointed. 'Where's the match?'

'Leicester. It's Leicester City against Nottingham Forrest. Ben and I are driving over to pick up Michael and taking him with us.'

'That's nice.'

'Maybe the following week. That's Michael's weekend to come down isn't it?'

'Yes, the first weekend in the month. He likes the routine. By the way, how's little Allie?' The newest addition to the family was a beautiful little girl with a mass of curly blonde hair and big blue eyes. Graham doted on her.

'She's fine. Teething, so we haven't had a lot of sleep lately.'

'Maybe I'll pop over tomorrow to see her. I saw this lovely little dress in town the other day and I just couldn't resist buying it for her.'

'Yes, no problem. I'll tell Judy. Well I've got to go. I'll ring you. Bye.'

'Bye darling.'

Aidan never mentioned them moving any more. He'd accepted, at last, that neither of them wanted to leave their lovely home, and especially now that the children had started coming to stay with them during the school holidays. They wouldn't be able to cope with those boisterous boys in a smaller house. For the first time in many years their house felt like a family home again. And, this is what surprised her, she loved it.

So they were taking Michael to football this weekend. Her father's love of the game had been transmitted to his son, his grandson and to his great-grandsons. Sometimes she thought that the game of football was the thread that bound her family together; it had certainly helped break down the barriers between Aidan and Michael.

In the end they'd taken a middle road with Michael. As Graham had so rightly pointed out, Michael had a stable life at Sunny View, with a job, a flat, friends and a girlfriend. Why tear him away from all that just so that she could feel she was making amends for her parents? He came to see them frequently and had his own part of the house. Sometimes he visited Aidan in London but, most important of all, he now had a family. They were all happy with the arrangement. If things were to change in the future then they would deal with that when it happened.

She switched off the radio and went into the kitchen to put on her wellingtons. It was too nice to stay indoors; she'd take Jess for a brisk walk along the tow-path and then maybe she'd drive over to the golf club and join Graham for lunch.

Made in the USA
Coppell, TX
11 December 2020

44046521R00157